BOYD COUNTY
JAN 1 8 2023
PUBLIC LIBRARY

Ice Maiden's Meltdown

ICE MAIDEN'S MELTDOWN

EMILY GREY

THORNDIKE PRESS
A part of Gale, a Cengage Company

Copyright © 2022 by Emily Grey.
All scripture quotations, unless otherwise indicated, are taken from the Holy Bible, New International Version®, NIV®, Copyright 1973, 1978, 1984, 2011 by Biblica, Inc.™ Used by permission of Zondervan. All rights reserved worldwide. www.zondervan.com
Scripture quotations marked KJV are taken from the King James translation, public domain. Scripture quotations marked DR, are taken from the Douay Rheims translation, public domain.
Scripture texts marked NAB are taken from the *New American Bible, revised edition* Copyright 2010, 1991, 1986, 1970 Confraternity of Christian Doctrine, Washington, D.C. and are used by permission of the copyright owner. All Rights Reserved. No part of the New American Bible may be reproduced in any form without permission in writing from the copyright owner.
Thorndike Press, a part of Gale, a Cengage Company.

ALL RIGHTS RESERVED
This is a work of fiction. Names, characters, places, and incidents either are the product of the author's imagination or are used fictitiously, and any resemblance to actual persons living or dead, business establishments, events, or locales, is entirely coincidental.
Thorndike Press® Large Print Christian Fiction.
The text of this Large Print edition is unabridged.
Other aspects of the book may vary from the original edition.
Set in 16 pt. Plantin.

> **LIBRARY OF CONGRESS CIP DATA ON FILE.**
> **CATALOGUING IN PUBLICATION FOR THIS BOOK**
> **IS AVAILABLE FROM THE LIBRARY OF CONGRESS.**
>
> ISBN-13: 979-8-8857-8350-7 (hardcover alk. paper)

Published in 2022 by arrangement with White Rose Publishing, a division of Pelican Ventures, LLC.

Printed in Mexico
Print Number : 1   Print Year : 2023

To my supportive family, friends, and writing partners. I love you.

To my friend, Elizabeth Noyes, who has the wit and wisdom to comfort or scold. Bless you.

1

Chills rippled down Suzanne's spine as she stepped from the taxi and tossed a soft, woolen scarf over her shoulder, a buffer against the raw February wind blowing in from the roiling Pacific Ocean. Her slumping shoulders exposed a state of weariness that threatened her sanity.

Spiky four-inch heels sank into the damp cemetery turf, much as reality plowed into her psyche. On tiptoe, she made her way along the right side of the crowd of mourners. Just then, twin bronze caskets appeared out of the drifting fog. She stifled a gasp, her need for comfort and a warm embrace so startling, she wrapped her arms around her body to stop the trembling.

Blankets of red and white carnations draped her sister and brother-in-law's coffins. The colors signified life and death. Could any of this be real?

Sue, I need you, whispered through the

towering Douglas firs, sending a frigid, eerie sensation through her.

Those same words, so often implored when her younger sister Pam asked for something, now clutched at Suzanne's heart. Her fingers curled into fists as the tears held back for so long threatened to spill.

Pain and anguish brought her feet to a halt. Grief slammed into her and threatened to drop her knees in the mud. The call, the notification — it all seemed surreal, until now. *Oh, Lord, help me.*

Blurred vision made it difficult to find a familiar face in the crowd of mourners, but then she spotted them — Karla and Vic, two of Pam's friends she'd met on a previous visit. Karla looked at her with a glare that made Suzanne's breath hitch. Her husband's lack of reaction confirmed their animosity.

A tall, thirtyish man with soft, dark curly hair and a face that could grace the cover of any magazine stood beside them. A fleeting thought of who he might be was interrupted by a loud harrumph as the pastor began the eulogy.

Half listening as he spoke with loving words about how much the couple meant to the townspeople of Emerald Point, Suzanne did her best to shut out the memory of the call about the accident.

A murmured prayer followed the tribute. People shook hands and hugged, seeking and giving comfort where they could. At last, the mourners departed and headed for their vehicles.

A trio of pelicans flew overhead, climbing and wheeling as a unit. Covering their heads, a few in the crowd picked up their pace.

She stood transfixed as the cemetery cleared. The funeral was supposed to bring closure, but it left her with open wounds far from ready to start the difficult healing process.

When only a few people remained, the tall stranger who'd stood beside Karla and Vic trudged to the twin coffins and plucked one red and one white carnation from the spray. Unmoving for several moments, he finally twirled the blossoms through the air in imitation of the set of wheels that ended Tad and Pam's lives.

Suzanne trotted across the grass to her sister's casket, the sucking mud capturing her heels. A low-pitched groan left her lips. Would she ever again catch a breath to fill her lungs? Her gut clenched and she shook her head in disbelief — tightness in her chest, and the physical pain of grief engulfed her.

With a cursory glance at the man, she lowered her eyes.

"You're Suzanne."

She forced herself to look up. The sharp angles of his handsome face spoke of weariness and pain — from personal loss? "Yes," she whispered.

His penetrating gaze searched hers, giving the moment a sense of intimacy. And then he took her hand, its warmth triggering a flutter in her stomach. "I'm Chase Garwood."

Tad's brother . . .

She swallowed hard, gave him a quick shake and withdrew her hand. "We never quite managed to be in Oregon at the same time with you in Tokyo and me in New York."

"True." A tinge of sadness crept into his tone.

Her attempt at a smile fell well short of its mark. Pleasantries seemed inappropriate, somehow disrespectful. Besides, related by marriage or not, regardless of her sister's respect for him, Suzanne didn't know the man.

Photographs were a no-no in her sister's home — an odd but lovable quirk. Pam wanted what she wanted.

"Both of our lives existed far from here. I visited when I could."

For lengthy moments, silence laden with memories swirled around them before Suzanne responded. "Me, too."

"Yeah, I know." His voice took on a rough, contemptuous edge he didn't try to hide. "I've heard a great deal about you."

Steel straightened her spine and lifted her chin, a spontaneous reaction she'd acquired when faced with hostility.

"Oh, I'm sure you have."

The uncomfortable silence stretched between them as she waited for his censure. Without asking, she already knew where his thoughts lay. Like so many others, he'd judged and found her guilty based on the lurid tabloid stories. Guilty until proven innocent was the rule of the news media today. Bitterness rose in her throat. Lies, all lies.

Beads of moisture dotted her brow, despite the bone-numbing cold. She dabbed at her forehead with a tissue, aware that he followed every movement. "You know, I've heard quite a lot about you, too."

He reached out to touch her face and when she didn't flinch, he drew his thumb down her cheek. "You look so innocent, hair like a cloud. Silken skin. I can see how a woman like you could lead a man to the very edge of —"

The heat of his touch surprised her. She stepped back, breaking the contact. "You're wrong, but then, it doesn't really matter now."

"Oh, it does, Suzanne." The air between them shimmered like a blurred reflection of the ocean.

She blinked at the abrupt change in his tone — taken aback by how his voice caressed her name. "I, uh, don't understand."

Hands by his sides again, determination seemed etched into his features. He offered his arm, and she accepted. He led her past the tombstones.

Balancing on her toes to avoid burying her heels in the saturated grass, she attempted to match his stride. Impossible. He hurried her along as if she were a bad-tempered child.

His high-handedness flipped one of her psychological switches. She jerked her arm free and stopped in her tracks. "Where are we going?"

He halted, gray eyes darkening as they drifted over her. "To get out of the cold. You're poorly dressed for this weather. We can talk in my car, or I thought we'd stop off at a diner someplace."

Her lower lip twisted. "Why can't we talk at the house?"

He swung around, a frown marring his perfect features. "I'd like to speak in private. Are you afraid to be alone with me?"

She tsked and looked away, peering at the gravestones and statues. And well aware of how isolated they were in this morbid place. "Don't be silly."

His deep-throated laughter jangled her nerves. "Fear is an emotion, Suzanne. I'd heard you're indifferent to them."

What? No emotions? Arrogant and domineering, this man brought out her emotions but fear was not one of them. Couldn't he feel heat rising off her like a hundred-and-six-degree fever? "Wrong."

"Not my judgment. It's your reputation."

"Don't worry, you're in good company. Most people set themselves up as judge, jury, and hangman."

His intense gaze narrowed, forcing her to glance away. "Have you even shed a tear for Tad and Pam?"

The telltale pressure behind her eyes rose once more. She'd spent the entire flight across the country choking back tears. She wouldn't cry now, not in front of him.

She turned away intent on walking the

short distance to her sister's home unburdened by the likes of this man. Rain threatened, but so what? She'd stuffed an umbrella in her tote. She'd get wet. "I'd like to be alone right now, if you don't mind."

"Of course, I'd expect the Ice Maiden to prefer solitude." He offered a sarcastic smile. "No. On second thought I don't think I'll give you that."

She should have recoiled when he took her arm again and watched her like a cat toying with a mouse. Ice Maiden. The label ballyhooed by the media and now from the lips of this man hurt. Despite the walls she'd built to protect herself, it cut deep.

A horn blared in the distance, enough to jolt her back to the present. Except for the rhythms of the incoming tide, this place chilled her spirit.

Conscious of his undeniable charisma, instinct warned her that given the chance Chase Garwood could wreak havoc with her heart. She called on every ounce of frost she could muster. "Please, just go."

"You're sure you won't come along?"

Her fists clenched at his low challenging tone. "I'm sure." His assessing gaze seemed to reflect the so-called sins of her past She'd seen it before in other eyes that had condemned her when scandalous headlines shouted BROADWAY STAR ATTEMPTS SUICIDE OVER WOMAN.

Carried along by a current of air, misty fog whispered over them. Chase's lips turned up in a half smile, half challenge. "You're having difficulty walking in this muddy grass. I wonder if I carried you, Suzanne, would you come without a fuss."

2

"Why are you acting like this? You don't know me."

Chase did a double take at Suzanne's response and the glare she sent his way. "Acting like what? Looking out for you? Trying to get both of us out of this miserable weather before you face plant in those ridiculous heels? It was a suggestion, Suzanne, that's all. An offer of help."

"It sounded more like a hostile takeover to me. Do you always go caveman on women you've never met before? Threaten to toss them over your shoulder to make them comply?"

He grasped the fact that he'd been rude to her — someone he only knew through others' point of view and tabloid headlines that revealed — what? Jumping to conclusions wasn't his normal way of dealing with a situation. A salesperson listened to his client and then spoke. But pain seared his soul, and he needed an outlet for his frustration, and from the look of her, she could take his ire.

He lowered his voice in a gentler approach. There was no sense in making her hate him, and he didn't want a spiteful woman dragging out the legalities. "Look. Tad and Pam's estate and their three-year-old son are at stake." At the mention of Jeff, all of his outrage disappeared. His shoulders slumped under the weight of the same terrible sadness she seemed to bear. "You're right." Her arms flapped once with a helpless motion. "There's so much to do and so little time to get it done."

"There's another reason we should discuss a few items away from the house. We don't want to upset Jeff or the housekeeper."

She winced and grabbed her stomach as if pain had settled in her gut. "Speaking of Lara, I saw her when I dropped off my suitcase at the house. She said she was heartbroken enough without attending a memorial service that would only shatter her further. She's been a wonderful addition to the household and loves that boy with a fierce protective quality that's so admirable."

"She's been the backbone of the family. How do we deal with her now that a major part of the family is gone?"

She shook her head.

Raindrops pelted his face, sporadic but with a promise of much more. He nodded toward his car. "Come on. Let's go before we get drenched."

With a sigh that splintered Suzanne's composure even more than it already had, she simply nodded.

Chase cupped her elbow as they headed toward an expensive black car, and she was grateful for the support.

The shivering had long ago turned into full body spasms before getting in the vehicle, but she looked back for a last glance at the coffins. Pam and Tad were gone. A fresh wave of heartbreak seared her. "Oh, Lord, help me," she whispered. But did God hear her?

If only she'd accepted Jesus as Pam had, the faith that had helped her sister deal with life's struggles would be hers now. *With His help, I can survive this tragedy and its aftermath.*

Chase opened the passenger door to help her in. Bam! Supernovas filled her vision and the top of her head exploded in agony as she rammed into the top edge of the window frame. She staggered and reached for balance.

"I'm so sorry, Suzanne. Are you OK?" Strong hands gripped her shoulders to hold her steady.

The pain, acute and throbbing, hurt like ice picks piercing her skull while someone pounded away with a sledgehammer. Not that she would admit it. "I'm fine. Whose car is this anyway?"

"Vic loaned it to me while I'm here."

After striding around the front, he slid into the driver's seat and turned on the ignition. The powerful, high-performance engine purred to life.

Beneath a furrowed brow, his compelling gray eyes took on an aura of deep concern. Though still in pain, she noticed how his smooth skin stretched over high cheekbones and the way the set of his shoulders exuded confidence. Why did his attributes tick her off? Suzanne stopped her hands from punching the air. Aargh. She'd never met a man so bullheaded, annoying, or physically appealing.

"Will the tavern in the center of town be all right?"

"Yes." At least he asked.

He maneuvered the car along the cemetery road, hands gripping the wheel like the steel claws of a bird of prey.

Suzanne's gaze flickered over the weather-beaten beach houses and small mom-and-pop stores that lined Emerald Point's Main Street, recalling that the tourist season was a few months away. Only a few locals milled around the business district, while boats rode at anchor along the breakwaters and many floated in the marina.

Chase parked at the curb in front of the tavern and stuffed the keys into his coat pocket. But before he could round the side, she eased out of the car and shut the door. A blast of wind whipped her hair, prompting a grab for the scarf.

With her hair secured, he tucked her hand into the crook of his arm and led the way across the street where he opened the door to Annabelle's Tavern.

The stale odor of liquor and beer set her empty stomach churning. At a table, he eased off her coat and laid it across the back of one of the chairs. Before removing his own, he cocked his head and searched her face. "Suzanne, are you OK?"

Her face heated when she realized she'd been standing there, just staring at him. Why did she respond to him when he merely murmured her name? How did he reduce her to a silly teen in her first encounter with a handsome guy? Was it the need for a strong shoulder to cry on? He certainly had those.

He settled into the opposite seat, loosened his plain dark tie, and unfastened the top shirt button.

An attractive, flame-haired waitress stopped at their booth, eyes flashing her appreciation, and her white teeth seemed ready to take a bite out of Chase. "Well, hello. My name is Tanya. What can I get for you, sir?"

Chase looked at Suzanne.

"Root beer." That was the first drink that popped into her head. Hot chocolate might do a better job of unsnarling the knot in her stomach, but no way would she change her order.

His eyes played over her face. "Root beer, huh?" When she nodded, he requested, "Give the lady a root beer and double bourbon on the rocks for me."

"You got it." The waitress scurried off.

His impeccably tailored, dark wool suit drew her gaze. Or was it the way the jacket fit snug across his broad shoulders, doing absolutely nothing to disguise his muscular physique? The tanned skin of his neck made a marked contrast to the flawless white shirt. Quality workmanship and expensive, he had excellent taste in clothing.

She worked her way to the strong line of his chin that projected a sense of power and his somewhat aquiline nose. Those nostrils had flared ever so slightly during their confrontation in the cemetery, a sure sign this man didn't bother to hide emotional distress.

After the waitress brought their order, Suzanne took a sip of her drink. "Root beer's refreshing." Did she really care what he thought about her choice? Heavens, no.

He turned that smoky, seductive smile on her.

Whoa. She looked away, fixing her gaze on an older couple who entered the tavern. They held hands and smiled at each other, the communication of long-time lovers. A pang of envy thrummed inside her. Still, it was lovely to see people who cared for each other.

"On a cold, blustery day like this, what a man needs is a bottle of liquor and —" Chase stopped short and tipped the glass to his lips.

And a woman, she mused as she mentally finished his sentence. Her mouth curved up. "Isn't fulfilling half a need better than none?"

While he studied her, he plunked down the glass with a thud and rubbed his hands together.

Those gray eyes seemed to penetrate her façade and look right into her soul. A sense of impending doom descended, an inevitable destiny. "Y-you're so different from your brother." She forced out a conversational tone. "Tad was affectionate and caring."

Chase covered her hand, his touch warm and almost intimate. "And you're nothing like your sister — but not at all what I expected. Pam was carefree and full of life."

Touché. Startled by his gesture and the subtle turn of his words, she withdrew her hand and shifted in her seat. "What *did* you expect?"

He responded with another half-smile, but this time it didn't reach his eyes. "Not this woman sitting across from me, that's for sure."

Her lips flattened into a smug line. "I was eighteen when we lost our parents. After that, I raised my fourteen-year-old sister alone. Responsibility like that modifies a person's behavior."

Chase's fingertips drummed in a staccato rhythm on the table. The look in his eyes said he'd gone somewhere else.

When he remained silent, she tapped her long fingernails against the glass. Whether it was the motion or the sound, she didn't know, but it drew his attention. "You said we should talk."

The front door opened, sending a brisk breeze through the room. Chase's potent scent of sandalwood filled her nostrils. Such a distraction. So not fair.

"How long do you plan to stay?" he asked. "Settling Tad and Pam's estate should be our top priority."

No. Jeff was more important, but that discussion could wait.

She folded her hands in her lap so he wouldn't see them tremble. What did he possess to rock her emotions this way? Crazy. If only he would stop looking at her as though she were blemished.

Ice Maiden. A date who'd expected more than she was willing to give had coined the name, one picked up by the tabloids. Why hadn't she flared up like a match in a pile of sawdust when Chase had said that earlier? No one got away with calling her that, no one. Yet, she'd given Chase a pass.

"I'm not sure." She pushed back in her seat to add more distance between them. "Mr. Pomeroy will take care of the necessary legal matters."

Chase nodded. "I suppose he might need input from us. I didn't see him at the funeral."

"His wife fell and injured her leg. He called Lara from the hospital."

"That's unfortunate. How is Lara holding up?" His voice held genuine concern for Tad and Pam's loyal housekeeper.

The abrupt change of subject left her mind abuzz.

She drew squiggly lines with her finger on the moist exterior of the glass. "I only saw her for a few minutes, but I think she's having a hard time accepting that Pam and Tad are gone." She shook her head, "Lara's a dream of a housekeeper, nurse, and friend, all rolled into one. They were so . . . blessed to have her." Pam's words filtered out of Suzanne's mouth. Whenever Pam talked about Lara, she'd gushed about how the woman was such a blessing.

He nodded, searching her eyes with a finesse that sent a chill down her back. "How come it took so long for you to get here from New York? Couldn't you drag yourself away from your business and the nightlife any sooner? After all, it's been four days since . . ."

Another abrupt change of subject. A dull steady throb had taken up residence in her skull making it difficult to keep pace with him.

She fingered the cool, silver handle of her

black leather purse, but the smoothness of its surface didn't provide the soothing effect she sought. Why had strength and logic deserted her?

A couple seated nearby burst into raucous laughter. Would she ever be able to do that again? Laugh with abandon?

Her life had gone into a tailspin for weeks before this tragedy occurred. Her only defense? Implement ironclad control over her entire life. That meant no tears, no reactions, and under no circumstances, any emotions. They only added fodder to an already over-fueled media firestorm. And now Chase dared to question her grief.

His blunt, rude, insensitive manner didn't deserve an answer, but she would give one anyway. "I was on a skiing trip in the French Alps. Iffy cell phone reception there, to say the least." She shuddered, remembering the horrifying news she'd heard. "I couldn't get a direct flight. Storms had rolled in and planes were delayed or cancelled. When I finally reached Mr. Pomeroy, he assured me that you'd given the funeral arrangements to him. It was a good decision, Chase, since neither of us knows much about the services available in this town."

She glanced at his fingers, large half-moons on each thumb. A sign of a sensuous person she'd read somewhere. Half-moons didn't affect her, but he did. Hadn't she had enough of men to last a lifetime?

She met his gaze and a sudden charge of electricity flashed through her. She lifted her fidgety hand, and touched her forehead.

"You think the French mountains lack cell phone reception?" His mouth twisted in a wry grin. "Try trekking into the interior of China."

What kind of business would take him to such a remote place? Or was it pleasure — according to Pam, Chase had no problem finding feminine company. Women flocked to him like ants to a picnic.

Now why did she think that? "What took you to China. A woman?" she blurted.

The candlelight from the red glass lamp flickered over his handsome features. His jaw tensed, but his smile reflected something else — a curious sense of satisfaction. "Not this time."

"My mistake," she managed to spit out while holding onto a shred of dignity.

At long last, his hands came to rest on the table in front of him. "When I got to Tokyo, I had to twist my boss' arm until he gave a final nod to my using the company jet. He's a hard-nosed guy. I got to Emerald Point late last night, so I didn't beat you here by much. I stayed at the motel."

A closer study of Chase's face revealed tired lines around his mouth, and dark shadows beneath his eyes. His fingers remained still, as though the smoothness of the table had quieted his mood.

A simple silence settled between them, not at all uncomfortable, until the perky waitress returned, body squirming in constant motion and eyes only for Chase. "Would you like anything else, honey?"

"Not for me." He glanced at Suzanne and smothered a smile when the woman leaned in toward him, "Nothing more, thanks." He dismissed the waitress without looking at her again.

"How long are you staying, Chase?"

"About a week."

"Will that be enough time?" She shook her head in disbelief. Pam. Tad. Jeff. And now she had to deal with this enigmatic man. "What will happen to Tad's lumber business? He worked so hard to establish it."

"Pomeroy mentioned a will, but until we know the contents, we have no legal rights. I suppose I could contact Tad's foreman to find out how things are going." He lowered his eyes. "Did you see Jeff this morning?"

She gritted her teeth, wanting to cry but

not allowing herself. "No. Poor kid. At three he won't understand his daddy and mommy aren't coming back."

Those relaxed hands clenched, the knuckles going white. "We'll work on that with him."

We? Right. He didn't have the sensitivity to console a child. "I'm sure I can manage by myself."

"I'm helping."

"Why?" If he stayed, she'd have to deal with the feelings he stirred in her, emotions best left dormant. "You didn't visit Tad and Pam very often."

His face tightened the slightest bit. Had she not been watching it would have gone unnoticed. "I came as often as I could." He stared at the carnations, picked them up and brushed them feather-like over the back of his hand. For a second, his eyes closed, and then he murmured, "Red for life, white for death."

Surprised that he'd voiced the same poignant thought she had earlier, Suzanne was mesmerized as he swirled the flowers until they blurred. A symbol of life — a blur of pain and remembrance of the two people she'd loved so much. That hurt so bad, she bit the inside of her cheek to forestall the ever present tears.

Slumped against the booth, she took another sip of the root beer. Cold, foamy, and definitely the wrong choice. A cup of steaming green tea would have warmed her. Instead, a chill corkscrewed through her. Because of the funeral? The cold, damp weather? Or the bewildering man seated across from her? Or maybe all three?

Behind her, the muted sounds of a newscast in progress could be heard. Chase stared over her shoulder; his eyes transfixed on something behind her. The chatty patrons fell quiet as heads shifted to the television over the bar.

Suzanne turned as the reporter's deferential voice filled the room. "The Garwoods were driving along the Ridge Route when their car spun out of control and plunged over the cliff. Authorities say there were no witnesses. At the funeral today —"

Suzanne froze. Her tortured mind silenced the reporter's words, but she couldn't block out the scenes of the wrecked car on the screen. Pam's favorite "red bug." Squashed. Mangled.

She turned away, unable to bear the terrible scene.

Chase stared at her, his lips white and tightly pressed. "You turned away too soon. The camera centered on you at the funeral, gave only a quick, cursory scan of the other mourners and caskets." He picked up his empty glass, fingers so tight she thought it might shatter. "You looked like a celebrity with those dark shades. But then . . . you are a celebrity, aren't you?"

"What cameras?" Her already racing heart kicked into a higher gear at the thought that the paparazzi had found her. "I didn't see any."

Scorn dripped from his voice. "Reporters were there."

Chase seem to see her only as a subject for the tabloids, that was all. At a time when her world had come to a sudden-death standstill, she craved sympathy.

Feeling the steel reassert itself in her spine, she let ice fill her voice. "Don't go there, Chase. You are what you are. I am what I am. If the camera focused on me, it was without my consent. I doubt they had any idea of my identity. Why should they? I have friends in New York who are celebrities, and trust me, I can't compete with them."

He leaned forward, his hand a hairsbreadth from touching hers. "I don't know why, Suzanne, but something about you sets me on edge."

She snatched back her hand, unsure

whether to laugh or cry. Unwillingly, the corners of her mouth curved up. "You know, Chase, disliking you would be very easy."

His frown revealed puzzlement. "Dislike — such an inane emotion. Now hate, love, those feelings make people interesting."

Tears pressed hard for release, but she would never let him know how much it cost her to hold them. She slanted him a frosty smile. "You're not very original."

He searched her face for lengthy moments before breaking the awkward silence. "Being sad and witty at the same time — not my style."

His style? She forced a laugh. To her ears, it sounded brittle. "Pam never mentioned you had a humorous side."

His left shoulder lifted and dropped. "Believe it or not, I do. But right now, humor is far from my mind."

Escape. She was trapped with him in Emerald Point until either he left for Tokyo, or she returned to New York. He'd said they should talk.

Well, she'd had enough of his nonspecific talk for one day. There was no need to stay in a place like this. With him. She shrugged and rose from her seat. "Let's go."

Chase caught her hand, the firm touch

sending sparks up her arm. "We should settle some things now."

She pulled away, her skin tingling. "I thought that's what we came here for today, but you've danced around anything of a serious nature."

Those blasted eyes never wavered. "There could be possible problems — legal ones."

He'd mentioned something like that before, but she hadn't paid attention. Neither of them had a legal background. If they were, indeed, facing legal issues, they would need a lawyer. Maybe one for each of them.

She sank farther back in the seat.

Chase leaned forward. "Don't tell me you haven't considered Jeff's future welfare?"

"Yes, I have," she retorted with a breath that almost choked her. "I've done nothing but think about him since getting that call and during those endless hours on planes and waiting in airport terminals."

"And?"

"He'll live with me."

A sense of foreboding swept over her as Chase's eyes narrowed. Fear squeezed her heart. Of course, Pam wanted her to raise Jeff. Until this moment, she hadn't thought about the impact the boy would make on her lifestyle. Or hers on him. She wasn't a coward, but right now, running as fast and as far as she could was the only logical action.

"Live with you?" he echoed, his voice sounding an ominous alarm.

Her chin shot up. "You have a problem with that?"

"You're always traveling. There's no permanence in your life. My nephew will not live in New York, cooped up in an apartment."

Did her face reveal the smoldering, baffling tension that had built up inside her from the moment they'd met? "You have another solution?"

He stared for what seemed an eternity. The message in his eyes meant what? That he'd made a decision, one that would alter her plans? She waited, aware of an acrid taste in her mouth and a chilly shroud surrounding her.

She laughed, the sound bitter to her ears. "You? You want custody? A bachelor who goes philandering around the wilds of China? What kind of life would that be?"

"In the boy's best interests, I feel he should be with me." Chase's fingers gripped the edge of the table. "If I'm not named guardian, I'll start court proceedings. One way or the other, I intend to have custody of Jeff."

3

Chase clenched his fists at his sides, tipping his head back to stare at the ceiling. He pinched the bridge of his nose. Jet lag. It had to be the weariness from traveling halfway around the world. Did he really think Suzanne would fall for his attempted intimidation with a custody battle? Honey worked with women. Threats and intimidation were for men.

He'd almost forgotten how to be nice to a woman. The statement he'd made to Suzanne that he'd fight for custody would enrage a saint.

Twin patches of crimson tinted her cheeks. Yep. He'd royally ticked her off and that would make her fight harder for Jeff.

Though lovely and gentle in many ways, she struck him as a person who seemed to have ironclad control over her emotions and reactions. Her soft, rich laughter nudged him from his resolve to stay free of entanglements. That reminder, in itself, should've punched his alarm buttons.

He narrowed his eyes. No woman would *ever* again lure him with a baited hook like Wendy had.

With a supreme effort on his part, he could win this argument with Suzanne and the battle for his nephew. He had to think about the child first, not this woman who sparked a desire he'd buried two years ago.

Fury charged through Suzanne's veins. "What did you say?"

A gleam of self-assurance filled those wicked silver eyes. "I'm taking Jeff with me to Tokyo."

Unbelievable. He had to be joking. "No."

"Why not? I'm sure that raising a child in the Orient might pose a challenge, but I'm up for it."

She had a vicious urge to smash the satisfied grin from his handsome face. A deep breath, then another calmed the impulse. "Is this a test of some kind? How is cooped up in Tokyo better than New York?" She waved off his reply. "There is no way I'm letting you take Jeff off to who knows where. He needs a woman, especially now, a mother's love, someone to patch up his physical wounds and comfort him. You can be sure he'll have lots of emotional issues in his future."

A force field crackled between them, one filled with electrical sparks and sizzling tension.

He muttered, "Yeah, doesn't every guy? Anyway, Jeff needs love and a father figure, too. I'll hire a nanny."

She looked him up and down, a sneer curling her lips. "That's not happening. What about Pam and Tad's wishes?"

Chase's expression turned frigid as the Alaskan tundra. Stubborn could have been written on his forehead the way his jaw clenched with determination. But then he sighed and covered her hand with his. "I don't want to fight with you."

His tone eased some of her distress, but his touch did little to quench the embers that smoldered between them.

Why did he keep touching her?

"I'm sure that's what both of them would have wanted for Jeff," he cajoled.

She yanked her hand away again, struggling to keep her voice steady. "I doubt that, but we'll see who they named as guardian. Whatever their will states, that's who will raise Jeff."

"They aren't here —"

The blunt, insensitive remark destroyed

her hard-fought-for calm. She leaped to her feet, hands on her hips, and shouted, "You'd dare go against their wishes? What kind of man are you, Chase Garwood?" Her stomach cramped until she thought she'd be sick. Serve him right if she puked over his expensive shoes.

His eyes glittered. "The kind you wouldn't understand."

Suzanne focused on his compressed lips, anything to avoid those penetrating eyes that saw way too much. "You're so right. I don't understand you and certainly not your motives."

For several uneasy seconds he measured her, and then tossed back the last of his drink. "Suppose Tad and Pam didn't name either of us as Jeff's guardian? Have you considered that?"

"Impossible. I'm certain they —"

"Right." He brushed a hand over his hair and, of course, the dark curls sprang into place. "This is all premature. We shouldn't even discuss it until we know Pam and Tad's decision."

The man was infuriating. What she would give to toss him out of her life. If she spoke even a single word right now, she'd blast him with all of her pent-up rage.

He stood, once again towering over her in

his proprietary way, his mouth twisted into a smile. "Let's go."

Share the small car's enclosure with him again? Breathe the same air and be privy to his self-serving schemes? No. She'd rather walk to her sister's house and get drenched in the downpour. A temporary solution at best since they would be living under the same roof until Jeff's future was settled. Besides, spite never won any battles, so why not be comfortable and ride along?

Suzanne pulled some bills from her purse and dropped them on the table before Chase could fumble in his wallet. Chin lifted in success, she tried to keep her smile from turning into one of his smirks.

The overconfident, arrogant man's nostrils flared. A moment now, then a quick nod, and he held her coat open.

Giving him her back, she slipped her arms in and tensed. His hands squeezed her shoulders. Heat prickled down her spine. Fine neck hairs stood on end. Why did he keep touching her?

Outdoors, the wind blew as hard as a category two hurricane. The cloud cover had thickened, leaving a chill in the air that only added to the conflicting, fiery and frosty sensations throbbing through her. Aggravated and more than a little distracted, without looking for approaching cars, she stepped off the curb and into the street.

Brakes screeched. A horn blared.

She gasped and stumbled back.

Chase grabbed her, whirled her around, and crushed her body against his. He blew out a startled breath. "Sheesh, woman. That was a close one."

The pickup truck that flew past had missed her by inches. Down the street, it pulled to the curb. A boy in his late teens hopped out and loped toward them. "Hey. Are you OK?" he squeaked, in an oxygen-deprived voice. "I didn't see you. I'm sorry."

Clasped against Chase's hard body, Suzanne sucked in air. Her limbs shook, and had he released her, she would have fallen to the concrete. She swept a trembling hand across her forehead. *I could have been killed.* Her breath whooshed out. "I'm fine. It was my fault."

"Are you sure?" At her nod, the teen trotted back toward his truck.

Chase grumbled, his voice taking on a cutting edge. "You're not in the city, Suzanne. There, no one looks before they step off the curb."

She gazed up at him, her body still pressed against his chest. If he dipped his handsome head a couple of inches, their lips would meet in a flash of fire.

She stepped back, shaking her head to rid herself of the inappropriate thought. It had to be all the stress messing with her brain. And her hormones. "Thank you," she whispered. "I feel so foolish."

And with a snap, his mood changed again. Gone was the cold, hard glitter in his eyes, replaced by something softer. Concern, maybe?

No, not concern. His earlier snide remarks made it clear he believed what the media had printed. Concern would be the last thing on his mind. Given the obstacle now posed regarding Jeff, Chase was probably kicking himself for pulling her to safety. A convenient accident would have cleared the way for him to spirit the boy away before she recovered.

"Devil," she muttered as he led her across the street.

When he opened the passenger door, and she eased inside, their fingers touched for one electric moment.

In the instant their eyes met, it was as if there was a magnetic pull. Again she pulled her hand away.

His eyes darkened. "You could tempt a man." He slammed the door so hard, her teeth rattled.

An inferno of need and want enveloped her. With ruthless determination, she smothered the feeling. Her mouth settled into a tightened line. Maddening man. Calculating, too. She wouldn't put it past him to try seduction to get his way.

He slid into the driver's seat, turned on the ignition, and pulled into a space in traffic.

She ran her hand over the leather upholstery of the seat and breathed in the car's scintillating scent. What an elegant interior. "Vic has good taste in cars."

He glanced at her. The intensity of his voice sent a chill galloping through her. "Yes, he does. He offered the use of this one when he picked me up at the airport. He's a kind and generous friend."

"I met him and Karen once." An unpleasant encounter she'd prefer to forget.

He drove with precision along the panoramic highway until the Garwood residence came into view. Perched on a bluff above the Pacific, framed by giant cypress, the imposing two-story English Tudor, with its rough-textured stucco exterior, reigned like a queen. Buffeted by the cold wind off the ocean and winter storms, most of the plants had gone dormant, leaving the house drab and sad, all vibrancy gone.

In the summer time, a profusion of roses and marigolds graced the manicured grounds. Thankfully, a new season would bring realization, and life would fall into a new normal. The world would go on.

People needed renewal, too. Suzanne certainly did.

Birds wheeled in the brisk air currents as Chase parked in the circular driveway.

Lara, the housekeeper, waited for them at the open front door. The shine of tears on her face belied her smile of welcome, but her greeting sounded sincere. "It's so good to see you, Mr. Chase."

"The same here, Lara." He folded his arms around her.

The woman swallowed hard. "It's been such a long time since you visited." Lara said in a quavering voice. Still, she exuded warmth. Slightly rounded, a more caring person for Jeff would be impossible to find.

Chase released her from his hug. "It's always too long."

Suzanne masked her surprise at Chase's gentleness with Lara, but fought back a flare of envy. Nothing she could do. He'd already made up his mind about her, but that didn't mean she'd allow his misinformed opinion to affect her. Once she and Jeff stepped aboard a plane headed for New York, it wouldn't matter.

He took her coat and hanged it in the closet before shrugging out of his own. His suit jacket followed, revealing a silky, white shirt clinging to a muscular chest. He folded back the cuffs as precise as though lining up for military inspection.

As he removed the somber tie, she couldn't drag her mesmerized gaze from his taut neck or the light dusting of hair that rested in the V of his shirt. A rubber band encircled his right wrist, digging into his flesh.

Hadn't she already convinced herself that men, all men, were trouble? The physical strength it took to look away drained her. She wouldn't stand a chance against him. The man was deadly, and she'd be wise to not underestimate him. Who was she kidding?

Lara wiped a tear from her cheek and announced, "Lunch will be ready in the dining room in twenty minutes. Oh, and Mr. Pomeroy called again. His wife will be released from the hospital later today."

"Thank you." Suzanne hugged the gray-haired woman, who then fled to the kitchen.

An idea flashed through her mind. Lara loved Jeff and knew him better than anyone else. Could she tempt the housekeeper to move with her and the boy to New York? A perfect solution, one that was too perfect, but worth a try. Once the lawyer read the will, naming her guardian, she'd go to Lara with an offer.

Suzanne glanced around the entry and living room with its luxurious pale apricot carpet, the mixture of contemporary and antique furniture, and copies of seascapes — among them a Homer and a Monet. The quiet elegance spoke of her sister's good taste in art. But no photographs graced the interior.

Ghost-like silence surrounded them and prompted a shiver. She half expected to hear Pam's laughter, Tad's chiding, or the childish prattle from Jeff. Where was the boy?

Grief, cold and dreary, returned with a rush. She choked and stifled a sob. Did Chase feel the same depth of loss?

"It's not the same without Tad and Pam." As if he read her mind, Chase answered her unspoken question. "When I heard they'd eloped, I was so glad he'd found someone."

She was alone in the world now. Her sister, her only relative, except Jeff, was gone. Loneliness and confusion mingled with her memories. Would the hole in her heart ever heal?

A war whoop broke the silence.

Jeff bounded down the stairs, his eyes sparkling like polished amber.

Suzanne kneeled and caught her nephew's sturdy young body in her arms. His uninhibited joy banished her sadness. "Hello, Jeff, sweetheart."

He planted a wet kiss on her cheek before wriggling away. "Unca Chase."

Chase swooped Jeff into the air, wresting a giggle from the boy.

A twinge of jealousy nipped at Suzanne's pride. From Jeff's childish, happy cries, it was easy to see the obvious enthusiasm for his only uncle. If he could choose, whom would he pick to spend his life with?

Back on his feet, Jeff took both their hands and led them up the stairs and past his huge bedroom. "Come see. Mommy got me teddy."

In the corner of his playroom stood a five-foot stuffed brown bear, wearing a yellow golfer's cap on his head and a silly, lopsided grin. Jeff wrapped his arms around the animal as far as he could reach.

In that instant of childlike innocence, Suzanne met Chase's eyes. One side of his mouth curved up. She smiled back. Oh, my, that devastating soft side was back. What would it be like if he turned it on her?

But then, her practical side returned. How

on earth could she take the bear *and* Jeff on a plane?

A brief safari through the rest of the boy's stuffed animals plus an exhausting inspection of every toy he owned, elicited appropriate *oohs* and *aahs* for Jeff's menagerie. Her heart melted at the giggles and a boyish grin that curved his sweet mouth.

Moving downstairs and into the dining room, Lara settled Jeff in his booster seat, and Chase and Suzanne sat on either side of him.

The main entrée, a crab casserole, smelled amazing, and made Suzanne's mouth water. But her appetite failed. She only nibbled a small portion. After a few bits of the accompanying salad, she declined fruit compote. Her thoughts kept straying to the prospect of uprooting Jeff and how she could minimize the impact on him. Provided Lara would come and continue to look after him, and with his array of toys, surely the transition would be manageable. Pam and Tad had often been away from him. Perhaps he wouldn't miss them too much. Huh. She could wish.

Jeff grinned and chattered throughout the meal, the lunch providing a much-needed reprieve from her sparring with Chase.

She studied Chase when she thought he

wasn't looking. He seemed different in the boy's presence, more animated, friendly, even. Could Chase be someone she might consider a friend?

Doubtful.

After all she'd been through in New York, a man in her life didn't rank very high on her needs list, not even as a friend.

After the meal, Lara took Jeff to watch his favorite television program.

Suzanne strolled into the solarium, unwilling to engage with Chase. The heady scent of flowers filled the room. Recessed lights cast delicate warmth on hyacinths and paper-white narcissus blossoms. Schefflera stood in the corners and flower print cushions on the wicker furniture added to the cozy atmosphere. Outside, dark clouds billowed across a leaden sky. Even inside, the weather here chilled the bones.

Suzanne reached for a black leather book on an end table with Pam's initials stamped in gold on the front. Her sister's Bible. With a smile of fondness and a heartfelt sigh, she flipped through the pages.

Grief struck her anew. The façade she'd kept in place all day threatened to crumple under this fresh onslaught of loss. A deep breath helped. Another, even more.

The well-worn Bible opened to a page

with stenciled stars in the margin and Pam's notes alongside the Scriptures. They must have been special to her sister.

John 11:25 *Jesus said unto her, I am the resurrection, and the life; he that believeth in Me, though he were dead, yet shall he live.*

The message pierced Suzanne's soul until she could barely breathe. Was finding the Bible a gift to her from the Lord? *Oh, how I wish...*

She returned the Bible to the end table and picked up a magazine.

When Chase entered, she was caught by surprise, but she refused to look at him even after he took a seat across from her. She pretended to be engrossed in the magazine article, but in truth the words defied translation, dancing across the page like an army of ants.

Undaunted by her disregard, he pulled up a land line and dialed. When his efforts to reach the attorney proved unsuccessful, he dialed another number. This one connected with the manager of Tad's lumber business. The two spoke for a while, then Chase hung up, and he leaned against the chair and closed his eyes. "Nothing urgent at the mill, thank God."

Twenty quiet minutes passed, and neither acknowledged the other, awkward and yet curiously not uncomfortable. The words in the magazine continued to elude her — how long since she'd turned a page? She soon found herself nodding off.

Chase didn't seem to have the same problem. His fingers moved with restless rhythm on the armrest. At long last he leaned forward, grabbed the phone again, and punched in another number. "This is Garwood again. Is Mr. Pomeroy available?"

Thirty seconds of silence followed before he spoke again. "Thank you for taking care of the funeral arrangements for us." He listened and nodded. "Glad your wife is better."

They spoke for a few more minutes about inanities, and then Chase asked, "How soon can we meet with you?"

While the conversation ensued, Suzanne's mind drifted back to the funeral and the crushing weight of sadness it brought.

Chase grumbled and dropped the receiver into its cradle.

Startled, she looked up.

"Tomorrow. Ten o'clock."

She nodded and lowered her gaze to the magazine once more. Her stomach rumbled, not from hunger but with a tingle of unease. And with Chase's gaze on her, when she looked up and met his gaze, she had to fight the hold of his stare-off. Men were such bold creatures.

As the grandfather clock ticked away the seconds, she sought for something to say. Nothing. She had nothing. Her brain had failed her again.

Rising from the chair, she dropped the magazine on the end table and headed for the door. If she couldn't do better in words, she would run. Better than remaining and get emotionally beaten to a pulp. "It's stopped raining. I'm going for a walk."

"I'll go with you." He jumped up and in two strides was at her side.

She sighed and put up her hand. "I'd rather be alone."

"Why?"

How could she make plans for Jeff and their future if he kept interrupting her thoughts? She needed her wits to contend with this domineering man, but his mere presence scattered her brain like dandelion fluff. "I want to clear my mind and think."

"What were you doing until now?" When she gave him a puzzled look, he nodded toward the magazine.

"Reading."

He laughed. "That's quite an accomplishment. I've known people who read backwards but not upside down."

She glanced at the magazine. He was right. Despite the emotions he stirred in her, she snickered. The guy was too observant and crafty.

She strode past him and climbed the stairs. Her wool pants, a royal-blue T-shirt and off-white, sherpa-lined leather jacket would be warm enough. She studied herself in the mirror before heading down the stairs with every intention of evading Chase.

And, of course, there he stood in the entry way, a brown paper bag in his hand, watching every step she took like a hawk eyeing its next victim.

Hysteria fizzed inside her. She steeled herself to ignore how handsome he looked in jeans and a bomber jacket. When she reached the bottom step, she whispered, "Can't you leave me alone with my thoughts?"

"I don't think I can." Confusion, interest, and some other emotion she couldn't identify crossed his handsome face before he schooled it into his go-to-look of insolent disdain.

"So, will your presence keep me from grieving?"

His gaze brushed over her. "No. That's something each of us has to do for ourselves. My goal of joining you is to try and figure out what you're really like."

Her laugh sounded hoarse and distressed. "I thought you had me all pegged, wrapped in old newspaper, and tossed out like day-old fish."

He snorted before leaning in to whisper, "No, never that. Pink plastic wrap maybe, so I can peek through and see what makes you tick."

The softened quality of his words created a quick tension in her body. "I wish I understood you, Chase. At times you're gentle, even kind, but then you turn tough as steel." She winced. "And as irritating as poison ivy."

He furrowed his brow and gave an open-handed gesture. "If I'm changeable, perhaps it's because of what I've heard about you over the past few years — doesn't mesh with what's standing before me."

"I don't buy that."

She caught a glimpse of vulnerability and uncertainty in the way his shoulders sagged. "I . . . looked in Tad and Pam's room. Right now, I'm hurting and don't want to bear it alone."

His confession took courage that she couldn't summon. Had she done that, her brain would shatter into a thousand pieces.

Chase puzzled and distracted her, but having someone who could understand and share the grief might be a comfort.

She jammed on a ball cap, the bill on backward. Certain she couldn't deter him, she murmured, "All right, let's go for that walk."

4

Chase opened the back door and allowed Suzanne to precede him. A feathery breeze tossed her hair. Fists clenched, he once again fought the urge to caress the soft, silken strands and bury his face in them. Why did she draw him? Would she purr or scratch out his eyes?

Emotions raced through him that hadn't surfaced in two years. Jealousy, hatred, desire. Love? Ha. That was a bit like death . . . and who needed it?

When he considered Suzanne's past, his thoughts were conflicted. His responses to her snapped from him like teeth on a rabid fox. She'd rejected the Broadway actor who professed his love for her. Tad had told him that after an explosive argument in a nightclub, she'd boarded a jet to get away. Derek, the actor, had shot up with drugs, and then attempted to put a bullet in his skull. The jilted man's life was saved by a friend's quick thinking, and he recovered, but he'd given a sordid, one-sided story to the tabloids. Fresh blood to the news media, they ran with the story.

Had she realized how desperate the actor had become? Chase pulled up short. No, he wouldn't make excuses for her. She probably deserved the bad publicity. And why should he care?

The path that led from the cliffs to the sand proved to be a challenge. Their sneakers slid as they bounded from one wet rock to another and then a final leap to the soft sand.

As she matched his lengthy stride along the beach, her chin lifted to catch the breeze. Though she appeared calm, he sensed underlying tension. Was she scheming right now for a way to get Jeff? Never back down from a confrontation — his byword for dealing with adversaries. A good fight, that's what he'd give her, even if she didn't want one.

He sneaked a peek at her sideways. She displayed strength in her body language, more so than in what she said. But inside, would she shatter like fragile crystal if he challenged her for the boy?

It puzzled him how Suzanne ignited a flame that simmered within him. She intrigued him more than any other woman, before or since Wendy. He couldn't interpret the signals she sent. As a rival for Jeff, that alone should keep him focused on the boy and not her.

He forced his mind back to the immediate problem — raising Jeff as his own, the son he would never otherwise have. He wouldn't marry, that was a given. Tad and their father's lives, as well as so many of Chase's colleagues had shown him plainly how a woman could make a man's life miserable. And he'd nearly married that witch, Wendy.

He shook off a renewed case of the shakes. He'd come close. She'd walked out on him, doing him a huge favor, he'd come to realize over time.

His mouth twitched, wanting to curl into a smile. He should send a case of Scotch to that rich, aging, stuffed-shirt English lord who'd carried Wendy off to his castle.

Suzanne glanced up and shielded her eyes as a gull flew low and flapped its wings. She laughed, breaking the silence that stretched between her and Chase. "Never look up when a bird flies by."

He cocked his head, met her gaze, and watched as they grew misty. Uninvited warmth infused his voice, freeing a bubble of laughter. "Pam and I walked along this beach a couple of years ago. A pelican splattered her hair."

Suzanne winced. "Ugh. And how did she react?"

He stared at the rock-strewn, wave-lapped shoreline. "She giggled. You know that silly little snicker that was so much a part of her? What I remember — I guess it's the little stuff she said and did."

The brief, almost intimate mention of Pam's devil-may-care attitude struck an added chord of grief inside of Suzanne. A sigh escaped her. "As a child, Pam often fell off her tricycle and bike. Though her knees and elbows stayed skinned and bloodied, she never cried. Our mom had no maternal instincts, so when I was seven, she insisted I take care of Pam, and I did. Until she left New York and married Tad." Suzanne continued on a wistful note that twisted her own heartstrings. "Did you realize Pam could hide her true feelings with laughter?"

His gaze vacant, a grimace flickered across his face. "I guess I never studied her that close. Do you know what went wrong with their marriage?"

"I never asked."

He gave her a lengthy stare, like peering

through shutters. "Since when don't women exchange confidences?"

"Not something that personal. If I'd been married, I wouldn't tell the world why my relationship had failed."

"Yeah, but she was your sister. You mean you and her never traded secrets?"

Puffy clouds billowed into strange formations that paraded across the sky. Was Pam looking down at them from beyond the Pearly Gates? Suzanne recalled their spirited arguments, leaving her filled with frustration. "At eighteen, I worked, attended college, and looked after my baby sister. I didn't have much time for secrets or anything else, but I did my best by her."

A clamshell crunched beneath his sneakers. "You think that's why life went wrong between her and Tad, because you didn't give her enough time?"

"Oh, yeah, blame me. I don't know what went wrong." She groaned. "Pam was a little wild growing up, but never got into any real trouble. And she was always loyal." She rounded on him. "Are you putting her life under a microscope? Whatever happened between them might have been Tad's fault."

Chase shrugged. "I need a lot of answers before I can rest again. One doesn't lose a brother . . ." A raw gust of wind carried away the rest of his words.

She ached from the agony of her loss and his. She no longer wanted to talk about dead people. "Wouldn't it be better if we changed the subject?"

When he touched her arm, she stopped to face him.

His hand slipped back to his side. "Do my questions make you uncomfortable?" His smoky gaze bored into hers. "Do you know something I don't?"

She'd always suspected Pam kept secrets. Drawing in a breath of salty, pungent air, Suzanne focused on the foam that splashed against the rocks. A lone black oystercatcher skittered about in its search for limpets and snails, and then hurried ashore ahead of a wave. "I doubt I could tell you anything that would ease your mind."

Chase extended the brown bag. "Lara gave us her fabulous potato crunchies."

"They're my favorite." She grabbed a few and sampled the delicious chips.

"Mine, too." He crunched on one. "Let's talk about you."

Yeah, interrogate her like the cops and journalists did in New York, skewering her with questions about Derek's actions. A spurt of irritation bubbled just below the surface. "Why? My personal life has been splashed across the tabloids. Why don't we talk about yours instead?"

He studied her, and then gave an offhand shrug. "OK. What would interest you about me?"

"I guess . . . everything."

"I weighed seven-pounds, nine ounces when I came into this world."

She snickered and jabbed him with her elbow — the first time she'd initiated any physical contact with him. "Not that far back."

His eyes shone with mischievous innocence. "You said *everything*, so I obliged."

He was so changeable — a quick flash of vexation or his mellow side kept her off-balance. If they'd known each other a dozen years, she'd still be unsure of how to react.

She munched on a handful of the crunchies, and then licked the residue from her fingers. "What's happened in your life, let's say the past few years? I heard something about a woman."

"She is ancient history."

They sauntered along the wet, hard-packed sand. A seal basked in the sunbeams that broke through the cloud cover on a distant rock. It raised its head to bark at them. Offshore, sea otters frolicked in the kelp.

Chase picked up a stone and skimmed it across the waves. "For the past six years I've worked for an Alaskan shipping company, first in Anchorage, and then I transferred with a promotion to general manager at their branch office in Japan. I'm in charge of contracts. Exports, imports, lumber, and supplies. I travel some."

She scooped up a shell, examined it, found it broken and let it drop to the sand. "And how often do you leave Tokyo?"

He hesitated. "Three or four times a year."

"Where do you live?"

He squinted at her as though dissecting the reasons for her questions. "I have a two-bedroom house outside the city."

"Oh." She peered at him and grabbed her bottom lip with her teeth before quipping, "Do you have your own geisha?"

His smile was anything but friendly. "Now who's judging. You don't know what a geisha does. Why don't you just ask if I have a mistress? That might convince a judge I wouldn't be a fit parent."

A twitchy sensation rippled through her. She despised and avoided manipulative people. He thought she was doing that when she merely offered a simple question.

"Did you think I'd give you ammunition in our private war?" he snapped. "Never underestimate the opposition."

"Is this war, Chase? I suppose Jeff is the spoils?" She had the urge to give him a swift kick. It was all she could do not to give in to the impulse. "If that's the way you want it, I would suggest you never underestimate a woman."

"Nor a determined man."

She snorted. " 'The female of the species is more deadly than the male'."

With a sarcastic grin, he leveled a firm gaze at her. "How did Kipling sneak into this conversation?"

"It was a memorable quote. I'm not trying to outwit you. That's not my style."

He stepped up his pace, as though working off energy or perhaps some form of agitation. "You shouldn't try so hard. Perhaps tomorrow we'll hear I've been named Jeff's guardian."

She rolled her eyes and strode on ahead of him. "Yeah, in your dreams. If Pam had any say in the decision, and I believe she did, then I'll be Jeff's new guardian."

His fingers pinched the bridge of his nose. A grimace flashed on his face.

"What's wrong?" she asked with a dose of compassion. What had gone right since she got here?

"I get headaches once in a while."

"Stress?"

He nodded, blew out a breath, and squeezed his eyes shut.

Wind whipped hair across her face. She yanked off the cap, pulled a crimson knitted hat from her pocket and tugged it to cover her ears. "Would it help if we sat on a boulder for a while? Would that ease your headache?"

"No. Only one thing works."

"What's that?"

He reached in his pocket, withdrew keys and a small plastic vial, and popped a tablet into his mouth.

Thoughts of Derek returned to haunt her. He'd turned her life into a fish bowl, and she was the lone guppy. Was Chase a junkie, too?

Ah. She'd jumped to conclusions. Controlling that bad habit would take concentration on her part.

When she spotted a polished jade stone attached to his key ring, she winced. A wave of jealousy surfaced, and she pulled a set of keys from her own pocket and held out a similar stone.

A pulse throbbed in Chase's throat. "Seems each of us thought we had a unique gift from Jeff, huh?"

5

Suzanne sidestepped the incoming ocean swells, almost bumping into Chase. "Yes," she whispered.

Chase nodded and kicked a shell. "Jeff found the stones on a beach up the coast a couple of months ago. Tad sent it with a funny crayon picture."

She sniffed and lifted her chin. "I'd assumed mine was the only one."

"Are you jealous, Miss Bratton? You thought the boy only cared about you."

He had that annoying look on his face again — the one that made her defensive, as though she had to justify her behavior.

"Jeff's very affectionate." Her voice spiked upward. "And I certainly love him."

The sudden contrast of white teeth against Chase's sun-bronzed skin struck her. His charisma like a weapon, he turned it on and off at will. Resentment rose swiftly, leaving a knot in her stomach.

His smile vanished. "So, you *can* display some emotion."

Without breaking stride, she dipped her hand into the bag, drew out more crunchies, and popped them in her mouth. "Heaven forbid. I wouldn't want to alter your biased opinion of me."

For a moment his mouth twitched, and then the tightness around his eyes returned. Was he hurting? At times he'd given *her* a pain in the neck. Too bad a pill couldn't take care of that.

His short, derisive laugh jerked her back to the topic they'd been discussing. "At least we've established that Jeff cares for both of us."

"Of course he does. Why shouldn't he?" A tiny temptation made her add, "You can visit him any time you're in New York."

"You mean when you're in Tokyo," he shot back.

A breeze ruffled Chase's hair. One dark lock spilled across his forehead, giving him a boyish look.

Suzanne glanced away. His too-tense features negated any youthfulness. The man was wound tight as a spring. He would never give up control of any situation.

When she'd first arrived, there'd been no doubt in her mind that Jeff would become hers. But the sheer magnitude of Chase's bravado and confidence had her dubious about the outcome. She feared he would do whatever it took to outmaneuver her.

Angry clouds loomed overhead. Sporadic raindrops splashed against her face and outstretched hand. "We'd better make a run for it."

He tucked the bag of chips into his jacket pocket, took her hand, and set off at a jog toward the path leading up the cliff.

Surging wind gusts stung her skin. Before they'd gone very far, her lungs were laboring. Over the past several weeks, she'd attended fashion shows in Paris, lazed about in a French mountain chateau, and never once considered skiing, even though the resort facilities beckoned to her.

The wet stones made their progress up the cliff difficult. After several missteps, they reached the landing. No way could she hide her heavy breathing from him, but neither would she give him the satisfaction of slowing down to catch her breath. Together they charged past the back patio to the kitchen door.

Lara hurried over to them, and took their wet jackets. "You should have taken a couple of umbrellas," she chided. "There are several in the elephant foot stand."

Suzanne's sneakers squished on the kitchen floor. She toed them off while pulling at the knit cap. Wet hair plastered her head. Not her best look. Was there time to blow-dry?

The thought caught her off guard. She didn't need to impress *anyone,* especially not Chase. She didn't care what he thought of her looks. Yeah, right.

She excused herself, grabbed the bag of chips from his pocket, grinned at his upraised eyebrows, and then bolted up the stairs, aware of each footstep on the treads. A prickling sensation tickled her shoulders. Halfway up, she turned. Chase and Lara watched. Lara, with her mouth open, and Chase with a look of puzzlement. A moment later, the stoic mask he usually wore returned.

Lara sent a considering glance to both of them. "When you come down, I'll have a warm drink for you. Do you want tea, coffee, hot chocolate?"

"Tea would be fine," Suzanne continued up the stairs. "Thanks, Lara."

Minutes later, her grateful body sank into a frothy tub of lavender bubbles. A semblance of peace settled over her and brought a respite from the rawness of her grief. Enough to allow her mind to mull over what had transpired since the funeral. Away from Chase's overwhelming presence, her mind cleared enough to consider what she knew of him. What had Pam told her?

Thought fragments filled her head, vague details of Tad's mysterious brother. Having never met him, he'd always seemed shadowy, unreal, a fictional character.

If only she'd seen his picture earlier, she might have had a better chance to deal with him. Sighing, she shook her head. No pictures would do him justice. A dozen adjectives couldn't have prepared her for a player of his caliber.

A half-hour later, dressed in a pale gold sweater and emerald woolen pants, she descended the stairs. A striped scarf at her neck, in darker shades of green and gold, complemented the gold and emerald. She'd featured the coordinated pieces in her boutiques and within days, the racks were picked bare.

Voices carried to her through the kitchen door, but the only thing she could make out was her name. Not wanting to eavesdrop, even though curious about what he had to say about her, she strode through the archway with her head held high.

Conversation ceased as three pairs of eyes looked her way.

"Jeff, how are you, sweetheart?" She stooped to kiss the boy's silken cheek and gave him a quick hug.

His cherubic face smiled up at her. "You bring present?"

"Oh, honey, I'm sorry. With all that happened," she glanced at Chase and Lara, "I forgot. How about we go to town tomorrow and let you choose a toy? Does that sound OK?"

"Unca Chase takes me after nap."

Her nemesis looked delectable — not smug — in a maroon sweatshirt and form-fitting jeans. A half-smile played at the corners of his mouth as he let his gaze take inventory of her.

Did he know Jeff had recuperated from a viral infection only two weeks ago? Had he ever considered the risk of taking him out in the cold, damp weather? Too late, Chase had already promised . . .

"OK. After your nap, we'll dress you in warm clothes and go with Uncle Chase." Suzanne turned to Chase, and propped a hand on her hip, lifting one eyebrow in challenge. *Make your next crafty move, buster.*

"Yay." Jeff squealed, his chubby little legs pumping in giddy eagerness.

Lara covered her mouth and turned away. "Talk about spoiling a child."

Chase lifted his coffee cup to her before taking a sip. "That's what uncles are for."

Jeff wriggled off his booster seat and trotted upstairs with Lara, his voice excited and sweet.

Suzanne took the seat across from Chase and sipped a cup of fragrant jasmine tea. An uncomfortable silence surrounded them, making her search for something to fill the void. Instead of witty and brilliant, what came out was anything but. "You like children. How come you never married?"

His eyebrows slanted in a frown. "Children I can take. Women I can't."

"Which means?"

He stared at the rose-colored linen tablecloth, his fingers tracing the flowered pattern. "I learned a few years ago, back when I was young and foolish, that women can't be trusted. I decided then that remaining a bachelor was an infinitely better destiny."

She laughed. "So, now you're *old* and foolish?" Sobering, she said, "She burned you pretty bad, didn't she?"

He shrugged. "I've seen too many unhappy couples who took a chance on marriage. Divorce is ugly." As though the words were wrenched from him, he added, "Personally, I don't need the trauma."

"Not all marriages end in divorce."

A tiny flame leaped in his eyes. "Why aren't *you* married?"

He had nothing in common with the men she knew. Did he expect sympathy from her? Was his projected air of mystery meant to charm her? "What's the reason for the headaches? And what are those pills you're taking?"

"I get tense at times." He held up the vial. "It's a prescription drug for migraines."

"Uh-huh," she said. "I heard that before." She'd never forget the toll illegal drugs had taken on Derek.

Chase's fingers clenched around the vial. His knuckles whitened. "You think I'm a junkie?"

"That's not what I said. But it's common knowledge that many addictions start out under the guise of doctor-prescribed medicines." She could add details about Derek that would make Chase's hair turn green. The way his mouth tightened stopped her.

The dark wings of his brows formed a straight line. "It's obvious you don't trust me."

Heavy silence loomed between them again, but she refused to look away.

Did he really expect a reply? "I hardly know you. Besides, why should I trust you? You threaten my plans for Jeff." When his eyes narrowed, she added, "At this point in my life, I find it safer not to trust most people."

"You mean men. You've given up on them?"

Even if his charm was a bit overpowering, she wouldn't admit it. "Let's just say I've shelved relationships for a while. A lot of other things keep me occupied."

"That's safe and unexciting."

"Unexciting is how I want it for now. And you're one to talk, Mr. Anti-women."

He seemed to weigh each of her words as though ready to pounce on anything that might be used against her. Fatigued and overwhelmed by the constant battle and the resultant uncertainty of a future with Jeff, a yawn crept up on her.

She stifled it behind a hand and got up to leave. "I have some business calls to make before we go shopping for Jeff's gifts. See you later."

Why was she explaining? She didn't owe him anything.

"Business calls, huh? Don't you mean thinking up a new counteroffensive?"

Halfway to the door, her steps halted. The tone of his voice sounded light, almost teasing, but the content sent waves of distress through her. With a look over her shoulder, she met those shell-gray eyes framed by sooty lashes, certain her face reflected the wound he'd inflicted. This man's constant attack left her scrambling for defenses.

"You heard right." He spoke softer, in a more mellow pitch, his eyes cast down.

She slumped back in her chair. "I am making sure my boutique managers are fine. And, for your information, it's only being responsible. The task of raising a child is a huge undertaking. I want to ensure that I will be able to provide for him. In a business, there's always a chance of failure."

"Life can be boring without taking some risks." At her snort, he looked up.

"Who says I haven't?" She didn't wait for a reply, but rushed on. "I took a risk when I opened my first store. That was a big gamble. I travel. These days, that's really taking chances. And I do have a social life, despite what happened in the past. Lord knows that's a crapshoot. I have experience caring for a child. Remember, I raised Pam. What are your qualifications?"

"So you say, but can you prove it?"

Heat stole up her cheeks.

"Go ahead, say what you mean. Or are you concerned you might bruise my sensitive emotions?" His mouth twitched. "That you might hurt me like you did that actor friend of yours in New York?"

"*Your* sensitive emotions?" she snapped. "A granite boulder has more sensitivity than you. And you have no idea what you're talking about regarding Derek." Why did the slightest reminder of Derek bring out the worst in her?

"You dish out the barbs," he said in a silky tone, "and you have a quick mind."

She took a sip of tea. "Yeah, lay it on thick, mister. I don't fall for such praise."

"Take it as a compliment." He placed his hand over hers.

Twisting free, she backed away, heart slamming against its ribcage.

His lips curled as if on the edge of laughter, and his gaze slid to her hands clenched tight at her sides.

A rush of restless, painful longing swept over her, the sensation so sharp, so poignant, an anguished moan passed her lips.

"Suzanne."

"Don't," she whispered.

"Don't what? Don't fight you? I have the energy for that and more."

Had she fanned the sparks between them without realizing it? "You might want to save all that pent-up drive for the legal battle."

Devilment danced in his eyes. "Your

concern about my stamina is touching," he purred. "I take vitamins."

Against her will, a grin tried its best to break free. "I'm not sure why I'm asking this, but how many other nasty pills do you take?"

He paused. "Ah. There's the real Suzanne Bratton."

Her stomach curled into a knot. Why did he affect her this way? "I guess you can take credit for bringing out the worst in me."

"From what I've heard, I'm not the first man to do that." A sense of urgency spilled into his voice. "I read some of Ramon Avelero's book."

An indictment. Nothing Chase said could have quenched the volatile feeling she had for him more.

Ramon — quick tempered and passionate. From the first time they'd met, she'd refused to date him. When flowers and expensive jewelry didn't work, he tried to influence her friends and clients to plead his case. Nothing broke her will, though he'd vowed revenge. One of Argentina's richest and most powerful men, he'd told the world about the "Ice Maiden" in his memoirs. Most of which were lies. After Derek's attempted suicide, everyone believed Ramon, even her so-called friends.

"I hope you enjoyed that fiction."

"Enjoyed? No, not really, but it revealed a lot about you. Tad loaned me his copy."

She wouldn't let him see how deep his remarks cut into her. "So now you know what you know. Are you disappointed?"

"I doubt you could disappoint any man." His mouth had softened. Had he forgotten his headache for the moment?

Feeling raw inside, she turned and started toward the solarium. "I'll be back when Jeff is ready to leave."

"Another time, another place, maybe the situation between us might have been different." Had a wistful note crept into his voice?

She stopped, planted her hands on her hips and turned to face him. "Another planet, a millennium, perhaps." She kept her tone even, though emotions strangled her. She should have been an actress, for she could hide her true feelings. At least she hoped so, this time. Ice Maiden, indeed.

6

Chase's hands clenched at his sides. Even as the friction between him and Suzanne built, on some level he was drawn to her. The momentary glimpse of fire in her eyes heated his blood. Did hidden passions flow through her?

As a rule, men didn't fall for women who displayed no outward compassion, but she'd affected both Derek and Ramon. And despite what he knew, Chase had let his defenses down, as a result, his own resolve had weakened.

Until Wendy, he'd pursued only women who looked on a relationship the same way he had — no strings, no commitments, and no emotional involvement. Wendy's perfidy had made him both break that philosophy, and then reclaim it.

Tad and Pam's unhappy marriage should keep him on the straight and narrow — and single. Farther back, another shattering example, his parents' angry clashes, with chilling threats and verbal abuse.

"I'll see you about three," Suzanne said.

For a moment Chase only saw her lips move. Then his brain put it all together. He nodded. She turned, and strode out of the room, her slim hips moving in a gentle sway. Long, well-shaped legs increased the distance between them.

Outside the glass doors, the storm's savagery left him with a similar tumult raging inside him. Lightning and thunder rattled the house. Fierce rain battered the windows. How much turbulence could the glass withstand? How much could he take?

He'd thought of himself as tough and strong, but headaches had plagued him the past few months and sapped his strength as well. His job and boss weren't his main problems at the moment.

With a shrug, he headed past the solarium, where the subject of his distraction made her phone calls.

More important matters demanded his concentration right now.

He trotted up the stairs and hesitated in the doorway of the master bedroom where his brother had shared their private sanctuary with the love of his life. One step inside, he stopped. Soft murmurs whispered greetings. Tad's voice and Pam's. Did their dreams and hopes linger here? Their fears and tears?

That thought left a leaden weight in his belly. The shaving gear and toothpaste in this room would wait forever for Tad's hand. His suits, shirts, jeans, and shoes in the huge walk-in closet would never again feel his touch.

Forcing another step forward, Chase's courage faltered. Devastation dropped him to his knees as a trail of grief rolled down his cheeks. He gritted his teeth and brushed them away. But they kept falling.

His brain had processed the shock of Tad's death, but his heart had gone into self-preservation mode. Autopilot had gotten him through the days to this point, allowed him to plan the next steps for his nephew's future.

Here, in Tad's room, now in this moment when nothing was expected of him, the fortress protecting his heart crumbled. Numbness receded. Grief, that insatiable devourer of emotion, exposed all the terrible, gut-wrenching, heartbreaking feelings he'd suppressed. Reality flayed him.

Time passed in a blur, whether two minutes or two hours, Chase had no idea. Eventually, the bottomless well of emotion slowed to a trickle and some of the insulating numbness returned. The big brother he'd adored, the one who'd looked out for him after their parents divorced, was dead. Even after Pam took priority in his brother's life, they'd remained close.

A fresh deluge of tears fell as he wondered what he would do without his best friend.

Holding himself in check, he went down the stairs.

Suzanne finished the calls to her business associates and took a much-needed moment to relax. Outside the storm unleashed its wrath, pelting the glass with wave after wave of furious rain. Inside felt like the eye of a hurricane. Calm. Serene.

On the table beside her lay one of Pam's Bibles. Did she spend time with the Lord here? More out of curiosity than for any other reason, Suzanne wanted to read the Scriptures her sister had marked.

Did she have the right to intrude on Pam's passion for Jesus? Did she have time?

Suzanne shook her head and glanced at her watch. Ten minutes to three.

Placing the Bible on the side table, she hurried back to the kitchen, hearing Jeff's giggles before he came into view.

Lara had bundled the tot into red ski

pants and matching parka that made him look like a tiny devil, which he could be at times.

Chase joined them a moment later. "Ready to go, buddy?"

"Yeah, ready to go." Jeff wriggled free of Lara's grasp and ran toward the garage door.

Minutes later in the car, he kicked the back of Suzanne's seat, his happy chortles sparking a smile from her.

Beside her, Chase grinned, but kept his focus on the road.

Ahead, an animal control truck blocked Seaward Avenue. A man in a white uniform scooped up the carcass of a cat.

Chase slowed to a stop. Suzanne looked back at Jeff.

"Poor kitty." His lower lip trembled at seeing the dead animal.

"Yes." This wasn't the time for the boy to witness such an unfortunate incident.

"Kitty goes heaven?"

She touched his hand in an effort to comfort him. "I hope so."

"See his mommy and daddy?"

She nodded. Her heart ached. There were no words she could say that would make the child feel better.

The truck moved on, and Chase turned

the car into a parking space. "Now," he said, "let's do some serious shopping."

Jeff clapped his hands. His childish mind leaped from grief for the cat to expectant joy.

She could only pray that when he heard about the loss of his parents, he'd react in a similar manner.

Exiting the car with Chase's help, Jeff skipped along between them while holding onto their hands. Anyone who watched them amble along the street would see what appeared to be a happy family.

In a toy store, Jeff chose an inexpensive stuffed alligator. He gave out a whoop when Suzanne nodded. She held onto it for him.

Chase picked up a complicated erector set with hundreds of intricate parts.

Jeff jumped up and down, shouting, "Want that."

"Too many pieces," Suzanne whispered. "It says on the box this is for children six years and older."

"He wants —"

Refusing to sound like a know-it-all, she laughed. "I suppose men buy toys *they* can play with."

"Because it isn't your choice, it's not appropriate?"

She glimpsed his annoyance and realized

she'd said more than enough. "Buy it if you like."

"Oh, no," he countered. "No way. And have you complain about it when we got home."

"So, I'll complain a little. What's more human than that?"

While they argued and sniped at each other like an old married couple, Jeff had wandered over to the bicycle display. With one hand trailing over the smooth finish of a red, full-sized bicycle, she could see he'd set his sights on one that would require years before he could ride it.

She should be guiding the child to more age-appropriate stuff, not trading jibes with Chase. She faced him, ready to suggest an intercession.

"Suzanne." His warning tone shimmered with exasperation. "That bike won't work for him. Let's try another store."

"I think you're right." She nodded and turned back to fetch the boy. "Jeff," she called.

No answer.

Her heart did a stutter step. Her hand swiveled side-to-side as she searched the immediate area. Before she gave them a conscious command, her feet moved. Scanning down each aisle of toys, panic reared its ugly head. "I don't see him. Where is he?"

"He was here a second ago." Chase loped past the bike racks and beyond. "Jeff. Jeff. Where are you?"

Suzanne picked up her pace, hurrying in the opposite direction to the aisles of puzzles, games and dolls.

"Can I help you, ma'am?" a young clerk offered.

"My nephew. He's three. I can't find him." Fear left her anxious. "Did you see him? He's wearing a red snowsuit."

"No, ma'am." The clerk's eyes widened. He went to a phone mounted on a nearby wall, one she hadn't noticed, and dialed a number. "Alert. Alert," he shouted, his voice resounding over the speaker system. "Lock all doors. Missing child."

Other store personnel rushed to assist. "A three-year-old wearing a red suit," the clerk added.

Frantic moments passed.

Oh, Lord, protect my little nephew.

More seconds slipped by. Sucking in a breath, she continued to race down one aisle and up another. "Jeff," she shouted. "Jeff."

At the far end of the store, a clerk stood waving his arms over his head, motioning to her. She broke into a full sprint, slowing as she spotted Jeff in a corner, his arms wrapped around a five-foot purple stuffed dinosaur.

Tears drained from her eyes. A blubbering sob broke free. Her legs, weakened in relief, almost collapsed under her. With a hand against her stampeding heart, she silently voiced prayers of thanks.

Chase skidded to a halt beside her, his face pale. He brushed back his hair with a hand that visibly trembled.

They stared at each other.

Suzanne turned and gaped at the boy for a long moment before turning back to Chase. "I was so scared," she whispered.

Chase finally pulled his gaze from Jeff to her. Using one finger, he wiped the wetness from her cheeks and then drew her into his arms.

Eyes closed, she pressed her face against his broad chest.

Leaning against him felt so good. Not always having to be the strong person was a blessed relief. She choked back a soft sob.

"We'll talk with him about this," Chase whispered.

With a jolt back to reality, Suzanne stepped back, and offered her thanks to the store personnel. They all smiled and scattered.

Jeff, oblivious to the turmoil he'd set in play, remained blessedly unaware, still hugging the giant plush animal and humming a song that seemed vaguely familiar.

"Yes, we will. I'm not sure I could go through this again," she murmured.

"Me, either. I don't think I'll ever forget this experience."

She wiped her hand across her cheek. "Never," she agreed. It took a while to bring her breathing back to normal rhythm again.

Jeff didn't want to leave the dinosaur, his arms still wrapped around it.

"We know you love him, but maybe you'll find something you like better in another store. And it's time for some hot chocolate."

Jeff made a face, but then he grabbed Suzanne's hand.

"Do you still like this alligator?" she asked, holding the toy.

"Yes." Jeff's enthusiasm almost relieved the fears she'd experience only moments ago.

She paid for the toy, and they left the store amid well wishes from some of the staff.

They stopped at a local restaurant with drinks all around. Jeff was smiling again.

A half hour later at the local department store, he chose a big garbage truck. He sang, "Goody, goody," elated with his choice.

Still uneasy over Jeff's disappearance, Suzanne didn't voice her thoughts.

Chase grumbled, "Go on and say it."

She shrugged. "We should have been watching him not sniping at each other about a toy."

Outside the store, they headed back to the car with Jeff chattering non-stop about his toys. He pawed at the packages, eagerness lighting up his eyes. "Thank you, Unca Chase. Aunt Sue."

She leaned down and gave him a swift hug, while Chase squeezed Jeff's hand, returning the boy's happy grin.

Their first mishap with the child. She said another silent prayer of thanks, deeply indebted to the Lord. How many more panic attacks would she have to weather before he could look after himself?

A half hour later in the dining room, Lara had fed Jeff, and his sweet head now rested against the table. "It looks like an early night for this one." Lara picked up the boy and headed upstairs.

Suzanne put a place setting at each end of the long table that could seat twelve. Even though Chase had declared war, dinner shouldn't become a battleground, but with

Jeff no longer offering a buffer . . .

Lara returned and put dinner on the table. She cast puzzled glances first at Chase and then at Suzanne, and grumbled under her breath.

Chase lifted one supercilious eyebrow at the housekeeper. Why did he have to be such a handsome scoundrel?

Suzanne picked at the tiny peas on her plate, shredded the delectable slice of prime rib, and managed only a few bites of the huge Oregon baked potato with parsley and chives. After the adrenaline rush, her system had yet to settle.

"I have lemon cake for dessert," Lara offered.

"I think I'll pass tonight." Suzanne was positive she couldn't swallow another bite of anything.

Lara turned to Chase with a question in her eyes.

"Me, too," he said. "Thank you for such a delicious and filling meal."

With a sniff of displeasure, the housekeeper bustled from the room.

Suzanne rose from her chair, gathered up their dishes and headed for the kitchen. "Excuse me, Chase. I have to make more phone calls."

His amusement manifested itself in a

89

smirk, but he helped in collecting the dirty dishes and followed her to the sink to deposit the dishes. Scooting around her, his fingers dragged along her arm, igniting a sizzle in her. "Always the busy entrepreneur," he needled with laughter in his voice. "Convenient, too."

"I run a business."

"You don't look like a business woman tonight," he said in a low tone. "You look soft and feminine."

Caught off guard, her eyebrows lifted in suspicion. "Thanks, I think."

He was a player in more ways than one. She didn't know the rules of his game, which put her at a disadvantage. Perhaps she could make up her own rules.

Holding the full skirt of the cocoa-colored dress wide, she did a little twirl. The flirty material floated above her knees. Purchased from a specialty house in Paris that made copies of originals and sold them at reasonable prices, the active sales had padded her bank account.

"I wear tailored clothes in my line of work," she said. "Women can be both feminine and tomboys."

"I'm not talking about other women, Suzanne. I meant you." His breathtaking eyes took on a silver sheen as he moved so close a single sheet of paper wouldn't fit between them.

Cool off. Back away. If he kissed her, she'd be lost.

Giving her a sideways grin, he moved back. "Will you join me later for a drink? I'll be in the solarium."

"Depends on how long my calls take." She moved past him, aware of the electricity that arced between them.

The woodsy scent of aftershave filled her nostrils. His mellow voice captivated her. The man had a monopoly on charm. Women must find him so appealing.

Though she fought her attraction to him, the battle seemed lost before it even started. Was this change of attitude meant to distract and throw her off-guard? She had to admit it was a pleasant way to lose.

Minutes later in her room, she shook her head at the reflection in the mirror. Heightened color on her cheeks and a lively sparkle in her eyes. Somehow, this time, she didn't mind his effect on her. And yet, she couldn't lose Jeff, no matter how alluring she found Chase. A momentary pleasure against a lifetime of love and devotion. No way.

She glanced at the Bible on her nightstand, the one she'd brought up from the solarium. She looked away, but her gaze returned, drawn by an invisible pull. *Should I read what you so lovingly symbolized? I know it's personal, Pam, but maybe the passages will help me understand you better. It's obvious I didn't do a good job of raising you.*

She glanced at her watch. Eleven-thirty in New York. She dialed her assistant's number, concerned about an overdue shipment of merchandise. A sleepy voice answered Andy Pollard's phone. Two years Suzanne's junior, a bevy of beauties always surrounded him.

"This is his boss," Suzanne explained.

He must have dropped the phone for Suzanne heard it clatter before Andy spoke. "Sue?"

"I hope this call isn't too late. I won't sleep unless I know what happened with the Eau Claire collection."

"You sound strange. Are you all right?"

"As well as can be expected. It's difficult being here under the circumstances. And Pam's little boy . . ." She couldn't discuss Jeff without having her throat well up and choke her. "Now, how about that —"

"Articles arrived today from Chicago. Inventoried and in perfect condition."

She brushed hair from her neck and realized her hand was damp. "When will you ship?"

"Tomorrow."

She could count on him.

"There are a couple of items you should know about," he said. "I'll get on my other phone and give you a rundown."

While Suzanne waited for him.

Over two hours later, she hung up the phone and sighed. Details. Details.

Would Chase still be up? She reached the solarium, but he hadn't waited. Not that she blamed him. The unexpected feeling of disappointment made her breath hitch.

In her room, she slipped into a silky lavender nightgown, and then looked out the window. In the distance, ringed by a fine mist, the harbor lights shed an eerie glow. A lonely sight, she was alone in a world without compassion.

Despite the comfortable temperature in the house, she shivered, the chill not physical, but emotional. She was always surrounded by people — but most of them didn't matter. After the disastrous weeks since the episode with Derek, she'd chosen solitude and avoided all men. But Ramon plunged into her world, wreaking havoc with her life. Until he finally gave up and took off for Argentina . . . leaving her to clean up his mess of lies.

A sound from the next room drew her attention. Chase? Was he asleep? Or perhaps he also looked out at the same scene beyond the window. Did some woman wait for him in Tokyo?

She crawled beneath the covers and girdled her heart with an iron belt. So why did that organ slam against her chest wall so hard, straining to burst its bonds? No more entanglements with men for her. Never again.

Was she relieved or frustrated by the way Chase played her? His nearness caused her pulse to race. Her mind buzzed with the memory of him, her imagination so vivid, she could feel his arms around her.

With a concerted effort, she re-directed her defenses. She couldn't afford to fall for a man like him. Ever.

But how would she sleep when those hungry eyes refused to leave her fickle mind?

7

Morning sunlight peeked through the cloud cover and minutes later, dazzling golden beams burst through the French doors in the dining room. Suzanne stood, her fingers stroking a glass pane. If only the same warmth could chase the chill from her body and mind.

She sat at the dining table, sipped a cup of green tea, and finished a dish of pink grapefruit sections. "Is Jeff up yet?"

Lara called from the kitchen. "He sleeps till nine lately."

An awareness intruded, an electrical current she'd come to recognize — Chase. She flinched at the thought of meeting his gaze.

The pale-gray pants and emerald-green blouse Suzanne wore gave her confidence. *Lord, help me muster all the self-assurance and strength I can.* She needed that in abundance to deal with him.

"Good morning." Chase took a seat at the

opposite end of the table, the greatest possible distance from her.

She murmured, "Hey."

Lara set a dish of apricots in front of him. "Maybe you two aren't far enough apart. Should I add a couple of leaves to extend the table?"

Chase gave her a wry smile. "I don't think that's necessary."

Lara mumbled something under her breath, shrugged, and left.

Chase peered at the fruit before he spooned some into his mouth, and then traded glances with Suzanne. "Did you sleep well?"

"Yes, did you?"

"I guess you could say that." He left the spoon in the dish and leaned back in the chair. "Did you have a nightmare?"

"No."

"I thought I heard you whimper about two o'clock."

"Oh? I . . . I don't remember my dreams."

Her response must have satisfied him, for one side of his mouth curved upward. "I considered knocking on your door, but didn't think I'd be welcome."

His palm brushed imaginary crumbs off the white linen tablecloth.

In rapt concentration, she watched his

hand movement and a tiny smile made a bid for freedom when she realized he was as uncomfortable as she. "I don't need —"

"No, I'm sure you don't." A touch of cynicism twisted his mouth. "You're one of those women who have no need for a man. Not as a permanent fixture."

"What I want or don't want is none of your business." Releasing a pent-up sigh, she continued. "Does it really matter?"

He went on as though she hadn't spoken. "I thought about you last night. I almost decided Jeff would be better off with you, since he's so young. Then I recalled what I'd heard about the men you've had relationships with. Too many men as role models can confuse a boy. Believe me, I know from personal experience."

His mother, that's who Chase referred to. Pam had told her that Elena Garwood left her husband and took up with numerous men. Chase probably saw more than he should have during the years he grew up in San Diego.

Suzanne cast him a sideways look. "I thought we agreed not to discuss Jeff until after we've seen the lawyer."

Lara returned at that moment; her mouth set in a grim line. She placed pancakes, eggs, sausages, and a batch of warm crescent rolls onto the middle of the table and headed back to the kitchen.

Suzanne's lips quivered. Valiantly, she got up with her plate in hand and served herself from the out-of-reach side breakfast food. Her appetite gone, she spooned eggs and flipped a pancake onto her dish. Nutrients would help with what lay ahead for her at the attorney's office.

Chase waited a dozen heartbeats before mimicking her actions, ensuring he went to the opposite side of the table to serve himself. Seated again, he speared a sausage on his plate, but it slipped off the fork and landed on the tablecloth. He muttered under his breath.

Suzanne picked at her pancake. "Are you always this grouchy in the morning?"

His jaw tightened. "Anyone ever mention that you can be exasperating?"

"No. Has anyone told you that you'd come in last in a Mr. Congeniality contest?" She bit into a buttered roll to hide the smile that curved her mouth.

"Not that I remember." He huffed and reached for the back of his head.

Was the gruffness a way to hide his headache pain?

Did she pity him? No. Attracted to him? Yes. Only a fool would deny that, and the last she looked, fool wasn't one of her character traits.

Unnerved by their constant bickering, she considered extending an olive branch, but not at the expense of letting him think she was weak. At this point, Jeff's future was her highest priority.

While they ate, she tried to imagine what kind of life the boy would have living with Chase. The exotic atmosphere Japan might result in Jeff's mind being torn between the cultures. No doubt he'd become a far different person than if he were raised in the States.

If she were honest, she could only see the good side of such an arrangement. Where he grew up shouldn't pose a problem. Who influenced him — that's what mattered. A young child needed love and understanding. Could Chase give him that?

Chase dabbed at his mouth with a linen napkin. Hard as he tried not to stare, his attention was drawn to Suzanne's lowered lashes and the frown that creased her lovely brow. At times she seemed fragile, and yet he suspected she had strength that far surpassed most women.

A small corner of his heart had melted. Could he tap into his suppressed desire to know her better? Lord help him, he'd like to. She stirred unwanted feelings and intrigued even as she irritated him.

He shook his head. Not a good idea. Suzanne Bratton posed a real danger to his peace of mind. Made him want things he'd left behind long ago and were better left unspoken. She seemed so calm. And according to what he'd gleaned, this woman had been born without feelings. Either that or she'd learned to subdue them. What had happened to create such icy disdain?

He didn't trust himself near her.

Last night she'd invaded his dreams. This incredible woman had crooked her finger. As he'd followed her, without hesitation, he'd leaped a chasm. Awakened later, he fought with the sheets. Over and over, before shadows enveloped him again, he'd argued with himself that he mustn't dream of her.

She finished her cup of coffee and relaxed against the back of her chair.

"Are you ready for today?" he asked.

"Yes."

She arose, each movement graceful. She had extraordinary fashion sense — she wore colors and styles that flattered her face, slim body, and long, flawless legs. No wonder her boutiques were blessed with success.

Pam had raved about her sister's foray into the business world, and how easily she'd financed additional stores.

He sought a chink in the woman's armor, one weakness that would make her readable. The only emotion he detected glowed in her eyes when she touched Jeff. Would gentleness work better than trying to provoke a response from her? Perhaps it was time to change tactics.

On the way to the attorney's office, Suzanne ignored Chase's sideways glances, grateful for his brooding silence.

When they entered the office, Oliver Pomeroy addressed them with cordial warmth. Tall, gaunt, and graying at the temples, he looked nothing like she'd pictured.

"I've heard so much about both of you." He shook their hands. "I'm so sorry I couldn't attend the funeral."

"We understand," Chase said. "How's your wife?"

"She's shaken by the accident. They kept her overnight in the hospital. Thanks for your concern." He waved at two chairs across from his desk and cleared his throat. When they were seated, he covered the preliminary items in Pam and Tad's will.

"They bequeathed their housekeeper, Lara, a generous sum of money. I'll inform her when she comes into the office this afternoon."

Suzanne nodded. "Lara certainly deserves it." She ran her fingers over the smooth, polished surface of the armrest.

"I want you to know that since no family was available, normally Jeff would have been taken into custody. Our judge, police chief, and I discussed the situation. Since Lara is an excellent caregiver, we decided that taking him from his safe environment would have been traumatic for such a young child."

Suzanne and Chase murmured their thanks in unison.

Pomeroy rambled on about less important contents of the will. Was he postponing the disposition of the house, business, and Jeff's custody?

A forklift load of bricks lay on her chest. Slow torture.

"The house, contents, and land," Pomeroy paused and met Suzanne's eyes, "will become yours."

She gripped the wooden armrest of her chair and hung on.

"The business . . . mill, logging contracts, and timberland go to Chase." The attorney eyed them each in turn.

Chase leaned forward. He gave no indication how he felt about the sudden acquisition of the successful venture Tad had created. What would he do with the business?

Her thoughts far-flung, Suzanne missed what one of the men had said. When Pomeroy mentioned Jeff's name, her gaze riveted on the attorney.

He ran a hand over his solemn gray tie. "Pam and Tad established a trust fund for the boy. Suzanne, you will have custody of Jeff Garwood."

She strangled the armrest.

Chase leaped up. "What?"

Pomeroy nodded, and rubbed his palms together, keeping his focus on the documents.

Chase's mouth became a flat, grim line. "Impossible."

"It was their wishes." Pomeroy finally looked up.

Chase slumped into his chair. "I can't believe it."

Comprehension dawned on Suzanne. *Jeff — he's mine.* The weight on her chest eased, but fear and uncertainty mingled with her joy. "It makes sense. You live halfway around the world, Chase."

The lawyer hurried on. "Soon after Jeff's birth, I convinced Tad and Pam arrangements should be made for his future. As young as they were, it didn't seem possible they might die at the same time. They believed themselves immortal."

Chase glared at Suzanne. "I'll bet they weren't even compatible on their decision about Jeff. It was more likely Pam's idea." Anger darkened his irises.

Suzanne's chin rose. Her heart thumped in her throat. "Tad must have consented."

"I assure you it was a mutual agreement," Pomeroy said.

"No." Chase raked his hand through his hair.

"I realize you're upset, Chase. Perhaps you and Suzanne could share time with the boy."

A gasp tore at her throat. "How could we possibly do that?"

"Yeah, as part-time parents." Chase scoffed. "No child should grow up that way."

Her emotions teetered on the edge of a cliff. "Sharing won't work. The geographical distance would be insurmountable."

"I want the boy." Chase's jaw was rigid.

"Only a judge can alter this legal document," Pomeroy said.

"Then I'll contest the will."

Suzanne's stomach flipped. "I'm taking

Jeff with me."

"I'll get a court order," Chase rasped and jumped up. "I won't let you take him out of the state."

Pomeroy studied them, his focus darting from one to the other. "A court case could take months. You would each need an attorney. Give it some thought before you make such a decision, Chase. Remember, the child's welfare comes first. This is what your brother wanted."

Swept by a mood of despair, Suzanne murmured, "This has to be settled."

The lawyer's palms flattened against the glass-topped desk; anguish written across his furrowed brow. "You're both mature individuals who should be able to handle the situation. Whatever you decide, any child of Pam's and Tad's will be resilient."

He made more sense than either she or Chase right now. More objective. Pam had spent much of her time involved in personal pleasures. Bowling. Golf. Clubs. Tad worked long hours at the mill. Jeff had thrived despite their absence.

"No." Chase grasped the back of his chair. "I want permanent custody of my nephew."

Suzanne rounded on him. "Wouldn't it be psychologically bad for him having to move to the other side of the globe?"

Chase's short bark of laughter startled her. "What about you giving him that woman-chasing South American as a father."

"You know well —"

"So do you."

Pomeroy stood, his sudden movement almost knocking over his chair. He grabbed for it, keeping it upright. "Enough." His sallow complexion took on a hint of pink. "Take some time, at least a few days." He clenched his fists as though anxious to escape the explosive quality in the air.

Yeah, in his position, she'd be plotting escape, too. "We'll . . . uh, talk about it." Suzanne stood and extended her hand. "Thank you for your help, Mr. Pomeroy."

"As far as I'm concerned, you can start the paperwork now to contest the will," Chase stated.

"This isn't the time for snap decisions." Suzanne's jump-to-conclusions habit — oh, but not this time. Too much at stake. That precious boy . . . "Besides, it would be Mr. Pomeroy's decision whoever he'd represent. If either of us."

For a moment Chase stared hard at her. "We can't resolve this."

"Give it a chance," Pomeroy urged. "A day or two, more or less can make a big difference in your outlooks."

Chase's eyes narrowed when he shook the attorney's hand. "Thank you. We'll be in touch."

"I hope you'll leave here with one thought." The older man spread his hands in a gesture of peace. "Those were Pam and Tad's wishes. You owe them some consideration."

8

Suzanne squirmed in her seat as Chase drove the car into the circular driveway of Pam and Tad's home. Her house now. A chilling thought.

"This arrangement with Jeff won't work," Chase grumbled.

"You're ready to give up before we even start? We should discuss the alternatives."

He spread his fingers, and then clutched the steering wheel with his palms. "What kind of alternatives are there other than you and Jeff move to Tokyo with me."

"Or you could move to New York with us."

"Sure." Pure sarcasm edged the single word. "Where would I find a job in my line of work with a comparable salary in New York?"

She hesitated. "How would I conduct a business in Japan when I don't know the language?"

Chase shook his head.

"What will you do with Tad's business?"

He lifted one shoulder. "Maybe sell it."

"Why don't you run it yourself? Emerald Point is a lot closer to New York than Tokyo."

"I'm not a logger. I have a job already and am not interested in a lumber mill."

"Lumber's in your line of work, and you know a lot about it." How could she convince him? "Since I already have a business established, you moving to Emerald Point seems the logical solution or move to New York with us."

He scowled. "If I went to New York, should I live near you?"

She shrugged. "It's your choice. At least it would be easier to share Jeff. Right now, you live on the other side of the planet. The trauma of a long trip by plane every six months would be difficult for him. As soon as his body adjusted to the different time zone, he'd have to move again." She slumped back against the seat. "Pam and Tad wouldn't want that for him."

Chase bore an almost helpless expression. "They had to have known I'd want custody of him."

"Jeff is very young. He needs a woman's love in his life right now."

"He also needs a man."

"Yes, well, the will states I have custody." Feeling smug, but not wanting to show it, Suzanne posed another question, "I wonder why Pomeroy suggested we share him."

Chase's eyes held a sudden mischievous gleam. "Matchmaking?"

She made a tsking sound deep in her throat. "If that's what he thought, he certainly couldn't have made a bigger mistake."

Chase's response was smooth, almost carefree. "Oh, I don't know. The attraction is there."

Her head spun toward him. "What?"

He studied her for a few seconds. "You mean you're not aware of the magnetic pull between us?"

A breathless silence followed. She couldn't deny she was drawn to him, the kind of awareness that simmered beneath the surface, but she'd run through the streets of Emerald Point in her pajamas before she admitted it.

He exited the car and headed around to open her door. With a hand extended to help her out, his gaze skimmed her face. "You didn't comment."

"You mean about the attraction thing?" She wouldn't lie. Why should she? "Yes, I'm vaguely aware that you're somewhat attractive and charming."

They climbed the steps, and he pressed the button beside the front door. The chimes rang. "I'm surprised you admit it. I didn't think you were capable."

A quiver shot down her back. She lifted her chin, her tone subdued. "Taking note of a player's attributes requires observation. I'm capable of a lot, Chase."

That stopped him for a second. "I'd need proof of that."

She tossed her head and a strand of hair brushed her lips. "I don't have to prove anything to you."

Lara opened the door, her sad yet smiling face a balm for Suzanne's frustration. "I put Jeff's latest crayon masterpiece on the refrigerator door. He asked for his mom and dad, but I didn't know what to say. How long until you tell him?"

"Soon," Chase replied.

Suzanne swallowed hard. "We'll make a big fuss over his art. Tell him what a good artist he is."

Chase nodded.

Just then, the cause of the friction between them flew down the stairs. Jeff hurled himself at them and hugged both at the same time. His childish chatter sounded like a happy tune. This young boy would enrich her life.

"Ooh," Suzanne murmured while she and Chase appraised Jeff's art work.

"Good job." Chase brushed Jeff's shoulder. "You want to be an artist when you grow up?"

"No, I wanna work on a garbage truck and be firefighter."

She hid a smile as did Chase.

Their efforts must have satisfied his need for attention, because he didn't bring up his parents.

"I wanna go Freddie's? Huh, can we?" Jeff's excitement beamed on his adorable face.

Freddie's Place, the local arcade, ice cream, and sandwich shop, featured clowns, fire sirens, and singing waiters and waitresses.

"I sort of promised if he ate all of his breakfast, you'd have lunch there." Lara winced. "I . . . uh, hope that's all right."

"I ate it all," the youngster shouted.

Lara nodded. "He did, indeed."

Suzanne smiled. "Sure, we'll go there, Jeff. After we get back, Lara, we'll tell you what happened at the lawyer's office."

Lara looked down and fidgeted with her nails. "Police Chief Trent called. He's coming by at four this afternoon."

That was unexpected. "Did he say why?"

Lara dressed the boy in a warm jacket and hood. "No. He only said to call his office if that time doesn't work for you."

Later in town, Jeff showed them the store where his mother exercised, his father's barbershop, and the florist where "Daddy buys Mommy flowers when she's mad at him."

Over Jeff's head Suzanne's gaze locked with Chase. "When should we tell — ?" she blurted.

Chase shook his head and lowered his voice. "Give it a few days. We'll wait until he asks us about them. The time has to be just right."

How would her darling boy take the news? Could a three-year-old comprehend what never meant? Even adults had difficulty accepting death.

She blinked. A week ago, she'd basked in the beauty of France without any unsolvable problems. Now she'd been catapulted into a traumatic situation.

At times she had the urge — to either beat Chase senseless or get to know him better. Now here he was doling out wisdom. How could one man be so infuriating?

The past few months she'd buried all her feelings, but this dark-haired handsome man with silver eyes created emotions in her best left ignored.

The drive to Freddie's Place only took a few minutes. They found the restaurant teeming with children and adults, most of them gathered around the video games. Chase chose a booth along one wall and took the seat across from Jeff and Suzanne.

Drums boomed in the background. The pleasant scent of hot chocolate and hearty grilled burgers filled the air. Costumed waiters sang "Happy Birthday" at a nearby table.

Jeff's eyes shone with delight while his small fingers beat a tattoo on the table.

On the other side, Chase's fingers kept time with his nephew's. A family trait?

A young man in a wolf mask crouched beside Jeff. "What would you like?" he asked in a deep voice. "We've got a special on Little Red Riding Hood chili dogs and Hansel and Gretel toasted cheese sandwiches."

Jeff recoiled, his small body straining against Suzanne's. "Dog," he burst out.

"I'll have the same," Suzanne added and slipped an arm around the boy's shoulders.

"Make that three," Chase chimed in.

She dropped a kiss on Jeff's dark curls, an unconscious expression of love.

"He's special, isn't he?" Chase's voice was low and husky as he looked between Jeff and Suzanne.

Warmth stole up her cheeks when she realized Chase's gaze remained on her. She nodded and squeezed Jeff's shoulder. "All the more now that he'll —" Be mine, she'd almost said. But what if a judge decided she had to share Jeff with his belligerent uncle? Or worse, give Chase full custody. Impossible. No judge would send a child to a foreign land with an unmarried man, not when his parents' will had specifically stated Jeff would be hers.

Unaware that he was the subject of their conversation, Jeff watched spellbound as a clown performed sleight-of-hand at the next table, producing dimes from behind a young girl's ears.

Uncomfortable beneath Chase's vivid gaze, Suzanne murmured, "Don't fight me for him."

He hesitated for one heart-stopping moment, and then the steely façade appeared. "I'm going for full custody."

How could Chase be sweet and gentle one moment, and then change in an instant? She almost asked him, but feared it would make him more defensive. "He'll complicate your life."

"And yours."

"I don't mind."

"Neither do I."

If she told Chase her plans, would that make a difference? She doubted it. "I've thought about asking Lara to come with us to New York. It would make the transition smoother."

A smile curved his mouth. "Excellent idea. She could join me and Jeff in Tokyo, or I can employ a nanny. I'm sure most Asian women adore children."

"I'm sure as in any culture most women do."

He raked her with his hot, silver gaze, but skepticism laced his voice. "What? You?"

"Of course."

The wolf reappeared with a tray, followed by a clown with a bass drum. The harsh sounds boomed in Suzanne's ears.

Jeff's eyes went wide. His mouth fell open.

The wolf whispered in Jeff's ear, prompting a giggle. The clown swiveled his drum around his back and pulled several colorful scarves from his sleeve. Magic tricks commanded everyone's attention.

Jeff clapped his hands when a bright red feather appeared from an empty hat.

Suzanne tapped Jeff's plate. "Your food will get cold."

The clown offered a smart salute. "If you eat every bit of your chili dog, the wolf will take you to the Magic Room," he promised Jeff as he moved on. "That's if your parents say it's OK."

Parents. Her antennae perked up.

Jeff devoured the food long before she did. The wolf wouldn't find a morsel on his plate.

"Ah, the joys of childhood." Chase rammed another bite of hot dog in his mouth.

The wolf returned to lead giddy Jeff, now somewhat hesitant, to the Magic Room. He looked back once, and, when she nodded and smiled, he grasped the young man's hand tighter and marched along with him.

Suzanne started to follow, thought better of it, and settled in her seat again. "Maybe we should have gone with them."

Chase picked up what was left of his hot dog. "We can't always baby him. Going to the Magic Room without an adult will build his confidence."

Suzanne met Chase's gaze. His square jaw held no sign of softness. Confidence, indeed. No lack there. The upturned lines beside his mouth proved he could smile, though rarely in her presence. But then, didn't this whole situation since she'd arrived warrant a serious demeanor?

"Should we talk?" Suzanne figured they

might as well take the opportunity while Jeff was occupied.

"Not sure it will get us anywhere."

"What?"

"We have no common ground." He stilled the restless motion of his fingers. "I've never known a woman like you."

"You said that before."

He ignored her snipe. "Have you ever known a man like me?"

She smiled, shook her head, and her heart compressed. "You're one of a kind, and sort of strange in some ways."

He cocked his head. "Strange meaning weird?"

She shook her head. "No, I didn't mean it that way."

When he reached across the table, she pulled her hand back. "I don't think —"

"Let's dispense with thinking for now. Just flow with the tide." He brushed her knuckles with his fingers and played a tantalizing rhythm on them.

No wonder he was a successful salesman. Part of her relaxed as a warm, tingling light shimmered through her.

He must've noticed she'd gone all honey-warm, for his vibrant gaze burned into hers.

Jeff came back at that moment, slid into the booth, his face flushed. Those spaniel-soft eyes, so much like Pam's, sparkled. "Magic," he murmured and bubbled with excitement as he pointed to the special room.

His giggles saved Suzanne. Her rapid breathing slowed. She wouldn't allow Chase to weave his own "magic" over her.

9

The chimes rang at ten minutes before four o'clock, and Chase strode across the foyer to open one of the double doors.

The tall, uniformed chief of Emerald Point's police force extended his hand. "Ray Trent."

Chase stifled a grin. The cop's rounded cheeks reminded him of a squirrel's chock full of nuts. "Chase Garwood." He shook the policeman's hand and opened the door wider, allowing him to enter. "Will you join us for coffee?"

"No, thank you." The chief removed his hat and peered around. "Will Pam's sister be joining us?"

"Yes, in a few minutes. Our nephew's a bit cranky, so Suzanne's putting him down for a nap."

Trent's eyes searched the interior. "Is Lara here?"

"No. She has an appointment with the attorney."

The clipped questions, short and to the point, set Chase's teeth on edge. Something was wrong. Something he wouldn't like.

He motioned Chief Trent to follow him into the living room. "Please have a seat."

Suzanne entered almost on their heels with a warm smile for their visitor. "I'm Suzanne Bratton, Pam's sister."

The chief shook her hand. "Ray Trent."

"Can I offer you a coffee or something cool to drink?" When he declined, Suzanne settled into one of the easy chairs.

The chief took a seat across from Suzanne, eyes focused on the hat in his hand, his fingers playing havoc with the brim. "I know this is a difficult time, but I feel I should inform you —"

Suzanne's face turned ashen. She leaned forward, her spine ramrod straight. "Inform us of what?"

Chase sat on the edge of the chair next to hers, the beginnings of another headache throbbing in his temples.

"Sorry, I didn't mean to upset you." Trent cleared his throat and looked at his hands. "The investigation into the crash is ongoing. We've found nothing to indicate why their car went over a fifteen-foot embankment. The roads weren't wet. Nor fog, and there was nothing wrong with the car."

Suzanne eased back in her chair. "I don't understand."

"We're like family here in Emerald Point." Trent scraped his hand through his hair. "We want to know why two of our citizens died."

Chase made a conscious effort to relax his clenched jaw. "Do you suspect foul play?"

"Not at this time." The chief straightened his tie and shifted in his seat. "But we did find a scrape on the front driver's side fender, which could be from the guardrail."

"Or from another vehicle?" Chase gripped the arms of the chair in an effort to control a spike of anger.

"You think another vehicle might have been involved?" Suzanne's hands were tightly clasped in her lap.

Chief Trent shrugged. "We won't have any information until the lab reports come back. I just thought you should know in case some reporter gets wind of it and comes snooping around."

"Thank you." Chase breathed through his nose, exhaling with exaggerated slowness, compelling his muscles to relax. To his surprise, the exercise did help with his migraine. When he felt in control again, he asked, "Other than the paint scrape, is there any reason to suspect the crash might be more than an accident? Something you're not telling us?"

"No." The admission brought pain to the chief's eyes. Perspiration dotted his forehead. "Most deaths here come from natural causes. We don't get many wrecks. When they do occur, everyone is upset and concerned."

"I appreciate that," Chase said. "I used to live here when I was a kid."

"I didn't know." Tension slipped from Chief Trent's body like a leaking balloon. "I believe Mr. Pomeroy told you about the decision he, the judge, and I made not to take Jeff into custody that night. The boy's so young that we didn't want to traumatize him. And we all know Lara. She's been a rock his entire life."

Chase nodded. "He explained about that. We can't thank all of you enough for considering the boy's personal welfare."

"That's about it." The chief stood, hat still in hand though somewhat worse for wear.

Chase and Suzanne rose with him.

"We appreciate the information," she said. "If there's anything we can do, please let us know."

Trent stepped toward the foyer. "I'll keep

you informed. Nice meeting both of you."

Chase hurried forward to open the door for their departing visitor. "Same here." He watched the officer get into his squad car before returning to the living room.

Suzanne remained standing by her chair, the faraway look in her eyes framed by the wrinkle between her eyebrows.

"For a cop, he sure was jumpy."

Startled, she turned to look at him. "Maybe things like this don't happen here very often. Remember, he said —"

"I know what he said." Chase's head tilted to one side, momentarily weighing the evidence. "I don't think he told us everything."

"Are you always so suspicious? I'm sure he'll tell us if he finds anything."

With a quick, disgusted snort, he challenged her. "It's obvious you've had little experience with police."

"So, it's bad to be a law-abiding citizen?" A nervous titter was followed by a delicate snort. "Sorry to be such a prude. I've never even gotten a traffic citation."

"Well, Saint Suzanne, *I've* had some experience." He reclaimed the same chair he'd sat in earlier.

Still standing, a hand flew to her chest. "You mean you had run-ins with the cops?"

He lifted his chin. "Yes."

An exaggerated eye roll told him exactly what she thought of that confession. "Maybe someday, when you stop trying to live up to your bad boy image, you'll tell me about your antics. Right now, I'm calling New York."

Chase waved his hand, dismissing her, but she'd already shown him her back and started up the stairs, two at a time.

Late that afternoon, before Suzanne left the solarium to give Jeff his bath and read him a bedtime story, she studied several articles in the local newspaper about various club meetings and the new historical museum. Emerald Point had a fascinating history of Native Americans, early Spanish explorers, and the migration of easterners.

Her sister had always been an enthusiastic supporter of civic affairs, and had often spoken about the art shows and moth-boat regattas she'd attended, all without Tad. He hadn't shared the same interests with Pam.

During his bath, Jeff made funny chicken clucking sounds and splashed soapy water on Suzanne. Then he giggled — the sweetest sound on earth. How easily this frisky little guy had banished her blues. He'd already given her a new focus, something more precious than hard work, more fulfilling than lonely hours.

Seated on the comfortable rocker in Jeff's bedroom, she perched the pajama-clad boy on her lap while she opened a book about a naughty squirrel.

He hummed along as she read, making little animal sounds to enhance the story, and midway through, his head lay nuzzled against her neck.

"There'll be lots of reading to him in the next few years."

She looked up. She hadn't heard Chase approach. "And you'd do that for him?" She held her voice to a whisper so as not to disturb her sleeping angel.

"Will you?" His deep voice dropped lower than normal, his hand jammed into his pockets. "Can you give up the social whirl of New York and the business dinners that go on till all hours of the night?"

"I adore spending time with Jeff. And for your information, I'm no longer active in the social scene. Haven't been for a while. As for business . . ." She arose, cuddling Jeff until she placed him in his bed. Covering him with a yellow blanket, she tucked his favorite blue bunny near his hand, and then bent to kiss his cheek.

Turning, she strode through the door past

Chase. "I'll schedule all my appointments at noon or have early dinners. My evenings will belong to Jeff. Can you say the same?"

Concern etched deep lines around his eyes as he followed her. "Since it's my job to get signatures on the dotted line, yes, there will be evenings when I'll be required to entertain, but —"

"Uh-huh." She squared her shoulders, ready for battle. "You're saying you won't have time to give Jeff his bath or read his favorite stories before bedtime? You'll delegate his care to a stranger?"

Tension filled the air between them, arcing like electricity.

Chase had a volatile temper, but so far, he'd kept it in check. Could she do the same?

"You don't think I can rearrange my life? If the promotion comes through as vice president in charge of sales, the new general manager who replaces me will take over the entertainment aspect for prospective buyers. Then I'll only spend an occasional evening with the most important clients."

"Having a child means giving up some things so you can share his laughter, love him, and make him happy that he has a family."

"Can I count on you to do that?" His

voice turned harsh and remote.

"Yes. I keep my word, Chase."

He cocked an eyebrow. "Does that mean in any relationship?"

She shifted her feet and nodded. "I inherited a few good traits from my parents."

Those silvery eyes penetrated hers. "Then Pam must've inherited some good ones, too."

Aware of the vibrations between them, Suzanne countered, "Yes, she did."

He didn't look convinced and offered no reply, just shook his head and marched away.

Mid-morning the next day, Chase jogged along the wet, sandy beach. In the distance a black Labrador paddled to shore, slid its shoulder along the wet sand, and then shook himself, showering a young girl.

She squealed, her laughter filling the morning with joy as the animal leaped back into the water, repeating the playful action.

Lost in the scene, Chase stubbed his toe on a half-hidden rock and yelped. After hopping about like a loon on one foot for several moments, he retraced his steps and limped until the pain subsided.

Before leaving the house, he'd shrugged on one of Tad's raincoats. A good decision since the heavy mist coated him within seconds. For the past hour his thoughts had been filled with the happenings of the previous day.

The skirmishes with Suzanne ebbed and swollen. She'd stood up to him and actually shown some emotion. The memory of the fire burning in her blue eyes made his body hum.

All he knew about Suzanne was what little he'd heard from Tad, plus a few articles from the tabloids, and Ramon Avalero's expose. How much should he believe, especially since none of it seemed to match what he'd seen for himself? What was fact and how much salacious fiction designed to sell? An Ice Maiden, cold and without feelings for any man. Discovering the truth — ah, he relished the challenge.

Playing hardball didn't work. Perhaps a low-key approach was called for instead. Catch her off-guard with a soft and gentle touch, and then slowly unwrap her like a cherished birthday present.

The thought had merit, but would require subtlety on his part. Not his strong suit. He'd always gone headfirst into presents, part of the excitement shredding the paper to bits to get to the hidden treasure.

At times since they'd met, he'd provoked

her on purpose. Not a wise strategy, but he did so enjoy playing in the fire he'd ignited. If she came to hate him, she could become even more determined to keep Jeff from him. Truly would any judge grant custody to an unmarried man who lived in a foreign country, executive position or not?

He blew out a breath, baffled by whatever went on in Suzanne's mind. Apparently, he could ruffle her proverbial feathers. Excitement charged through his veins.

His pace slowed, and his aching muscles thanked him. Shoving aside thoughts of the aggravating woman, he focused on the more serious problem — Jeff's custody. He had to make a decision about Tad's lumber mill.

Own a business? The challenge of working for others, making deals, and emerging a winner was in his blood. Known in timber circles as a tough-guy negotiator, he'd always hidden his vulnerable side. A carrot dangled in front of him with the promotion and stock options that went with it. Sure, he could always walk away, but not so easily done with the amount of money involved with his job in Tokyo.

For now, Tad's efficient foreman could run the mill. Hands-on management was Chase's motto, so there was no way to perform his job and run the business at the same time. Nine-thousand miles separated Tokyo and Oregon. An overpowering fear of failure gripped him.

He halted, looked around at the waves heading ashore and said a silent prayer for courage. Minutes later, his mind now cleared of distress, he slowly made his way up the cliff.

A thought stopped him in his tracks. Could he discuss his problems with Suzanne? An astute businesswoman in her own right, the success of her boutiques suggested she might have some savvy intellect that could prove useful to him.

It felt odd to realize that he would consider asking her advice . . . and possibly even heed it.

Something about her — the concern she showed for Jeff, the inflection of her voice, the gentleness in her lovely eyes touched his heart — a heart he'd encased in an iron box.

Should he explain about Wendy? No. He didn't want Suzanne's pity. And why in the world would she be interested in what or who had added to his distrust of females?

Memories engulfed him, too many to hold back. The floodgates had opened. Until now, he'd only allowed thoughts about his recent past. His heart remained hardened and untouched. What had caused the melting process? Suzanne? That didn't seem possible.

A tiny fishing boat left the harbor to brave the choppy surf. It was all alone on the ocean that could turn treacherous from one moment to the next. Much as he felt — alone.

He lifted his face to the fine spray. Wiping his cheeks, he found, intermingled with the mist, a hot, burning dampness.

10

Suzanne held Jeff's little hand as they walked along the cliffs above the Pacific. When the boy started to fidget, she guided him down the rocky path to where sea foam kissed the beach. A gentle breeze, tinged with the scent of salt and full of promises of far-off lands across the horizon, teased their hair. She'd never seen anything as beautiful as the morning sun gilding the waves with bright gold and pink reflected from the rich colors of the sky.

Arms outstretched, Jeff darted across the whirling, twirling sand.

Bemused by the sheer joy of the moment, she tracked his every move. This one small boy, so innocent and yet so full of life, soothed her ravaged heart like nothing else could.

Satisfied that he'd yelled at the birds enough and left his mark on the sand, Jeff grabbed Suzanne's hand and grinned up at her. Mischief sparkled in those eyes. He kicked at the shells left by the ebbing tide, and now and then picked up one still intact.

"Lara not likes music now?" Jeff studied another shell, his frown a vivid reminder of his dad's expression when he focused on something.

"What do you mean, honey?"

"She used to sing."

Understanding dawned. Lara hadn't turned on the radio to her favorite western station since the funeral. "She's sad. Sometimes when you feel that way, you don't want noisy sounds from the radio."

"I like music."

What was the harm in having joyful sounds in the house, especially if it made Jeff happy? "I'll talk to her. I like music, too." First, though, it might be best to discuss the matter with Chase. She had no idea how he felt about music, especially now with their recent loss. But Jeff shouldn't be deprived of his mental and spiritual benefits.

Later that afternoon, she smiled as country-western music again filled the kitchen, Lara humming along with her favorite male singer. It seemed the astute housekeeper had figured it out for herself.

Suzanne groaned and slumped into a

kitchen chair opposite Lara. "This issue seems insurmountable. Chase is determined to fight me for custody, all the way to the highest court if necessary."

Her finger caressed the Early American blown-glass vase filled with fresh roses and carnations. Delivered each week by a local florist, the flowers had been Pam's favorites. Now they served as a poignant reminder of the sister Suzanne had loved and lost.

"I can't believe two intelligent people can't find a solution. Jeff's welfare — that's most important."

The tremor in Lara's voice snapped Suzanne's attention back to the housekeeper whose eyes brimmed with tears. She'd been so focused on her own grief, on her own problems, that she'd lost sight of how much Pam and Tad's deaths must have affected Lara. The woman had been with them for years, long before Jeff came along. They were her family, and she grieved now as much, if not more than she and Chase. Jeff's future had to be hard for her to contemplate.

"You're right, Lara. Mr. Pomeroy said the same thing. Jeff's future is all I've been thinking about since I learned of Pam and Tad's deaths. If Chase were to get full custody, he'll raise Jeff in Tokyo. I don't think the boy should be bounced back and forth between two continents."

Lara dabbed at her eyes with a tissue. "Chase is a fine man, but a child needs a mother as well as a father. Unless he's planning marriage . . ."

For some unaccountable reason, Suzanne felt she'd been jabbed with a hot poker. "Has he mentioned anything like that?"

"No. He can be closemouthed. Of the times he's been here, I only remember he spoke once about his life. The woman he'd been going with married someone else, a rich, influential older man, someone with an English title." She paused. "I don't really feel I know Chase, but I do like him."

She squeezed Lara's hand. "He likes you, too. Me, I'm not so sure. I think he sees me as a threat."

Lara tapped her pursed lips with a finger. "Maybe so, but he's still a fine-looking man. He'd make a good catch."

Suzanne's mouth twisted. "Maybe for a woman who's looking to snag a husband?"

The twinkle in Lara's eyes faded. "You don't want to marry?"

"I have no plans."

"Then Jeff would grow up without —"

At the sound of footsteps on the tile floor, Suzanne turned.

"A father," Chase finished for Lara.

The woman's hand jerked to her chest. "Oh, Chase, you startled me."

Suzanne stiffened. How much of their conversation had he heard?

"I'm sorry." He planted a kiss on Lara's cheek and turned to Suzanne. "Have you considered that Jeff won't have a male role model? I had a father until I was twelve, but even that wasn't long enough."

Suzanne lifted her chin. "Many children survive with only one parent. You did."

"Is that all you want for Jeff, survival?"

She fingered a loose tendril of hair and took in his earth-toned sweater, brown pants, and muddied sneakers. "Are you saying that living with your mother left you unfulfilled?"

He met her gaze and blinked several times. She sensed his withdrawal.

Taking a deep breath, he reached for a chair and straddled it. Was he ready to do battle in front of Lara?

Instead, he confronted her with a voice low and even-tempered. "Having only one parent doesn't necessarily leave a kid unfulfilled, but I missed things. Camaraderie, the warmth and perspective a young man gets from an older male sibling or father. And that's what a boy needs."

His admission revealed a sensitive side to his nature that seemed to be genuine. Even though she'd suspected he possessed those traits, she hadn't actually seen them before. Adrenaline rushed through her at this new discovery that he could be vulnerable.

"What you're saying is true, Chase, but what about the warmth and affection of a loving mother, or in my case, a loving substitute mother?" She noticed a single freckle on the bridge of his nose. This wasn't a time for noticing such things.

The conversation had turned serious, enough so tears burned behind her eyelids.

"Lara's done very well in that capacity," he said. "If you recall, Pam wasn't home much. And I understand Tad was always at the mill."

Chase was up to something. Whatever it was, she knew she wouldn't like it.

"Yes, I agree. Lara's been a wonderful mother figure to Jeff."

Lara twisted her hands and squirmed in her seat, her gaze shifting from Suzanne to Chase over and over.

Chase nodded. "Let's get out of the kitchen. Lara doesn't want to be involved in our discussion."

Suzanne rose and went around to Lara's side of the table. "There's something I'd like to ask before we leave." She hesitated for a moment, and then plunged ahead. "Jeff needs your love and caring. Would you consider coming with us to New York to look after him there?"

Lara blinked. "Why . . . I don't know. I could think about it. All my relatives and friends are here."

"Take some time." Suzanne touched Lara's arm. "For me, it would be a wonderful solution, and maybe yours, too."

Lara's hands spread in a gesture of loss. "I love that little boy. I'd like being with him."

"And Jeff loves you. Because I've asked doesn't mean you have to agree." Suzanne stepped back.

Chase stood and rested both hands on the housekeeper's shoulders. "At the same time, consider my home in Tokyo." He grinned wide. "Marry me, Lara."

The housekeeper's face reddened, and her hand flew to her mouth. "Tsk, tsk, Chase." Her eyes glowing, she murmured, "If I was thirty years younger . . ."

Suzanne wanted to clobber that miserable, wily fox. He'd pulled the rug from under her.

Lara pressed her hands against her cheeks. "Oh, my, all this is a bit overwhelming."

"If you have any questions, just ask," he said.

"Thank you both."

Lara gave no indication which offer might interest her. Either one must have seemed earthshaking to someone who'd reportedly never traveled beyond the Rockies.

Before Suzanne could exit the kitchen, Chase caught her arm. "It doesn't seem this is the time to discuss our problem."

She spun around, pulling free of his grip. "And what made you come up with that brilliant conclusion?" Her voice carried a brittle edge.

"You're ticked off about my offer."

She jammed her hands to her hips. "You'd better believe it. Shouldn't I be?"

"No more than when *you* asked her. If I hadn't made an offer, you would have had an unfair advantage."

He was right, but that didn't make her feel any better. She rounded on him. "You actually think a judge in his right mind would overturn the will? That he or she would alter a custody choice made by the parents to give a toddler to a single man who lives in a foreign country?"

He cleared his throat. "Maybe we should get out of this house for a few hours. I don't believe either of us is thinking very clearly right now. Too many memories and too much grief. Would you consider going somewhere for dinner with me?"

Her pulse kicked into higher gear. Logic said, *Run, fool,* but her heart argued that maybe getting away for a bit would ease the animosity between them, at least for a while.

Several long seconds of searching his eyes for deceit or some other devious plan left her believing him sincere. "I suppose that would be nice. Any place in particular?"

Did he feel the same crazy zap of attraction laced with distrust?

He gave her a strange smile. "Let's play it by ear, OK?"

"Right."

He checked his watch. "Give me thirty minutes. I need to talk with Tad's foreman about a problem at the mill."

"Right." She headed upstairs, relieved to get away from him for a breather. The man radiated vitality, a deadly draw for her.

Suzanne settled into her seat at a tiny table in a shadowed corner of the Emerald Point Lounge, and tried to enjoy the ambiance.

A small, subdued crowd occupied the room. The attractive, dark-haired singer, her voice mellow and throbbing, finished a set of love songs and departed amid a smattering of applause. While the vocalist took her break, a guitarist played instrumentals.

After a sip from the snifter of bourbon, Chase leaned back against the chair and swirled the liquid in his glass.

Dressed in a charcoal-gray suit, white silk shirt, and a crimson-patterned tie, he appeared dashing, handsome, and cosmopolitan. That only began to describe him.

A waiter took their orders and within minutes brought their food.

Suzanne dipped her fork into the shrimp linguini. "Delicious," she murmured.

He picked up his now empty drink, peered at the ice cubes, and set the glass aside. "I don't usually pour these down."

"Do I make you nervous?"

He laughed, but it wasn't a happy sound. "I don't think nervous is the right word."

She waited, wondering if he would elaborate.

He didn't. Instead, he covered her hand with his and scooted his chair closer.
What —

Smoky grey eyes did a slow perusal of her jade-green pantsuit. "You look lovely."

"Thanks." Her heart thudded against her ribcage. Something had mellowed him and loosened his tongue.

A half-smile turned up one side of his

mouth. "You must know it's true." He waited, his steady gaze fixed in silent speculation.

Had he expected a denial? "There are many attractive women, Chase. I've learned that if you look, you'll always find one who's better looking."

"I'm not looking." His gaze softened as though his eyes carried a message of sincerity.

She set aside her fork. Twice in one day she'd witnessed that arresting trait. When he displayed a sense of honesty, she looked at him in a different, more complimentary light. Could she afford to do that with Jeff's future at stake?

The vocalist had returned and now sang country, soft rock, and oldies. The songs drew a number of couples to the dance floor.

"Shall we give it a whirl?" He quirked one eyebrow at her.

Suzanne nodded, taking the hand he offered. He wove past the tables, and then wrapped his arms around her. His lead smooth, he whirled her in an intricate dance step that she followed easily.

"My fantasy's been fulfilled."

Not sure what he meant by that comment,

she blithely tossed her head. "Well, that was quick."

"You've been keeping me at bay."

She studied his lean, tanned face, and the potent challenge in his eyes. "You can be very charming when you choose. And also, I believe very dangerous."

His hand slid up and down her back. "And if I choose to be charming now, would you have any objections?"

"None I can think of."

He hummed to the music, letting his warm breath fan her neck. And then his lips brushed her cheek, hesitant at first, as though he expected a rebuff.

She smiled. The muscles of his shoulder rippled beneath her touch. Would his next move be a kiss? Well, maybe she'd once again jumped to conclusions.

Chase stared at Suzanne. He'd thought her cold and insensitive, but couldn't shake the idea of her lips beneath his. Approaches he'd used in the past with other women wouldn't work with her.

His thoughts fragmented; dormant feelings gnawed his insides. He was not only aware of her, but also of the warm caressing air encircling them, the oak floor beneath his leather soles, and the tom-tom beat of his heart. He should release her, back away.

With great effort, he shook off the emotions that gripped him. Sure, she intrigued him, but that was only one of the reasons he needed to challenge the Ice Maiden. More than anything, he wanted to know what simmered beneath that cool façade.

But this wasn't the time to find out.

On the way back home, Suzanne peered over at Chase. She couldn't figure him out. He made all the right moves, charmed and flirted with her, but hadn't kissed her. Now, as she drove them home, he stared at the dark road ahead and ignored her. The wipers swished back and forth, clearing the light drizzle from the windshield.

Men she'd figured out a long time ago. They shied away from relationships, but loved a good challenge. Chase did, too, except he didn't follow through. He balked at the next step. Why?

More confused than disappointed, would his pendulum moods swing back once they reached the house? Even more, she wondered if she'd welcome the attention after his advances at the lounge.

He parked the car, strode around the front, and opened her door.

She thanked him and walked into the

house without a backward glance. Soon, she thought. After they took off their coats.

"Did you enjoy the restaurant? And the dancing?"

"Yes. Thanks. It was a good distraction. We needed that."

"How about a cup of hot chocolate?" he suggested.

"Sure." She frowned. Would he kiss her in the kitchen?

They located the ingredients and set the cups in the microwave. The clock ticked. The refrigerator hummed. Rain spattered the window panes. Still nothing happened.

"Do you have plans for tomorrow?" He removed the cups and set them on the table.

She cradled her mug in her hands and took a cautious sip. Warm chocolate always soothed her. "I want to spend some time with Jeff. And you and I still need to talk. What are your plans?"

"I have calls to make, but I'll set aside some time for us."

Her suspicions perked up. She didn't trust him when he was this calm and polite.

Her foot tapped the tile floor. She stopped when she realized the sound was louder than the noise from the refrigerator and rain spattering the window. "I think I'll turn in."

She got up and rinsed her cup in the sink,

trying her best to ignore the glittering mischief in his expression.

"OK."

Fat chance. She was ready for him, but not in the way he probably expected.

They climbed the stairs side by side and stopped at her bedroom door.

"See you in the morning." He sounded cheerful as he strolled to his own room and slipped inside without glancing back.

Suzanne stared at his closed bedroom door and tried to figure out what had just happened.

She could've sworn he wanted to kiss her. So, why hadn't he? No man had that much restraint.

Puzzled, exasperated, and a little angry, she turned away with a huff and barely stopped herself from slamming her bedroom door.

Chase leaned against the door with a low chuckle. His idea was working. Those gorgeous blue orbs had signaled Suzanne's bewilderment when he'd made no move beyond holding her hand.

What if he had kissed her? Would she have withdrawn into her icy interior, or blossomed like a crocus in snow?

Such a fascinating creature.

Uh-uh. Those kinds of thoughts would get a man into trouble. Deep trouble.

She'd be gone soon, back to New York and her boutiques, her playboys, and mad social whirl. The inactivity here in the current surroundings — this house, the small town, made him feel boxed in. He needed crowds, noise, and a bustling metropolis. Tokyo.

He had only a few more days to convince Suzanne that Jeff would be better off with him, which would eliminate the hassle of a court case. Before he left with the boy though, he needed to determine what this strange pull toward her meant.

A wall separated their rooms. Not a sound came from the other side. On a whim, he tapped three times and waited.

Suzanne stood at the window when she heard the soft taps. Chase must have had second thoughts about not pursuing his amorous mission. She grinned and was satisfied she'd been in tune with him.

He tied her in knots, and she had only herself to blame. When he'd first pressed his hand over hers at the nightclub, she should have put a damper on his action. Something about him shifted her emotions into overdrive.

A moment of panic filled her. Only a wall

separated them. Was her response brought on by the change of pace, or the need to throw her into work?

Two could play this game. Before she headed for the shower, she paused for a moment and slid her hand down the yellow-flowered wallpaper.

But she didn't tap back.

11

At the dining table, Suzanne smiled at Chase and turned her attention to the scrambled eggs and toast with marmalade on her plate. She took a bite of each, savoring the food, her appetite intact for this early morning breakfast.

The housekeeper's eye twitched as she flitted between the dining room and the kitchen, brushing her hair off her face time and again.

Suzanne focused on Lara. Something was out of sorts, which gave her deep concern.

When Lara offered refills of coffee a third time, Suzanne was certain something was wrong. "Is everything OK?"

Lara wrung her hands. "Not really." Her voice quavered.

Chase stopped eating and watched the interaction between the women. His brow furrowed, and he sat back. "Please sit down, Lara, and tell us what's wrong. If there's something we can do —"

Lara sat on the edge of the chair and wiped a trembling hand over her cheek.

Suzanne put down the toast. "You know you can tell us anything."

Beads of perspiration dotted Lara's brow and she folded her hands as though in prayer. "Something I heard has been bothering me. I don't know if it means anything —"

Chase set aside his napkin. "Feel free to share whatever it is with us."

Lara gripped a corner of the table, as though seeking a lifeline support. "Before Tad and Pam left the night of the accident —" She took in a deep breath and tears pooled in her eyes "— they argued."

Chase leaned forward. "Please go on."

"Mr. Tad accused her of carrying on with some guy and that it had to stop or he'd move into the cabin at the mill." Lara wiped her hands on her apron. "When I looked at Mrs. Pam, her smile could only be described as . . . pleased."

"Wicked?" Suzanne grabbed her bottom lip with her teeth. "Guy? What guy?"

"I don't know. I shouldn't have said anything." Lara covered her mouth, pain etched in her eyes.

Chase glanced at Suzanne. "Could it be true?"

The meaning of Lara's announcement took several moments to sink in. Disbelief came first, and then a smidgeon of doubt crept in. Her sister wouldn't — would she? "Pam never mentioned another man to me." She turned to Lara. "Could you have misunderstood?"

The housekeeper's hands went up in a defensive gesture. "I'm just repeating Mr. Tad's words. I never heard him say anything like that before that night —"

Suzanne reached across the table and touched Lara's arm. "It's OK. Thank you for telling us."

"Did I do the right thing?"

Suzanne's voice softened. "Of course, you did. Was that all he said? Did Pam say anything?"

Lara shook her head.

"If you recall anything more that would point to what he meant, please be sure to tell us."

Chase's hands had curled into tight fists. His strained smile did little to hide his anger over the betrayal, the same emotions his brother must have experienced and that Suzanne now felt.

"Yes, yes. I'm just so sorry." Lara stumbled

out of the chair, still wiping tears from her eyes, and hurried back to the kitchen to her safety net.

A long silence followed, broken only by the rattle of dishes from the kitchen as the housekeeper filled the dishwasher.

"If she had a lover, it's no wonder they didn't get along." Bitterness and anger deepened his voice.

Suzanne pushed back her chair and stood to glare at Chase, fists leaning on the table. "We don't know that. Maybe Tad was teasing."

"That's not his way. Besides, Lara said they'd been arguing."

"Well, we don't know —"

"No, we don't." Chase dropped his head, shaking it side to side. But then he looked up, his stare intense, penetrating. "Was your sister cheating on my brother?"

"Stop jumping to conclusions." She should take her own advice. "The better question is, how can we find out?"

"Vroom. Vroom."

Stretched out on the rug in Jeff's playroom, one hand supporting her head, Suzanne imitated the sounds of the toy garbage truck and maneuvered it around the block building.

Opposite her, Jeff ran an armored tank back and forth. With an ear-piercing screech, he rammed the miniature vehicle into her hand. Ouch.

The truck toppled over, the crash worthy of a Hollywood action stunt.

"You're a rough driver," she scolded as she sucked her injured thumb.

"I won." Cocking his head with childish arrogance, he raised one chubby fist and gave a slow pump.

"Winning isn't everything, Jeff."

He pouted. "Daddy drives rough."

His words made her flinch, the emotional pain still raw.

Tad and Pam had loved fast driving, making it all too easy to picture them in the low-slung car, plunging over the cliff, tumbling into the ravine.

A shiver skidded down her back. Eyes closed, she took in a deep breath. Grief sat too close to the surface. Probably would for a long time. "You know dads sometimes make mistakes," she whispered.

"Mommies, too?" Sweet innocence softened his delicate features.

"Yes, mommies, too. Everyone does."

He picked up the tank and flipped it over and over, and then tossed the expensive toy on top of a pile. His small brow furrowed.

"Let's play blocks, OK?"

They stacked blocks into a pyramid, and then, with a forceful push, he toppled them into a scattered mess on the floor. "See what I did?" He flung himself down and beat his fists against the carpet.

The fury with which he performed the action gave her a moment's pause. Did he have anger issues?

Footsteps sounded on the carpet.

"Unca Chase." Jeff jumped up, his outburst over; he kicked aside robots and plush toys in his eagerness to reach his uncle.

Chase leaned against the doorjamb, an amused expression on his face.

"Come, play with us," Jeff pleaded and grabbed his hand to pull him into the room. "Please."

Chase's eyes twinkled as they swept over Suzanne. "Depends on what you're playing."

"Jeff likes old-fashioned games better than creative learning toys." Giving Chase a determined stare, she blurted, "What would you like to play?"

"Post Office." His voice dropped as he winked at Suzanne. "Spin the Bottle."

Her stomach leaped.

Jeff pouted again. "Don't know those."

Hinting at more than kids' games, Chase

purred, "Aunt Suzanne and I can show you."

Jeff scrunched his face and grabbed a tube of pick-up sticks. "Play my game, OK?"

Chase crouched beside Jeff. "We'll play your game, tiger."

"Tiger?" A huge smile lit the little boy's face. "Me tiger?"

"Yep." Chase grinned at Suzanne. "And I know a real tigress."

Jeff's brow wrinkled. "What's that?"

"A lady tiger."

"Oh." Jeff picked up the truck and crashed it into his uncle's arm.

"Ouch. Ouch." Chase whipped his hand out of the way. "Careful there, tiger."

"I sorry," Jeff blurted, his bottom lip quivering.

"I'll forgive you, Jeff, but don't do it again. It's not nice to hurt other people."

The boy put his little hand on Chase's arm. "Won't do it. Promise."

Chase looked up from the boy with a grin for Suzanne.

Surprised by Jeff's response to Chase's scolding, she felt unsettled — and hurt — that the child didn't apologize to her when he rammed the toy into her thumb.

Chase sprawled onto his stomach, like a lazy leopard biding his time. The aura of

156

energy that constantly surrounded him hadn't dissipated one bit, which only added to Suzanne's nervous reaction in his presence.

She clenched her teeth and swallowed hard.

A card game later, Jeff gave a loud whoop and pointed at Chase. "You an old maid."

Chase tickled Jeff. "First time anyone's called me that."

When the roughhousing subsided, the boy yawned and rubbed his eyes.

Suzanne glanced at her watch.

Moments later, Lara appeared in the doorway. "Time for lunch, Jeff."

"Tired." He thrust out his lower lip. "Don't wanna eat."

Certain that Lara could handle Jeff better without onlookers, Suzanne got up and left the room.

Chase followed, predator matching his pace to hers as they traversed the hall. "I guess we tired Jeff out."

She paused at the top of the stairs and took a step to one side to face him. Space was required between his tall, muscular body and her own traitorous one if she had the chance of staying out of his clutches.

"That took a lot of energy."

When heat flared in his eyes, she wanted

to back away.

"But a very pleasant weariness," he said from deep in his throat.

Pulse racing, she started down the stairs only to hear his heavier footfalls close behind.

At the bottom, he threaded his fingers through hers. "Let's talk in the solarium. Who knows? Maybe we can find an amicable solution."

She shrugged, anything but indifferent to his touch. He didn't release her hand, and she made no effort to pull away. In the solarium, she sank into a cozy, chintz-cushioned wicker chair.

Chase stood before her, staring down at her as if fascinated. A handsome, dangerous guy, dressed in navy trousers and a lightweight cream sweater that hugged his chest. A curl fell over his forehead, softening the lines of his face.

What was he thinking? This man didn't bend for anyone or anything. He would view vulnerability as a weakness . . . and use it for his own devious intent. She would do well to keep that knowledge uppermost in mind when dealing with him about Jeff.

Or anything else.

Still standing in front of Suzanne, Chase

studied her and tried his best to understand what about her appealed so much to his inner caveman. He considered her a strong-minded woman, which garnered his respect. She was beautiful with that copper hair and dewy, rose-petal skin. A femme fatale that would make any man's heart pump faster. She'd certainly destroyed his peace of mind.

Chase shoved his hands in his pants pockets to keep them from reaching out to caress her cheeks. Around her, his emotions overrode his good sense to the point he no longer trusted himself not to touch her.

"Won't you sit down?" she invited in a low, sultry voice.

With a groan, he plunked into a chair opposite hers. What if they just got married? What would it be like to wake up beside her every morning, to hear her voice heavy with sleep?

The image teased for only a moment, eradicated by the memory of the Ice Maiden's photo from the tabloids. Cold. Disdainful. Regal in all her frozen glory.

He squared his shoulders and forced his thoughts to Jeff. The boy's future hung in the balance. Time to move ahead with his plan. "Jeff loves you."

"I know. He loves you, too."

"I noticed how you focused on each game

when you play with him. I like that. And I agree with what you said about his being rough."

Their gazes met and a glassy sheen appeared in hers. "I'll throw this out as a possible solution. Could we share Jeff on a yearly basis?"

With some trepidation, he'd softened his resolve to remain aggressive.

"Too unsettling. Switching his home and loyalties so often, he'd no sooner adapt before he'd have to move again. And who would travel with him?"

"I suppose we could take turns."

"If Lara cared for him at both your place and mine, she could accompany him. The best of both worlds for all of us."

Suzanne nodded. "She would remain a steadying influence in his life."

He eyed her worn, snug-fitted jeans, pastel striped shirt, and then traveled up to her face. "It's a possibility."

"Or you could stay here and run the mill." She repeated. "That's a lot shorter flight between Oregon and New York, and the culture would remain the same."

Change his lifestyle? No. He had no plans. "I could suggest that you sell your boutiques and open a chain on the West Coast, or better yet Japan. American fashions are popular over there."

"No." She shook her head and curled her legs beneath her. "I've sunk far too much time, money, and effort into my business. It's too risky and impractical. I couldn't consider such a move."

The play of emotions on her face could mean anything, but while he was no mind reader, he did know a little about pushing buttons. "Not even for your nephew?"

"I could ask you the same question."

Chase glanced away, unable to meet her gaze.

Beyond the plants and windows, gray skies dominated the view. Not a soul in sight. Quiet. Pastoral. Serene. And vastly different from his house in Tokyo where ships and tankers plied the bay. The singsong sounds filled every moment, leaving no room for quiet thoughts.

"Any alternatives?" she asked.

"There's one." He shifted in the chair. "But I won't consider it." Instinct told him she wouldn't agree. "Leave Jeff here with Lara."

"Of course she's capable; but we couldn't ask her to accept such a responsibility for any length of time. Jeff needs at least one of us with him."

He sat back and his thumbs made nervous

circles. "So, unless Lara agrees splitting time between Tokyo and New York, we have a court case?"

Her gaze snapped back to his. "It appears that way."

Chase slapped his knees with his hands. "OK. Let's check with Lara."

Suzanne arose and grasped Chase's forearm. The touch of his skin, the soft sprinkle of curly hair and unyielding muscles sent an electrical charge through her. She let her hand flutter back to her side. "We can't rush Lara. She deserves time. Let's see what she thinks of our original offers first."

"Time is what we don't have." He shuffled his feet. "My boss is roaring for my return. Work's piling up. He doesn't have a lot of patience, and I'm losing mine."

"Sometimes it's good for a boss to fret a little. It makes him appreciate a valuable employee, and that the winner is on his team."

He leaned forward. "You think I'm a winner?"

"I have no doubt of it."

He huffed. "I'm not a winner at the moment. Webb, my boss, is unrealistic toward expansion. I've expressed my thoughts about his establishing too many satellite offices and warehouses in the Far East. The one thing we don't have is liquid assets in the event of a downturn in the economy. Companies go bankrupt by overextending themselves."

Surprised that he'd offered that much information, her lips curved into a smile. "Maybe it's time to take a walk and find a new career."

"Can't. I'm up for promotion that includes a lot of perks. As long as Webb wants me, I won't give up on him."

She nodded. "A loyal employee."

He weighed her remark for a few seconds. "Maybe too loyal. I'm aware of your competence in the business world, too."

Her eyes widened. "Thanks. Coming from you, that's a compliment."

Lara waved the phone. "Chase, this is for you."

He headed toward her, took the phone, spoke for a few minutes, and then reclaimed the same chair. "Would you mind following me in the truck when I return Vic and Karla Lamb's car? We can use Tad's new pickup."

Yeah. That should be a joyful reunion, but she had no choice. "Sure."

Later, as she followed him in the truck, Chase turned onto the road where Pam and Tad's car had gone over the cliff. Suzanne's hands trembled on the steering wheel. Pine scent permeated the interior, and she glanced at the wood chips on the floor mats.

Who had driven Pam's car? She shuddered, not really wanting to know, yet the question nagged her.

Chase pulled into the driveway of a large rambling one-story redwood set against a backdrop of giant, blue-green Douglas fir.

The Lambs stepped from their porch and ran toward him. He parked the car, and then Karla threw herself into his arms.

Suzanne groaned.

Hoping to avoid another unpleasant encounter with the couple, she waited in the truck with the motor running. No such luck.

The three of them approached, and Chase opened her door.

With a sigh she tried to hide, she cut the ignition, and stepped out onto the lush grass. "Hello, Karla. Vic."

Tall and attractive, Karla wore her dark hair in a thick braid. Her soft brown eyes held sadness, the shadows beneath them attesting to her grief. "Hello, Suzanne. We wanted to visit, but decided you had enough problems. Vic and I are devastated," she whispered, a sob making her voice hitch. "Poor little Jeff."

"They were our —" Vic choked; his voice

thick with emotion. "Best friends."

Six-feet-five inches of well-honed masculinity; he epitomized the kind of gentle giant that would have captured Pam's teen-aged heart. *Could he be the other man Lara had mentioned?*

"Pam and Tad spoke of you often." Suzanne's throat grew tighter with each reference to them.

Karla's attitude hadn't changed since the first time they'd met. Standoffish seemed an apt description. And yet, the Lambs had embraced Chase like a long-lost brother.

She gave Suzanne a brief tour of their lovely home.

Suzanne looked around the room. "Your house is so warm and homey. I love the open areas, the carvings on the supporting pillars, and your Navajo rugs." She could play the polite game.

"Thank you."

As though laughter would relieve their distress, they sat in the living room and spoke of lighthearted memories. "Once we were at a fair." Karla paused. "Tad fell off the merry-go-round. He'd had a couple of drinks. Thank heavens he didn't get hurt. Later, he was mortified for being a klutz."

"Remember the time Pam lost her skirt when it caught on one of the horse's stirrups?" Vic's deep laughter filled the room. "Gallant Chase took off his jacket and wrapped it around her. After that, she blushed every time we reminded her about it."

They'd shared some wild experiences. Somehow Suzanne felt left out of their fun.

Chase's laughter came easily. Relaxed, he lounged in one of a pair of ornate wooden rockers.

Suzanne smiled when appropriate, but didn't contribute much. And yet, she couldn't help but admire the three of them. Several times Chase had caught her gaze, and each time one side of his mouth had lifted as though they shared a secret.

Karla waved her hand, encompassing everyone, though she spoke directly to Suzanne. "Did you know Chase made these rockers?"

Caught off guard, Suzanne's mouth fell open. "Really?" Intrigued, she looked around the room again and studied each of the rocking chairs. "Beautiful workmanship. I didn't know you had such talent, Chase."

"I have a lot of talents you don't know about."

She managed a nod and a smile, while Vic let out another hearty laugh.

"Chase, come with me." Karla took his

hand and coaxed him toward a desk in one corner, leaving Suzanne alone with Vic.

Quiet and confident, the big guy brushed back his long russet hair before angling his body to face Suzanne. "Pam always talked about you. Told us how you had a number of boutiques on the East Coast."

"We were close. I appreciated her support. She was a very special sister."

Vic's eyes clouded. "Maybe more special than you know."

"Pam mentioned you in her last e-mail." A thought struck her. "Something troubles me, Vic. Maybe I shouldn't bring this up, but was there any truth to the rumor that she'd become involved with another man?"

Vic leaned forward and narrowed his eyes. "Are you implying — ?"

"I'm not sure what to think."

"Well, if she did have someone, it wasn't me." He opened his mouth to say something more, but Chase and Karla returned.

Suzanne hadn't meant to throw out an unfounded accusation. Why had she mentioned the other man?

Chase held a small velvet bag. His face had paled, and a solemn expression replaced his previous jocularity. With unexpected abruptness, he started toward the door. "Thanks for the loan of your car. We need to be going now."

Hurrying after him with even more hasty goodbyes, Suzanne stopped short when Chase did an about-face.

"I'll drive." He held out his hand for the truck key.

Irritated by the extreme swings between bossiness and charm, she nonetheless handed over the keyring.

Better to fight coming battles that meant something than batter herself for nothing against the rock that was Chase Garwood.

Minutes later, he maneuvered the truck over the back roads. Staring ahead, pensive, he asked without glancing at her, "Do you want to see the spot where Pam and Tad went over the side?"

She blanched. "No."

A muscle clenched along his jaw. "Might help us come to grips with reality. Make the grieving period shorter."

She rubbed her temples. "Yes . . . No. Please. I'm not ready."

He nodded. "Tad and Pam were on their way to see the Lambs that night."

She bent her head and studied her hands, not wanting to think about the accident. "I got the impression from your conversation with them that they led a pretty full social life. Yet, whenever I visited them, they did very little."

"Not much goes on in a small town. They found their fun where they could. Maybe they thought their entertainment was tame compared to your social life in New York."

He tossed the bag onto her lap. "Open it."

She pulled out a jewelry box and hesitated before lifting the cover. Two gold necklaces lay inside — one serpentine, slim and feminine, the other a heavy quadruple herringbone, purely masculine. The pendants were half hearts. Puzzled, she fondled the jewelry. "Each heart has a jagged edge."

Chase sucked in a deep, unsteady breath, but kept his eyes on the winding road ahead. "Yeah, they fit together. The smaller one was for Pam from Tad for their fifth wedding anniversary next week."

She choked back a sob and had to turn away as hot tears threatened to fall.

"Tad tried to save their marriage."

"How do you know that?"

"Tad told Vic when he asked him to hold the necklaces. Pam always went through closets and drawers before anniversaries and birthdays looking for gifts. She never could wait." His face took on a grim look when he added, "Like a child."

"She was also a wife and mother," Suzanne whispered, stealing a slanted look at him.

His chest heaved. "She was spoiled, Suzanne."

She clutched her abdomen. "And I suppose I'm responsible for that?" Compelled to provide some semblance of a defense, she went on. "I did the best I could. I was little more than a child myself when our mother died, and then our father was killed in a barroom brawl. I had to be mother, father, and sister all rolled into one, while I held down a part-time job, attended college, cooked, and took care of the apartment."

No comment.

"Pam hated New York, hated working for me. As soon as she saved enough money, she returned to Oregon to spend a few weeks with a friend. Then she met Tad."

Chase nodded. "I remember the quick romance. Tad said eloping was the answer."

"I'm sure they loved each other — then. Do you believe that?" When he nodded, she went on. "So, what went wrong?"

"Who knows? People jump into the fire, get singed, and then leap out. Lots of marriages end up the same way these days. It's one reason I've remained a bachelor."

"That can get mighty lonely, more so as

time goes by and you get older."

"Better than going through a horrible divorce." If he clenched his teeth any harder, there'd be a dental visit in his near future.

"Maybe you're right."

He shrugged. "It doesn't matter now. Nothing does except Jeff and doing what's right for him."

She kept her eyes on the road ahead. What had Vic started to say about Pam? He'd denied any involvement with her. Could *he* have been the reason Tad and Pam had fought that disastrous night? Jumping to conclusions again.

"Would you wear the necklace?" Chase asked.

"Wear it?" Her throat was so tight, the words emerged as a croak. The close intimacy of the truck taxed her exhausted spirits and her strength as well.

"I thought you might want to, since Tad intended it for Pam."

"Half a heart," she murmured.

"Fits some people."

"You mean me?"

He gave a nonchalant shrug.

Renewed testiness stirred in her, and she sat up straighter. "You should wear the masculine one. That way *you'd* at least have half a heart."

He searched for something in his pocket. A pill for another headache? Well, he'd given her a few.

He braked in front of the house. She opened the truck door as soon as the truck stopped and hurried inside.

Halfway up the stairs, Lara called out, "Suzanne. Wait."

She retraced her steps.

Chase halted in mid-stride just inside the door.

"I've made my decision." Lara clutched the edges of her apron, fingers wrinkling the fabric. "I can't accept either of your offers. I want to stay here in Oregon near my family and friends. With the money left to me from the estate, I can take my time finding another job." She hesitated. "I'm really sorry."

Suzanne's shoulders slumped with disappointment. Only a judge could resolve their issues now. She pressed the woman's arm in a gesture of understanding. "We hope you'll stay until we can make some arrangements about Jeff."

"Of course, I will. I wouldn't dream of —" Her voice broke, and she made fast tracks to the kitchen.

Suzanne and Chase stared after her.

She grasped her collar. *I should take Jeff*

and go. Would Chase try to stop her?

"If you want Pomeroy as your attorney." Chase seemed to hold himself in check. "I'll ask him for a referral."

She hesitated, not knowing why. "That's fine."

They ascended the stairs side by side, their bodies close. At her bedroom door she turned to him. "Meet you in court."

Chase's eyes clouded. From frustration about Jeff or something she didn't dare consider?

12

Delayed shipments. Incomplete orders. Wrong products. Enough problems to make a person rub her forehead and grimace. While speaking with first her new cosmetic supplier, and then her assistant, Suzanne wasn't ready to face what had to be done.

Chatter from the other room coaxed a smile to her lips for the first time that day. She stepped to the door and peered around the corner to where Chase and Jeff sat cross-legged on the floor, cutting and fitting together pieces of balsa wood and bright red paper. Buying a ready-made kite would have been much simpler, but Chase chose to involve the boy in the construction of it.

Chase's long, lean fingers guided Jeff's pudgy hands over the kite's material, encouraging the child to take a hands-on approach. Though the finished product was less than a masterpiece, the boy jabbed his thumbs into the top of his T-shirt, his face aglow with pride.

"Goody, goody. Best kite ever."

"What do you say we go down to the beach and give her a test run?" Chase pushed from the floor and gathered up the kite and its long tail.

"Yeah, yeah, yeah. It'll go way high like a jet." Jeff jumped up and down in his excitement, hands clapping all the while.

"Go tell Lara you need your coat. I'll meet you at the back door."

Envious of the fun they'd already had and yet to come, Suzanne watched them leave. Why couldn't she join them on the beach? Her work calls were complete. Sure, reports filled her inbox, but those could wait another day.

With a spring in her step, she hurried upstairs to change her shoes and grab a coat.

A gusty breeze blew in from the ocean, tangling her hair and sweeping away her frustrations. The sun warmed the air, making the day as perfect as any could be.

Ahead, she watched the red kite flutter and dance while the two guys — one small and one grown — raced across the sand. Jeff toppled forward in a faceplant, picked his body up, and charged after his laughing uncle.

When her sweet nephew spotted her, he

waved and ran forward, joy beaming on his adorable face. She scooped him up, his small arms pin-wheeling, excited screeches echoing off the cliffs.

"Unca Chase."

Displaying his own brand of boyishness, Chase turned with a wide smile.

Quite a guy, she admitted with great reluctance. Jeff might never find another man so like his own father. Tad had been special. Now, caught in a tug-of-war between the two people who loved him most, what kind of values would Jeff grow up with?

First and foremost, he needed to learn about Jesus, about receiving Him as his Lord and Savior, and about eternal life. So many Christian values to impart to a youngster. Could Chase maintain an exemplary lifestyle as an example for the boy?

Could she?

Religion hadn't always played a part in her life, though it did now. Almost sure her sister's hand warmed her shoulder, Suzanne shivered.

"I flied the kite. Unca Chase let me."

With a chuck under his chin, she hugged the boy's warm, squirmy body close. "Are you having fun, sweetheart?"

"Yeah." He squealed in her ear.

She recoiled, moving one hand to cup her

ear. Good heavens, she'd have trouble hearing for a while.

Beckoning to Jeff, Chase waved the kite reel. "Want to fly this again?"

"Yes. Yes." Jeff wriggled free and hit the wet sand with a solid thud, his pudgy legs pumping as he raced after the kite.

"Stay close," Chase cautioned the boy.

At a more leisurely pace, Suzanne followed.

A swift gust of wind thrust Jeff forward into the sand. He squealed. A momentary flash of terror crossed his face, and he almost dropped the reel.

Chase was there to grab both Jeff and the reel. "He's OK."

"He's . . . safe with you," she called back, catching up with them.

In a low voice, Chase whispered, "Thanks for believing in me."

Yeah, he'd make a great father, which meant her loss. Throat and heart so full, she couldn't speak for a few moments. "He's a blessed boy to have you." Pam's word again.

Jeff jabbed a thumb to his chest. "Me bwessed?"

"Yes, sir, you are." Suzanne hunkered down in front of him. "Are you tired? It's almost nap time."

"No. Not tired. Want more," he pleaded,

and yanked on the string. The kite did several jerky aerial loops, and his brown eyes glittered like starbursts.

"OK," Chase said. "This is your day, tiger."

She studied the man, wondering at the strange, almost misty quality that filled his eyes. Was he remembering times like this spent with his brother?

In silence, she trudged alongside Chase, keeping a sharp eye out for her tiny nephew.

Late that afternoon, after they'd all worn themselves out on the beach, Suzanne stopped short at the solarium door. Chase paced back and forth inside the room, his cell phone clamped to his ear, his voice harsh and demanding. After the call, he grabbed his coat, told Lara he had an appointment, and stormed out without a word for Suzanne.

She pulled out her own cell phone and punched in the digits to the attorney. At least she'd have some privacy for the conversation.

"Chase called and I gave him the names of several lawyers," Mr. Pomeroy said. "We'll wait and see what he does. I wouldn't worry. As things stand now, he doesn't have a chance of overturning the will and getting custody of the boy."

"Maybe so, but one never knows how a judge might rule."

That evening, Lara called them all to dinner to share her fabulous pizza and Caesar salad, with a yummy German chocolate cake for dessert.

Not surprising, Jeff didn't balk when Lara announced his bath and bedtime. He drooped a bit from his romp on the beach, and now stumbled up the stairs with the housekeeper at his side.

Replete with good food and a loving glow, Suzanne relaxed in her chair and sipped tea.

Chase aped her movement and let his lips curve into a slow, devious smile. After wiping his sculpted mouth with an Irish linen napkin, he announced, "My lawyer thinks I can get custody of Jeff."

A stone settled in her stomach, panic gripping her for a long, debilitating moment. He'd dropped a bombshell that left her reeling.

No, no, no. Mr. Pomeroy said . . . A deep breath and a slow release eased some of the constriction around her heart. She had to believe, to have faith. Chin lifted high, Suzanne met Chase's gaze straight on. "Dreams don't always come true. You, of all people, should know that."

179

His grin faltered, but then he rapped his knuckles on the end table. "I won't reveal the lawyer's battle tactics; though he made an interesting suggestion I hadn't thought of."

No way would she ask. And he wouldn't tell. Time to turn the tables. "I understand you requested a leave of absence from your job. Why did you do that?"

His eyebrows arched. "News travels fast."

A sip of delicious green tea warmed her. "I overheard you on the phone in the solarium."

Stark eyebrows drew together into a single intimidating line, his tone rough. "Eavesdropping?"

"Hardly. I'm sure the folks in Emerald Point heard you, too."

He gave her a narrowed glance. "It's not a secret."

"I thought your boss wanted you back right away."

"I gave him an alternative," Chase snapped. "Either grant the leave or I'd quit."

Suzanne sensed his decision hadn't come without a great deal of thought. *Deflect. Change the subject.* "Lara said Jeff asked for his parents a couple of times this afternoon when she put him down for his nap. We need to talk to him. Soon."

The gleam in his eyes dimmed. "Yeah, we do, but how do you explain to a child his age that his mommy and daddy aren't coming back?"

She swallowed hard. "I don't know. Now that you're staying on for a while, do you think we might put it off few a few days?"

A trace of suspicion surfaced in his darkened eyes. "Why wait?"

She crossed her arms and leaned forward. "I need to make a quick trip to New York."

He poured coffee from a carafe. "You already made plane reservations?"

"Yes."

He lifted the cup to his lips. "Problems?"

"A large shipment of skirts and tops arrived from Paris. My assistant doesn't think the workmanship meets my standards. Some of the fabric is inferior. I need to examine the merchandise and confirm his opinion."

One eyebrow lifted. "You question your assistant's judgment?"

"He's worked for me less than a year. I could lose my supplier. I should be the one to make a decision as important as this." Her confidence soared when she discussed her business.

Lara entered the room at that moment. "Would you like me to refill the carafe?"

Chase shook his head.

"I hope you're not angry with me for not accepting your offers," she said.

"Of course not." Chase patted her shoulder. "We're grateful for all you've done for Jeff and his parents."

Lara bit her lower lip and hustled to the kitchen.

Suzanne pushed back her chair and rose. "I need to finish packing."

Chase moved around the table toward her. "Need any help?" At the gleam in his eyes, she sensed danger.

"No. I'm just taking a few things for the trip." She edged past him.

At the foot of the stairs, he caught her arm and turned her toward him. Removing the jewelry bag from his inside jacket pocket, he tugged at the drawstring. "I asked you before if you'd wear this."

"I really don't —"

"Gold will look beautiful against your flawless skin. You'll do for this necklace what no other woman could. And I'll bet the pendant will dangle right there." With his index finger, he touched the hollow on her neck.

Her lungs stopped working.

The sound of his voice sent heat rushing to her face. She reached out to push him away, but missed, her hands flailing.

His fingertips brushed her cheek.

"Don't," she pleaded.

"Do this for me," he murmured.

She peered down at the bag that held the two necklaces and whispered, "Only if you wear the other one."

Several long, tension-filled moments passed before he nodded.

"Allow me."

He brushed the wisps of hair from her nape, and then draped the pendent over her head. His warm touch burned into her skin as he fastened the clasp and then caressed the delicate skin under her ear.

Tiny shivers raked her body. The jagged-edged pendant nestled in the hollow just as he predicted.

"Thanks." Suzanne made a quick turn toward him. "Why are we doing this?"

"A reminder of Pam, Tad, and Jeff."

She touched the pendant and squeezed until it dug into her palm. "I don't need this to remember them. They're in my heart."

He studied her for endless moments and then moved closer, his eyes gleaming like polished silver. "Maybe wearing it will help you remember me, too."

What was his motive? And why did she

question everything he said or did? Then a thought jolted her mind, recalling the night she'd expected him to kiss her.

Now? Would he kiss her now?

"Since you'll probably leave early for the flight from Portland, I should send you off with something more than words."

Oh, oh. Her heart picked up speed.

His arms encircled her waist, and he drew her toward him.

She inhaled a quick breath, his look so intense, she had to tear her gaze from his. "Don't do this, Chase."

With his finger he tipped up her chin. "Why not?"

"Because I know the way you feel about—"

"Hush."

Part of her desperately wanted to pull away, but another part of her didn't.

His face lowered to only inches from hers, and he squeezed her body tighter. "I won't say goodbye. That's too final. We both know you'll be back."

"In a few days," she murmured.

His mouth covered hers.

For an instant she didn't react, but then she relaxed and allowed him to coax a response. Her hands slid up his chest to grip his shoulders. Nothing in her life had ever felt more right.

He pulled away, stared at her in awe, and claimed her mouth again. When he paused once more, she tried to wriggle away, but his arms were bands of steel.

Drowning in him, she whimpered, "Please stop."

Standing close, bodies touching, Chase couldn't think. How sweet Suzanne's mouth tasted. Something flitted in her eyes that puzzled him. Was she afraid of him? And then she asked him to stop. Maybe it was a good thing.

Disconcerted, he eased his hold but didn't let her go. "I feel as if I'm being washed down a churning river, and can't swim away from you or strike out for shore." And now he'd gone and admitted to the power she held over him.

Unable to process his insane reaction to her, Chase let his arms drop away, turned, and walked to the stairs.

13

Early Sunday morning, Suzanne awoke to the crash of surf at high tide. The open drapes let in a view of the whitecaps slamming against the rocks while the sun played with the high clouds, a welcome contrast to yesterday's coastal rain.

Envy rippled through her when an eagle flew past the window. The bird had no cares, no worries, unlike the burdens she faced.

A quick shower later, dressed in a blue tunic and skirt, she entered the kitchen and popped a slice of toast. "Morning, Lara."

"Morning." The housekeeper fussed with a ham and cheese omelet, and moments later, ladled it onto Suzanne's plate.

Suzanne spread butter on the toast, and then nibbled on it. "Where's Chase?"

"Tad's foreman called about a problem with a contract."

Hmm. Chase was knowledgeable about stuff like that. "Is my little tyke ready for church?"

"I woke him a little while ago. He's rattling around in his room." Lara placed the flour sifter on the counter top. "Just because I'm caring for my sick sister today, doesn't mean you have to take Jeff to the service."

"You said he's been a precious angel the past few Sundays. Tad and Pam would want this."

"Yes, they would."

Suzanne twisted her mouth. "I only started to attend Sunday services a few years ago. For Pam's sake, I feel I should do all I can for her son. A child needs consistency in his life, so I might as well start now."

"Of course." Lara checked her watch. "The cab's due in thirty minutes. I'll get Jeff fed and dressed."

"Thanks. We'll sit in the back pew. If the bell tower hasn't fallen by the time we leave, I'll say an extra prayer."

Lara tsked. "All you have to do is pray and sing along with the choir."

Suzanne grinned.

Lara squinted in the sunlight now gleaming through the French doors. "Have you asked the Lord for a solution to Jeff's problem?"

"It's Chase and I who need Divine intervention."

"Ask the Lord. He will listen if you welcome Him into your heart."

Lara was right, and was also a great spiritual influence on all of them. But still — "That's a long trail to ride."

"Not if you're sincere and seek Him out."

Could *she* be that fortunate? "I'd meet Jesus with open arms if I thought I could make up for the spiritual years I've lost."

"A good attitude always helps."

"Now I know why Tad and Pam thought you were the perfect addition to their family."

Lara blushed. "Pshaw."

Jeff skipped down the stairs, all smiley-faced. He dug into a gingerbread boy pancake, complete with chocolate chips for eyes, nose, mouth and buttons down the front.

After every crumb was cleared from his dish, Lara bundled him into a warm, hooded jacket. Minutes later, he and Suzanne climbed into the waiting taxi.

The white church with a large bell tower came into view. The building overlooked the ocean, its huge double doors welcoming. Her lips curved into a smile.

With no desire to be anywhere else, she

held Jeff's hand as he skipped along beside her.

A couple stopped at the entrance and stared at him. "Jeff?" the woman whispered and hunkered down. "Of course, it's you." She stood and faced Suzanne. "You must be —"

"Pam's sister."

"I'm Melody Kelly. And this is my husband, Grant. We are . . . were friends of the Garwoods."

Suzanne grasped the woman's hand. "Suzanne Bratton. Nice meeting you both."

Grant nodded. In his early forties, he resembled the kind of hunk Pam would've flipped over. Well, she would have before her marriage.

Suzanne winced at the reminder of another man in her sister's life. But her sister was a Christian. She knew Pam wasn't perfect, but to have broken her marriage vows. It just didn't seem a woman with a dog-eared Bible would have had an affair. Would that thought cast suspicion on every male in town?

Melody glanced around. "Our son's here somewhere. Ah, there he is. Rick?"

A tall, lean teenager, loping across the parking lot, looked up. As he drew nearer, his eyelashes shifted down to hide his eyes.

"Suzanne, this is our son, Rick."

He nodded without looking up and mumbled, "Hello."

"Nice meeting you, Rick. You know Jeff?"

The lanky teen offered a half smile. "Hey, squirt."

Jeff grinned at him.

A puff of wind blew Melody's dark hair across her face which she brushed aside. "Come, sit with us."

Suzanne nodded. "OK. Thanks."

The Kellys headed for a pew on the left side aisle.

Suzanne followed with Jeff's little hand wedged firmly in hers, and slid in beside the family.

A warm, cozy sense of connection to life with the Lord drifted over her as she gazed around the small church. The altar stood in relief against a wall of windows while the sun's golden rays created a pattern on the wooden floor.

"We have a new minister," Melody whispered. "His name is William Masters. And that stained-glass window?" She waved toward the side of the altar. "That's new, too."

"It's beautiful." Suzanne lifted Jeff's hood and he wriggled out of his jacket.

On the pew between them, he ran his tiny

car back and forth and then up and down her hand. He spotted someone at the altar and put his finger across his lips, settling back against the seat.

She placed her arm around him, thrilled when he snuggled close against her side. Such a sweetheart. Joy bubbled inside.

At the glorious sound of the organ, another thrill shot through her. The soloist sang "Count Your Blessings" in a contralto voice that lifted Suzanne's spirits. She closed her eyes and tipped her head back.

The pastor began the sermon, and after a few moments, Jeff began to squirm in his seat. She gave him a children's book of Bible stories she'd found in his playroom.

He flipped through the pages and pointed to the glossy pictures of Jesus. How much had Pam taught him about the Bible? He had so much to learn . . .

She did, too.

Similar situations would pop up in the future. There'd always be new circumstances to tackle. At times like this, the thought of caring for a young child almost overwhelmed her.

Most of the songs the choir and congregation sang were familiar. She joined them, the words coming freely from the recesses of her mind while Jeff's little head nodded and his body relaxed beneath her arm. Safe in dreamland.

The service over, she tickled his chin until he woke up. Gathering their things and donning their coats, they made their way out.

Jeff, lost in his own little world, stomped his feet.

"Little gentleman walk in church." Suzanne leaned down to whisper, "Be grownup, like Uncle Chase."

"Gentle." His brow furrowed, and he stopped stomping his feet.

Ahead, the people moved rapidly through the line where the pastor greeted his congregation. When she and Jeff reached him, Suzanne extended her hand. "I'm Suzanne Bratton, Pam Garwood's sister. Thank you again for the beautiful words you chose to eulogize her and Tad."

He grasped it with firm hands, welcomed her, and introduced himself. "It was my honor. We miss them." The pastor reached for the boy's hand. "Hello, Jeff."

Shyness made an appearance. Ducking behind her, Jeff grabbed Suzanne's leg and peeked around it.

She patted the boy's head and sent the pastor a knowing smile, which he returned with a nod.

The Kellys waited for them outside.

"I'm so glad we met," Suzanne told Melody.

Pam's friend hugged her. "If you have time, let's get together."

"I'd be delighted." Suzanne shook Grant's hand.

Their son, Rick, barreled across the parking lot. For some reason, the odd way he kicked out his feet tickled a memory in Suzanne's mind. "How old is Rick?" she asked.

"Seventeen." His father grimaced. "No, thirty-five."

Suzanne laughed. Pam's teen years came to mind. "Normal behavior for that age."

"Really?" He raised his eyebrows. "I guess I've forgotten."

Melody hugged Jeff, before turning with her husband and heading toward the parking lot.

"I'm hungry," Jeff announced.

"Lara left lunch for us in the refrigerator." Spotting the taxi she'd called waiting at the curb, she led the boy to their ride.

A nagging thought of something brought a frown to her brow. Was it Rick or his parents that seemed a bit off?

Jeff jumped into the waiting taxi. "Unca Chase here?"

"I don't know." She sat beside him, her

focus switching to her upcoming trip back east. The Kellys slipped off her radar.

Weary from a long and uneventful overnight flight, Suzanne entered her business loft in Manhattan. Andy Pollard, her twenty-six-year-old assistant, waited. He picked her up and spun her around with multiple kisses for her cheek.

"I'm glad you're here, boss."

"Put me down." She grinned. "We have lots of work to do."

He deposited her in her seat behind the desk, clicked his heels and saluted. "At your service."

Wow. What a guy.

"You know what?" Giggles still quivered in her throat. "If you weren't such a hunk, I'd fire you for whirling me around like a rag doll."

He expanded his broad chest and thrust out his chin. "It isn't just good looks, brawn, and humor I offer, my lady. I've got brains, too."

She laughed at this overgrown boy whose playful nature enhanced his charm. From his curly, wheat-blond hair to size 14 triple E shoes — six and a half feet of solid masculinity. One might think his brain was composed of bubble wrap. Not so. Andy possessed intelligence and shrewdness in everyday decisions. Though he'd only worked for her a short time, he'd already proved to be a loyal and valuable asset.

She massaged her temples. "Let's check the shipment from Paris."

In the warehouse, she inspected the newly delivered racks of tops, pants and skirts. "You're right, Andy. These garments look as though they've been sewn by two different groups." She shook her head and tsked at the shoddy workmanship. A waste of time, money and effort.

He nodded. "Any delay is critical for the spring showing. I couldn't accept this shipment without your approval."

"It just proves what I've known all along. You have a knack for this business."

He grinned, his male ego — and there appeared to be lots of it — now bolstered. "Shall we call Pierre?"

She glanced at her watch. "He should be in his office. Tell him what you found. If he gives you any trouble, I'll talk to him." Oh, yeah, she'd more than talk. She'd demand.

Andy grabbed the receiver and dialed the number in Paris.

While Andy spoke to Pierre, Suzanne went to the pile of substandard clothing, placed it back in the packing material it came in, and went online to print a shipping label. She made quick work of taping the box and affixing the label, carried the package over to the door, and set it in the space reserved for the mailman to pick up.

From the seventh-floor window, she scanned the world below. Her warehouse and office were located in Manhattan's garment district. Tiny workers loaded and unloaded boxes of fabric and supplies and pushed racks of clothing along the sidewalks.

She'd first rented the loft three years ago, her thumb on the heartbeat of the industry. But the thrill she'd experienced then escaped her now. What was missing?

His hand over the mouthpiece, Andy motioned to her. "Pierre insists on speaking with you."

She plucked the receiver from his hand. "My handsome Frenchman, how are you?"

"If you are not pleased with my shipment, I am not at all well, *ma Cherie*," he said in thickly accented English.

Suzanne stifled a laugh at the image that formed in her mind of featherweight Pierre, seated behind his huge, leather-covered desk, twirling his thin, black mustache. "No, I'm not pleased, but I'm sure you have a logical explanation."

"*Mais oui.* I have troubles with my sewing staff. They clamor for more money. They call in ill or give all sorts of reasons why they cannot work."

"So, you farmed out my order?"

He faked an asthmatic cough. "I had no choice."

"Why don't you pay your employees what they're worth?"

"No, no. I cannot do that." He wheezed, but failed to sound convincing. "You see, I would have to increase my prices."

"Take a little less profit," she said. "Postpone the purchase of that expensive Italian car."

"My wife —"

Suzanne leaned forward. "No increase in price. The fabric in at least a third of the skirts is not what we agreed upon. Also, a dozen tops. Remember, we have a contract." Before he could respond, she rushed on. "We're returning the unacceptable garments at *your* expense. Andy will e-mail the list. Now, when can we expect a replacement shipment?"

Pierre sputtered. "You cannot do this."

"The unacceptable portion of the shipment is already on its way."

Andy's eyebrows shot up, but she motioned to the packed order waiting for the mailman. It was only one box of the many received, but it was a start in the return shipping process. Andy nodded.

"But —"

"When?" she demanded, tapping her pencil on the desk while Pierre's muffled expletives filled the line.

"You are *tres difficile*." He hesitated, but only for a few moments. "Four weeks."

"Make it two. I'll expect a written confirmation today. Don't let this happen again, Pierre, and double check the fabric and workmanship yourself."

"*Mon amie* —"

"Going forward, know that my assistant speaks for me. I trust his judgment. *Au revoir,* my friend." She dropped the receiver into its cradle.

Andy combed his fingers through his golden hair. Women must adore running their hands through its softness. "Pierre wouldn't listen to me," he grumbled.

"He will from now on. The next time a problem like this happens, and there will certainly be a next time, Pierre will know you're in charge. Even if you and I have to reinforce it with a quick trip to Paris. He may have a gift for style, but it's good we buy mostly American made clothes."

Andy grinned. "Thanks, boss. I needed

that." He stood straighter, an added measure of self-confidence in the set of his massive shoulders.

She nodded in dismissal and turned her attention to the huge stack of papers on her desk. A long day lay ahead of her.

14

The endless flight from New York caught Suzanne either napping or reading Bible Scriptures. One Psalm resonated with her, uplifting her spirits. *He shall cover thee with His feathers, and under His wings shalt thou trust: His truth shall be thy shield and buckler.*

So many questions remained unanswered in her life. She craved the Lord's comfort. Here especially, in the airplane, so far from earth, she felt closer to Him than ever before. It came as no surprise for the feeling to amplify when the plane's tires touched down on the runway.

Late afternoon sun filtered through the windows of Portland International Airport terminal where she could see Chase waiting in the lounge area. "Oh, no," she groaned, "I don't think I can handle another dose of that man's charms."

Even if he hadn't been waving his arms, it wasn't difficult to pick him out of the crowd

— a giant sequoia in a forest of Western hemlock. Dressed to kill in a beige sweater and brown woolen trousers, the turning heads of every woman under fifty gave testament to the fact that he was the best-looking man there. More than one admiring glance went his way.

She frowned. "I told you it wasn't necessary to meet me."

His gaze traveled over her face. "After I spoke with you, I called the weather bureau and the airline. All flights are cancelled because of heavy fog south of here. There's no way you could have gotten home tonight. Let's pick up your luggage."

He said the word home with odd, almost tender warmth. Was he thinking of Emerald Point as home? Was she?

His hand on her elbow set her heart revving like a racecar. "Thanks." She lifted her overnight case. "I travel light."

He took the small bag, looped it over one shoulder, and led Suzanne toward the parking lot. An almost frosty silence filled the space between them.

Suzanne brushed an imaginary wrinkle from her short-cropped jacket. "Are you sure the roads are clear?"

"We'll manage."

He unlocked the truck and held the door

for her to climb in. And then, he sprinted to the driver's side. Moments later the engine sprang to life. Was it her imagination or did he seem in a different mood from when she left for New York?

He must have read her thoughts, for a bark of laughter left his lips. "What?"

"I don't know. I expected you to revert to your less-than-friendly disposition. This concern," she gestured toward him, "is disconcerting."

A faint glint of humor lit his eyes. "I'm trying."

She felt her mouth curve up in response. "Yes, you can be very *trying* when the mood suits you."

His eyebrows shot up. "You're badgering me, ma'am."

"Not really. I'm just tired. A cozy bed in Emerald Point is what I need." She settled back. "How are Jeff and Lara?"

"He fusses when I don't give him an answer about his parents and clings to Lara. And she often wipes tears from her eyes."

"Poor baby, and Lara, too," Suzanne murmured. "I hope the three days I've been gone haven't been too hard on all of you."

With a few deft maneuvers, Chase cleared the airport traffic. "I doubt you could have done much. Right now, in Jeff's childish mind, maybe he associates us with the reason his parents aren't here."

That could be true. Who knew what a child's mind conjured up?

They fell silent while the scenery whizzed past. Immersed in her own thoughts, she jolted when Chase finally spoke.

"Did you resolve the problem with the French couturier?"

She gave him a brief summary of her conversation with Pierre.

"Sounds as though you know how to handle the man."

Maybe so, but she sure couldn't handle *this* man. "Pierre was wrong and had no choice in the matter. He called me a tough lady."

"Tough lady," he repeated. She glared at him, and he laughed deep in his throat. "I only repeated what you said."

She sniffed and tossed her head. "You're determined to provoke me."

"If you say so." His glance said more than his words.

Thirty minutes south of Portland, pockets of fog appeared. They soon thickened and swirled around the truck, at times impairing visibility. When oncoming headlights lurched into their lane, he jerked the wheel. The truck skidded, bumping onto the shoulder of the road. He jammed on the brakes as a tractor-trailer thundered past.

The shadow of death had crossed her path. Her pounding heart sent a rush of adrenalin through her veins.

"Crazy idiot." Chase slammed his palm against the wheel. "This fog is getting too heavy or that kind of speed. Maybe we should stop for a while."

"Is there a restaurant around here?"

Chase looked over his shoulder and pulled back onto the road. "We'll stop at the next one."

Neon lights flickered ahead. Two cars in front of them signaled and pulled into the diner's parking lot.

Her heartbeat had slowed at last, but now she felt sluggish. A bad time for jet lag to kick in. But that wasn't her kind of blessing lately.

Inside the crowded diner, Chase steered her toward the last empty booth. "We might as well make ourselves comfortable."

She draped her coat beside her.

On a nearby wall, a TV showed a weather forecaster bundled up in warm gear and standing to the side of a road. The camera panned across the area, focused on the soupy fog while the reporter issued a travel warning.

■ ■ ■ ■

Chase drummed his fingertips on the tabletop, nerves on edge. Silence stretched between him and Suzanne, one he didn't know how to break. At long last, a harried waitress came over to take their order.

"Sorry for the wait. We're crazy busy. What can I get for you?"

Chase waited for Suzanne to voice her order, and then gave his own. Twenty minutes later, their burgers arrived.

"About time." He rubbed his hands together and grabbed the ketchup. "I'm starved."

Her mouth twitched, but she didn't speak.

"I have a question." When she looked up, he continued. "Do you still hate me?"

A pensiveness shadowed Suzanne's eyes. "I don't hate you, Chase. But even after those kisses, I don't believe you want to change anything between us."

"Really? What about our attraction? Can you accept it?"

She stirred in her seat. "I've been attracted to many men, but that doesn't mean I acted on it."

"You're known as the 'Ice Maiden.' Is there any truth there?"

"Yes, with certain men."

"Am I, by any chance, one of those men you're attracted to?"

The shadow in her eyes deepened. "Perhaps we should talk about something less explosive."

Every fiber of his body became attuned to her. "Let's get this out in the open. I know I'm tough and arrogant. Does that turn you off?"

"You're tough in some ways, but you also have class. And arrogance is often confused with confidence. Your attitude, on the other hand, could use definite improvement." She picked up her burger and took a bite.

"Class? Should I live up to your expectations? Prove I'm arrogant?"

Her food held in mid-air, she finished chewing, swallowed and sighed. "You sure ask a lot of questions. What's this really about?"

"It's the only way I can find out the answers to what's bothering me."

"If you don't already know." She snorted, not a delicate, ladylike sound. "I doubt I can enlighten you."

He scarfed down the last of his burger and drained the cup of coffee.

Dark circles under her eyes gave her a bruised look. Not the best time for this conversation.

He got up too fast, almost knocking over his glass of water. A quick grab set it aright again. "I need some air. There's a store across the highway. Would you like anything?"

She leaped to her feet. "Crossing the highway in this fog is too dangerous. Visibility is bad. You could get hit by a car or one of those big rigs."

He stepped toward her and lowered his voice. "Well, that would solve our problem with Jeff. With me out of the way, there'd be no question about custody."

Her face paled with astonishment. "I don't wish you harm."

"Not even if it got you Jeff?"

"Not even for Jeff." Irritation filled her voice as her eyes gave off sparks.

He shrugged. "I'll be careful."

She extended slim, feminine fingers with pink lacquered nails toward him.

Tossing a bill on the table, he slipped out the diner door, and strode toward the road. Misty fog swirled around him, the hard concrete beneath his shoes. Here and there the fog dissipated a little. After a logging truck swept past, he jogged across the road.

Minutes later, a bottle of brandy stuffed in his jacket pocket, he listened to the hum of motors approaching. Stepping back off the pavement, he waited, ventured forward, and then retreated again. Vehicles whizzed past from both directions.

"Idiots," he muttered as taillights disappeared.

Out of the mist, a caravan whooshed past and a semi-trailer zoomed by with four cars close behind.

Tires screeched. Milliseconds later —

Boom. Boom. Boom.

Rending metal and anguished cries filled the cool night air.

Crashing sounds echoed in Suzanne's ears. Heart pounding, she knocked her coffee cup aside and jumped up. The cup clattered against the table. "Oh, Lord. Please, not Chase." She shrugged into her coat, and dashed for the front door.

Shouts and screams erupted from the road. Then an eerie quiet descended.

Taking a deep breath, she clamped down on her rising hysteria and peered through the billowing fog, frantic to find Chase. He'd been gone — she glanced at her watch — twenty minutes.

Barely able to make out the store's neon lights across the road, she whispered, "Chase, where are you?" If anything happened to him — No, he would've been between the store and the truck, not down the highway where voices shouted.

Ahead, flashlights cut through the fog. A ghostlike form emerged from the twilight. A car, overturned. One wheel still spinning.

Two men raced past. She rooted in her purse for a tiny flashlight, chased after them, and then peered through the darkness. Nothing.

She smelled the pungent odor of gasoline, and a child's cry echoed in the gloom. Then the tinkle of breaking glass, and someone pounding on metal.

"Need a light over here," a deep voice commanded. "Get the boy to the side of the road."

Moments later, the same voice yelled, "Don't light those flares. There's gasoline everywhere."

Could that be Chase?

In the distance, the spine-tingling sound of a siren reverberated through the fog. Shouts became mingled. Muted. A light flashed. Someone lifted a tiny girl through an SUV's smashed window and placed her on the pavement. The vehicle was crushed between a car and a tanker truck.

"Mommy," the child wailed. The tiny face

and body showed she couldn't be more than four.

Flashlights lit the area, giving the scene a surreal impression. A man picked up the child and carried her well away from the road. Suzanne rushed to them.

Can I control my tears?

She shone her tiny light on the girl's bloody face and gritted her teeth. Kneeling, she draped her coat over the fragile body, brushed aside dark hair from the girl's cheeks, and caressed the damp forehead. "You're OK," she whispered.

The child sniffled, and one tiny hand grasped Suzanne's and held on.

"What's your name?" Suzanne asked.

"Emma."

"Emma, do you know the Lord's Prayer?"

She sucked in a sob. "A little."

Suzanne squeezed the child's hand. "Say it with me, OK? Our Father, Who art in heaven, hallowed be Thy name."

She recited the rest of the prayer, and Emma joined her with a hesitant word here and there.

"Who was in the car with you, sweetie?"

"Mommy." The little one whimpered.

"God will help her."

Emma wept softly.

Suzanne sat back on her haunches to peer

around. *Chase? Where are you?*

Praying for him and all the souls involved in the accident, she remembered sending thoughts heavenward earlier today. Strange how that struck her now.

Sirens blared, louder this time. Closer. Half a dozen more flashlights arced, signaling the way for the vehicles. Red lights flashed through the soupy fog. Amid a flurry of activity, two paramedics checked the injured.

When one of them aimed a light on Suzanne, she shielded her eyes with her hand and stood.

"Are you hurt, ma'am?"

"No. I wasn't in the accident, but this little girl was."

He dropped to the child's side, pushed aside the coat, and ran his hands over her body. "Hey, sweetheart, can you tell me where you hurt?"

Emma sniffed. "I want my mommy."

"Appears to be scrapes and bruises," he murmured. "We've requested more ambulances. Look after her, OK?"

"Sure." Suzanne hunkered down again, shivering without a coat.

The paramedic ran toward the vehicles, his flashlight centered on the grisly scene. Two rigs with a car sandwiched between them. Other cars sat at odd angles, as if they'd ricocheted off the semis. Like Jeff's cars and how he crashed them into each other.

Moments later, another beam of light landed on her and the child. Chase.

With a muffled cry, Suzanne jumped up and hugged him. "Are you all right?" she whispered. "I was so worried."

"I'm fine. I can't say as much for some of the others." A touch of gruffness in his voice, he added, "With the condition of the vehicles, it's a miracle this little gal wasn't badly hurt." Stepping back, he pulled off his sweater and slipped it over Suzanne's head. "Put your arms through the sleeves," he ordered.

"I'm OK," she protested. "Aren't you cold?"

"I'm moving. You're not."

Several oncoming cars inched toward the crash site. "I need to help the others," Chase said. "Stay off the road. If some lunatic comes barreling along, anything can happen. I'll be back." He and the flashlight disappeared into the billowy fog.

A new man's voice had joined the others on the scene. "There's a woman pinned in this car."

Suzanne focused her flashlight on the girl

before she touched the little face. When she whimpered, Suzanne murmured, "Shhh, honey. I won't leave you."

Much later, Emma and her mother were whisked away in an ambulance.

Chase returned, no longer holding the flashlight. "The police and firemen have arrived in force. We can't do any more here. Let's go." His arm draped around her shoulders, he steered her back to the diner.

"Did you speak with the police?"

"I told them what I could. I didn't see the accident happen."

Patrons milled about in the diner's parking area, asking questions and expressing concern. Chase answered a few, emotion threading his words.

Inside the diner, they squeezed into a smaller booth toward the back.

Suzanne spotted crimson smears on his shirt and the sweater she wore. "Oh, Chase . . ."

"I think we both could do with a drop of this." His voice was barely audible as he held up the bottle of brandy.

"I don't drink."

"It might help."

"I'd rather not."

A breaking news alert interrupted the television program playing on the wall across from them. Pictures of the terrible scene outside filled the screen, but thankfully the fog obscured most of the gory details. A bevy of flashing lights from the rescue vehicles added to the sense of catastrophe. "Here's what we know so far. Dense fog is being blamed for a vehicle pile-up. Some fatalities have been reported, but names are being withheld at the moment. There are a number of injuries of those being transported to local hospitals. Stay with us for updates."

Unable to drag her eyes from the TV screen, Suzanne offered a silent prayer for everyone involved. Pam and Tad's car looked like the mangled SUV Emma had been rescued from.

Chase drummed on the table, a nervous habit she'd come to recognize. "I'll go to the counter and order us some warm drinks. I heard a waitress say it'll be hours before the road is reopened. We could spend the night in the truck. I have blankets. How do you feel about that?"

"There's no other choice."

When he poured brandy into his empty cup and sipped on it, his hand shook.

They left the diner and made their way through the fog. He opened the truck's passenger door, adjusted the angle of her seat, and then stood back so she could climb in. "I'm afraid it won't be comfortable."

She curled up. "That's OK."

He handed her a blanket and a bag of Lara's chips. "Don't drop any on the seat," he teased. "Broken chips make me cranky." His footsteps echoed on the pavement as he strode around the front of the truck. The driver's side door shut, and the overhead light went out. A car's headlights brightened the scene, and for a moment she spotted Chase's profile as he adjusted his own seat.

"I need to call Lara to let her know our predicament." Suzanne rummaged for her phone, scrolled to the right number still listed as 'Pam–house phone', and hit the icon. The glow of the backscreen popped to life, lighting her grief for her sister for a bare moment. After a few assurances from her, and Chase on speaker, Lara wished them both a good night.

Darkness closed in around them.

In view of the horror, the nightmare they'd shared, the problems between them seemed insignificant. She shuddered at the thought of him crossing the road in the fog. How easily he could have been a statistic.

A shroud of silence descended. Time passed.

She caressed the pendant Chase had given

her. Did he wear its mate?

Though she didn't look at him, she realized he was no more asleep than she. Swallowing hard, she pressed her cheeks to hold back tears.

"Suzanne?"

Her eyes widened and a chill charged through her. "Yes?" she whispered.

"All those broken bodies tore me up. I feel like crying, but I'm not ashamed of that." His words held a slight slur, the effects of brandy, no doubt. "Would you do something for me? I need the warmth of another human. Please, may I hold you, Sue?"

15

Suzanne mentally repeated what Chase had said. He asked if he could hold her.

How could she comfort him with the truck's console jutting between them?

She ran her hand over the leather upholstery. The interior still smelled new, other than the added scent of wood chips. She glanced back at the extended cab, only big enough for Jeff's car seat and a few packages.

She fumbled with the blanket Chase had given her, unsure if she should cover herself. He might misconstrue her action as closing herself off, putting a barrier between them.

Tapping her fist against her lips — was that to avoid a reply?

She tugged on her earlobe and it came to her that she must have lost the inexpensive piece of jewelry. A small matter.

Her mind a jumbled mess, she fought with herself, agreeing one instant, refusing the next. Run, common sense told her, but for some crazy reason, she wanted him closer.

An invisible band constricted her chest. Could she turn him down when he might be suffering from mental shock over the horrific injuries, the stench of blood, and the general chaos at the accident scene? He wasn't in the medical profession, nor used to seeing broken bodies. No, she couldn't refuse.

A passing car's lights flashed on the windshield giving her a glimpse of his shadowed face and sad eyes that touched her heart. She sucked in the anguished feelings she really couldn't cope with. Then she heard herself murmur, "Sure."

Chase moved closer, near enough that she could feel his upper body heat, his fingers firm on her back. "Thanks."

Her arms went around his neck. The pleasant scent of mint drifted to her nostrils. "When I heard the crashes, I was so scared you were hurt."

"Fear scared me, too, of what I'd find in those cars and trucks." He groaned, despair dropping his voice into bass range.

The languid movement of his hands across her back increased the tempo of her heart. "Were you the first one on the scene?"

"Yes. I couldn't see much until someone

brought a flashlight." His shoulders shook. "I smelled gasoline and thought about fire. Agonized over my decisions — whether to move the victims or wait for the EMTs."

Swamped by visceral feelings cartwheeling through her, she refused to let her mind dwell on the accident any longer.

Her fingertips traced the jagged edge of the heavy gold medallion around his neck. With the other hand, she clutched her matching half-heart.

Silence enveloped them.

"You have soft hands. Soothing. Winsome."

She froze. "Don't say those things."

"Why? Because we're adversaries? Can't we forget that for now?" Seconds passed before he spoke again in a velvet-edged voice. "I need you, Suzanne."

"I do," she whispered, shocked at her own admission.

"Then what's the problem?"

She pulled away. "You think I'm cold and unfeeling. So, what's your motive? Curiosity?"

Chase's muscles tensed. Right. He'd thought of her that way when they'd first met, and had given no indication he'd changed his mind. "I didn't know you then."

"You don't know me now."

He sensed her hurt. His conscience told him his attitude had caused her pain. "Can you think of a better way to find out other than discussing it? I care about you."

She let out an audible sigh. "You care about me?"

"I'm not a monster, Suzanne."

"I didn't say you were."

No, she hadn't. He needed her tonight, if only to have her comforting arms around him. Unable to break down her barriers, he'd settle for whatever she'd give.

"I suppose we could try working on a friendlier attitude tomorrow."

He nodded.

Her fingers splayed across his back. "Good night."

"Good night, sweet one," he murmured, and pressed a soft kiss on her forehead. "Sleep tight."

She nestled against his neck. A perfect fit.

"A long, restless night," Chase muttered as the morning sun filtered through the wisps of fog still enveloping them. Their world seemed so small in the truck's interior.

Arms wrapped around Suzanne, his attempts to force sleep had resulted in little success. Now weariness drained his strength.

Straightening, he slipped from the truck, and strolled along the road in the opposite direction from the accident. No way would he look at the mangled vehicles again. Instead, all he saw was a line of cars on the southbound lane, all at a standstill. A reminder of what lay behind him, of what he'd seen the night before . . .

He backtracked toward the parking lot.

Suzanne sat upright, her hands combing her hair. A moment more and she pressed her face against the window. Was she searching — for him?

His pace quickened until he reached the passenger side and opened the door. Her shadowed eyes brought back memories of the long night he'd spent just holding her. "Are you OK?"

She yawned. "I will be as soon as I get my first jolt of coffee."

Sharp needle pricks stabbed behind his right eye. Not again. Not now. He lifted his hand and rubbed his forehead out of habit. Not that it helped. Only a pill could.

He clenched his fists. This time he'd ride out the pain.

Minutes later in the diner, with conversations buzzing around them, they ordered breakfast.

After fifteen minutes of silence between them, their food finally arrived.

She sipped at her coffee, and then scooped up a forkful of scrambled eggs.

He followed each movement of the fork from the plate to her lips.

"You look tired," she said. "Did you get any sleep?"

He couldn't leave that alone. "You, too. Did you get any rest?"

She poured strawberry syrup on her pancakes. "Sitting up all night in a truck isn't my idea of rest. Or maybe you played a part in it."

His hand shook as he sipped the coffee. "You were toasty warm against the chill in my soul."

"Don't go there, please," she whispered.

"I didn't even kiss you."

"Chase, our lives are complicated enough without that."

During the night, close in each other's arms, had she felt the ripple of passion charge through him?

She'd appeared so kissable, her mouth relaxed, long lashes fluttering on her cheeks.

Her acceptance of his embrace had erased the battered bodies from his mind. But he still ached from the fantasies his mind had woven in the early morning hours, images

222

of her beside him, working together through a lifetime ...

Two men entered the diner, one carrying a TV camera. He asked one of the waitresses about the Good Samaritan. "You know — the guy who helped rescue the injured before the paramedics arrived."

Chase ducked his head and stared at the remainder of his food.

"I don't know," the waitress replied. "We were so busy that we didn't know what was going on out there. Some of the customers called him a hero, gung-ho to save more than one life."

He looked up. Suzanne studied him, concern in her gorgeous eyes. "Won't you talk with the reporter? You might get some free publicity for your company."

"Forget it. I did what anyone would do." He threw down his napkin, and took a final swig of coffee. Dropping some money on the table, he grumbled, "Let's go."

Suzanne's brain didn't function during the two-hour roundabout drive to Emerald Point. She kept casting furtive glances at Chase, but he kept his gaze on the road and his hands on the steering wheel.

Well into the drive, he finally spoke. "The accountant called yesterday. He sent the statements of Tad's business along with the house account. We discussed the financial condition of the mill. It's heavily mortgaged. Tad's foreman, Zach, said equipment replacement was the reason. I looked through the checks. It all seemed in order. But the house account —" One hand splayed the air. "Excessive expenditures."

"Running a large home like theirs must take a lot of money. Housekeeper wages, food, health care, maintenance, incidentals."

"You'll find the envelope in the solarium, along with a batch of letters for Pam."

She eyed him. "What aren't you saying?"

"The house is mortgaged, too. I went over the balance sheets. Wow." He shook his head. "Check out the five boxes in the spare bedroom that arrived while you were gone."

She frowned. "Maybe I've jumped to conclusions, but Pam craved lovely things. Growing up we didn't have much." She paused, and her mouth turned down at the corners.

"We lived up the coast from Emerald Point," she continued, lost in memories. "Our dad was a drill press operator when he could hold a job. Mom didn't help, always harping on how he couldn't provide for us. She made his life miserable and ours, too."

"I know all about difficult moms." He rubbed the back of his neck. "You should look at the statements as soon as possible."

"I'll do that. You have me worried." She stared out the window. "And we still have the difficult task of telling Jeff about his parents."

Chase signaled and turned off the main road. "Let's compare notes after you've checked out everything."

She nodded.

At the house, he collected her overnight case from the backseat and followed her through the double doors.

Jeff flew down the stairs, straight into Suzanne's arms. He gave her a swift hug, and then pulled away and turned to Chase.

Chase scooped the boy up, rewarded with a resounding kiss on his cheek. "How's my tiger?"

"Fine."

Lara emerged from the kitchen, wiping her hands on her apron. "I'm so glad you called and let me know you were safe. The TV reported a terrible accident on the highway."

"You probably heard about the Good Samaritan who helped all those people." Suzanne gestured toward Chase. "Meet our hero."

225

Lara's hands fluttered. "Oh, Chase, I'm so proud of you."

He frowned at Suzanne, and his irises darkened.

"Unca Chase hero," crowed Jeff. He beat a tattoo on his uncle's shoulders and shouted, "Hero. Hero," until Chase set the boy down. "Play games?" he pleaded.

Chase cupped the child's cheeks. "We'll do that later. I have to make some calls first."

Jeff nodded.

"That Mr. Yamamoto called again about buying the mill," Lara said.

Suzanne's head snapped up. She stared at Chase as she took Jeff's hand and stomped up the stairs. Someone wanted to see the mill?

"We should tell him today," Chase called.

She turned, looked down at him, then at the child whose world had changed forever. "I know," she whispered.

16

Suzanne gathered Jeff onto her lap and hugged him close. A frown puckered the child's little face, his confusion plain to see. The concept of death, the fact that his parents weren't ever coming back, was too much for his young brain to comprehend. His small chest hitched on a sob, breaking her heart.

She let him cry, the slow back-and-forth motions of the rocking chair in the playroom soothing both of them.

A half hour passed before Jeff's hiccups subsided. He turned his wet face to hers, and chubby hands held her cheeks as he leaned in nose-to-nose. "Mommy and Daddy go way. They come back."

Seated in a chair across from them, Chase's face was a study in misery.

How could she soften Jeff's pain? Nothing would. From now on she would only tell the boy the truth. "Not this time," she whispered.

Jeff's head popped up, defiance in his eyes. "Yes." He pounded on her shoulders. "They come home. You lie."

Chase lifted him away. "Aunt Sue didn't lie."

"You lie," Jeff shouted, then wrenched out of Chase's arms and dashed for the hall.

Waves of nausea washed over her. She started after him, but Chase caught her hand. "Maybe it's better if he's alone for a while."

"He's so little." Helpless tears slid down her face.

"He'll be all right, but I'm not so sure about you." Chase extended his arms.

She stepped into them and leaned her head on his shoulder. Tense, confused, she couldn't think. "What can we do?"

"I don't know," he murmured. "When he's ready, we'll be here for him."

Her eyes closed. Chase's comforting warmth pressed against her. "If he needs anyone right now, it's Lara."

Later, when they entered Pam and Tad's room, the housekeeper stood at the window, staring at the bleak landscape. She turned and pointed.

Inside the closet, Jeff lay curled in a dark

corner, eyes closed, mouth clenched, his expression a reminder of Tad when he was ticked off. He clutched one of his mom's fluffy slippers and his dad's tie in his pudgy hands. Maybe the scent of his parents' clothes offered him some sense of relief.

They agreed to wait until he came out of the closet.

Suzanne reached for the Bible on Pam's nightstand. She thumbed through and read several passages her sister had underlined. Psalms 25:4 *Shew me Thy ways, O LORD; teach me Thy paths.* And Proverbs 22:6 *Train up a child in the way he should go: and when he is old, he will not depart from it.*

Pam had sought guidance for raising Jeff and several other Scriptures pertaining to marriage.

Suzanne took Chase's hand, tugged him from the room and down the stairs.

When an hour passed and they returned to check on Jeff, the small, bewildered boy emerged from the closet, rubbing his eyes and went straight to Lara, who sat in a rocking chair in the corner. He climbed onto her lap, thumb tucked securely in his mouth. It wasn't two seconds before his eyelids fluttered closed. Lara waved them away as she rocked him.

Back in the solarium, Chase opened his

hands. He looked as bewildered as she felt. "Maybe our problem is bigger than we thought. Jeff's immediate well-being —"

Distraught from lack of sleep and Jeff's reaction, tension increased in her chest. It was like climbing a mountain and not being able to breathe because of the thin air. "We can't let Jeff's problem simmer on a back burner."

"Of course we can't." Chase's eyes clouded, and a vein pulsed in his neck. "It isn't *my* fault."

She slanted her body away from his highly emotional reaction and lifted her chin. "I'm not blaming you, Chase. It's no one's fault."

He cracked his knuckles, the sound like popping corn as he paced like a caged lion. "Sure seems like it."

Suzanne wiped her brow, surprised to find moisture there. "Good heavens, Chase, I'm as upset and baffled as you are."

"Yeah, right."

Uneasy beneath his scrutiny, she blew out a breath. "Why are we arguing?"

He stopped his pacing, turned and glared at her before throwing both hands in the air. "Who knows?" he yelled.

Her spine hit the back of the chair as she recoiled. He'd shown his moody side more than once, but this volatility was excessive.

"Look." She forced a softer tone and attempted to diffuse the situation. "The tension between us doesn't help. If we dispense with that, maybe we'll cope better."

He groaned and held his head. "It's not just Jeff. We're fighting whatever's happening between us, too."

Her nails bit into her palms. "No. I can't deal with this. Not now."

The look he gave her bordered on sheer agony. "Neither can I, but how can you deny this . . . this attraction, whatever it is?" His voice fell to a whisper. "I don't know why, but I need you."

Oh, Lord, make him stop. She shook her head again. "It's not real. Physical attraction fades with time."

"Not this time. Believe it."

She froze and felt the blood drain from her face "It's too fast, too soon."

"The Ice Maiden. I get it now." His passion-filled eyes shed their warmth and hardened into solid ice. He stood and backed away, pivoted, and strode from the room.

Ice Maiden. That hated term. A strangled sound left her throat. She wanted to pummel Chase for the level of callousness she hadn't expected.

Lara appeared in the doorway of the

solarium. "I'm leaving now."

Suzanne's head jerked up. Lara took off Thursday afternoons. Had she heard them arguing?

"If you want, I could take Jeff with me," Lara added. "He likes my grandson. It might help him forget for a little while."

"Maybe that's for the best, if he wants to go. You must take time off to make up for this afternoon."

Lara nodded and headed for the stairs. "I'll ask him. Another child and a change of scenery can make a difference."

"Thanks."

Minutes later, the front door closed behind Jeff and Lara. Suzanne took the stairs two at a time, needing the solitude of her room. The patter of rain on the glass drew her toward the window. The rhythmic sound should have soothed, but it didn't.

Her head buzzed — Chase, the powerful tension between them, Jeff's future and his trauma. And the difficult times that lay ahead for her or whomever became his guardian.

She pulled off her aqua cable-knit sweater, dropped the woolen skirt on the floor, and stood before the full-length mirror. Her fingers caressed the gold chain and pendant, and she replayed the scene that just happened between her and Chase.

Donning a long T-shirt, she slipped between the blue floral sheets. Her insides clamored for answers. *Forget what smolders and sizzles between Chase and me. Sleep it off.* That was the only way she might find relief from the tension and constant state of turmoil.

A sound came from the adjoining room. She raised her head and strained to listen, but the house was silent.

Suzanne searched through the mountain of receipts spread across the table in the solarium. She studied the balance sheets and vouchers, and held her aching head. The monthly bills were staggering. Catered food and decorations for one party alone totaled more than twelve thousand dollars. Orchids imported from South America. What had Pam served? Petrosian caviar in teacups?

Next item on the ledger was the mortgage payment on this house. It was twice the rent for her apartment in New York. Mental numbness set in. *Lord, help me.*

Unable to stomach the sight of any more bills, she headed for the spare room and the boxes Chase had mentioned.

In one, tucked between folds of tissue

paper, she lifted a dress from a fashion house in Portland. The exquisite floor-length creation — a golden gown for Princess Pam. She wiped a tear from her cheek.

The next box contained a gorgeous enameled vase one might see on *Antiques Roadshow.* The enclosed bill of sale took her breath away.

More clothes filled the rest of the boxes, thousands of dollars of designer apparel, but none from Suzanne's boutiques. The clothes she sold didn't carry exorbitant price tags.

Had Pam thought the mill was so successful, she could throw money away?

Suzanne crumpled a sheet of paper, and then smoothed it out again. She needed to talk to Lara, time to get some facts.

Lara stood at the kitchen counter, chopping veggies for a chicken casserole.

Suzanne slumped onto a chair. "Level with me, please. There are things I need to ask. Difficult things."

The woman's eyes shuttered. Her shoulders sagged, though her hands stayed busy.

"Did Pam have a lot of big parties?"

Lara's hand halted in midair. "Yes."

"How many?" Did she really want to know?

"Five, six, a year."

"All catered?"
Lara nodded.
"Booze?"
"Cases."
"You said Tad and Pam argued?"
"About money and expenses. He said many times he couldn't make enough to pay the bills. I . . . usually went upstairs when they started arguing. It always ended with Pam crying, and Tad slamming the door and leaving."
"What about her and the man you mentioned?"
Lara shrugged. "Before they left that last night, Tad accused her of being involved with another man. That's all I heard."
"The boxes in the bedroom, are those normal kinds of purchases?"
"Yes. There were constant arrivals." Lara sagged into a chair and rubbed a hand over her face. "Mrs. Pam attended lots of parties, each time in a new dress. She always looked beautiful. And pride always lit Mr. Tad's face."
Suzanne pressed a hand against her abdomen. "Where are the other dresses?"
"In the spare room closet. She ran out of space in their bedroom."
"Pam sounds . . . almost driven."
"She often told Mr. Tad, 'I'm worth it.'

Then he'd cave and throw up his hands."

"I'm sorry you witnessed that. When I visited, they never did anything special. Homey stuff — barbecues, playing games with Jeff. You know. You were here."

Lara flattened her lips. "I couldn't tell you —"

Suzanne captured Lara's hand. "I would never expect that. The family deserved your loyalty." She grabbed her lower lip with her teeth. "Maybe this is my fault."

"Oh, no, you didn't cause it."

Suzanne paced the floor, little sighs of regret leaving her lips. "Maybe I did. I raised Pam since she was fourteen. The values I tried to convey — apparently I didn't do a very good job."

"Don't blame yourself. They weren't children. Well, Mrs. Pam could be childish —" She covered her mouth. "I shouldn't have said that, and shouldn't speak that way."

"You didn't say anything bad, just the truth."

"But —"

"It's OK, Lara."

"We shouldn't speak badly of the dead. Jesus says —"

"I know. Sorry I'm putting you through this. Forgive me for that."

Lara threw up her hands, an anguished look on her face.

"I have to go through more papers the accountant left. And I'm going to rewrap those boxes and return them." Seeing Lara's pale face, sorrow filled her that she'd caused the woman pain by asking all those questions. "Why don't you go for a walk on the beach? Clear your thoughts."

"Dinner —"

"I'll feed Jeff. Chase and I can have the casserole later. Was Jeff crying when you put him down for his nap?"

"No. I don't think he fully realizes his parents won't be back." Lara brushed her hand through her gray hair. "When he plays and gets excited, he forgets."

Suzanne gave Lara a quick hug. A boulder lay on her chest. More and more the pressure of Pam's and Tad's deaths weighed on her. *Cry. Release your anger. Smash something precious.*

Since the news of their deaths came, her life had spiraled downward. But that was only the beginning of an unreal scenario. She stared at her empty palms and felt so alone.

A stomping sound from Jeff's room alerted her that the little guy had awakened. She charged up the stairs, and at his door, she feigned a smile. "Hi. Are you hungry or thirsty?"

"Nuh, uh."

"Wanna play?"

"OK."

"Maybe we can finish that race we started the other day. Your red car almost won. I had the blue one."

"Purple," he corrected.

"That's right. Let's head for your playroom. Last one there's an old maid."

He giggled and raced for the door. "Gonna beat you," he taunted.

"Think you can do that, tiger?"

"Yeah." He waded into the pile of toys and tossed them about until he found the two cars.

Suzanne sank to the carpet, masking tears that threatened, and made the vroom sounds that had become a new part of her life.

17

Noisy gulls squawked and circled in the clear ocean air. Pelicans dove into the surf and emerged with their beaks full of lunches. Despite the warmth of the mid-day sun on Chase's shoulders, a chill spread through him.

Troubles, there were too many of them. He'd come out here to consider the practicality of buying replacement equipment for the mill, but now he had to put his hand to his head to stop it from throbbing. This wasn't working.

After a quick climb up the cliff, he jogged to the kitchen door and strode inside.

Suzanne sat at the counter, nibbling on a sandwich with a cup of green tea at her side.

"Can I get you anything?" She started to rise, but he motioned for her to stay.

"Enjoy your food. I can make something for myself." He found the leftover vegetable soup in the refrigerator, scooped some into a bowl, and heated it in the microwave. While the minutes ticked down, he made two sandwiches piled high with beef, lettuce, tomatoes, avocados, and a generous slathering of mustard.

Her eyes lit up. "That's quite a snack."

"I have an enormous appetite."

Her mouth quirked at the corners. "I never would have guessed."

Seated across from her, he eased aside the vase of flowers.

Her brow lifted.

"The better to see your lovely face, my dear," he said.

Suzanne poured herself a second cup of tea. Chase's presence made her lightheaded, as though she'd drank an entire bottle of sparkling wine. Heat shimmered through her, a result of his nearness.

She offered him a tiny smile. "That was a nice compliment."

"One for a lovely lady." He took a huge bite of his sandwich, leaving a smear of mustard on one side of his face.

"Thanks."

He swallowed and wiped his mouth before replying. "I have a problem at the mill and I'm not sure I can solve it. And I intended to tell you about Yamamoto. There's no reason to withhold that information."

"Well, it's your business."

"Not the point. We're in this mess together. Both of us have secrets that we can't or don't want to share, but we can stay aboveboard. I need your trust." He put down the sandwich. "I told my boss I'd inherited the business and thought I might sell. An hour later, his friend Yamamoto was blowing up my phone. He called again this morning. Wants to see the mill and the timberlands"

"You'd sell?" She couldn't hide the catch in her voice.

"That's a tough question, probably as difficult as you putting this place up for sale."

What would she do with the house her sister loved? The nice décor and sense of comfort it brought brushed away some of her regrets. Another puzzle piece she'd rather not think about. "I understand. The business is one of your last links with Tad."

He nodded. "I'm also responsible for his employees. How can I oversee the mill, run the logging operation, and still maintain my job in Tokyo? It's either one or the other."

"Long distance doesn't work in business or romance." Now why had she added the latter? Had her subconscious considered a relationship with Chase, one that would require traveling halfway across the world?

She shook her head. Impossible.

"If two people matter to each other, distance is only an inconvenience." He stroked his finger along her wrist. "It's what you do with the time you have that's important. Quality, not quantity is my byword."

Flustered, she drew away from his scorching touch. Could he possibly guess how much his action and words affected her? They needed a change of subject quick. "Are you planning to show Yamamoto the mill?"

Chase's expression turned dark and remote, as though the bleakness of a winter storm had settled on him. "Yes. He arrives Friday evening."

"Will he stay here?"

He blinked. "What? No. He booked a room at the motel in town."

"What about entertainment?"

The sneaky man again captured one of her hands, distracting her. Flustered by her response to him, she blurted out, "Invite him here Saturday evening."

"What? Lara doesn't cook Asian dishes."

"I can handle the arrangements. I have some experience, and if I run into a problem, my Japanese friend in San Francisco will help."

He arched his eyebrows. "You're a lady of

many talents. A special effort would certainly impress the man. Are you sure it's not too much trouble?"

"Not at all. Don't worry about a thing."

"Thanks, Sue. I appreciate that."

The gentle whisper of her name on his lips made her giddy, as though she were whirling through space on a moonbeam.

Her phone rang, spoiling the moment. "Hello."

"Hello, Suzanne, Pomeroy here. I spoke with Chase's lawyer earlier. Your case is on the court docket for a month from today. That's much quicker than I thought possible. Will you be available?"

Strength seeped from her body at the thought of a legal battle. "I'll make it a point."

"Good," he said. "Asking for a postponement might result in a long wait. Chase's lawyer will call him."

Her stomach lurched. Jeff's future had slipped her mind, thanks to the twisted complexity of her feelings for Chase.

She no sooner hung up than her cell phone rang again. Andy. With good news, she hoped. Forcing a happy tone, she asked, "How's my handsome assistant today?"

Across from her, Chase shifted in his seat.

"I'm in need of a lengthy discussion with

you, Sue." Andy lowered his voice. "And how is my gorgeous boss tonight?"

"I'm fine. I take it you've run into a serious problem?"

"A few convoluted personnel problems. I prefer to go over them with you item by item, and it will likely take a few hours. Any chance you could fly here this weekend?"

"I can't, Andy. We're entertaining a prospective buyer for my brother-in-law's mill."

Chase rose and stood behind her, so close his breath brushed her nape. "If this is important, don't worry about it. I can handle Yamamoto." He stepped away and leaned on the table.

"Give me a minute, Andy." She covered the mouthpiece and turned to Chase. "I keep my promises." When he made no reply, she spoke into the phone again. "I have a better idea. You come here. Hop a plane this weekend."

"Cool. OK, boss. I'll let the managers know I'll be gone."

She disconnected the call, set her phone down, and turned to Chase. "The first call . . ." She folded her arms across her chest. "Mr. Pomeroy said the custody hearing has been scheduled for a month from today."

Chase's head jerked up. His hands

clenched into fists. "OK. I haven't given Jeff a thought. Well, today anyway. And that's not right. Not fair. He's the reason I'm here." He muttered and shook his head.

She flinched at his anguished tone. "Forgetting for a few hours isn't a crime, especially when you have other concerns of importance. Aren't you a little hard on yourself?"

He dragged a hand through his hair. "My nephew is my number-one priority."

Suzanne winced at the harsh inflection of his voice. He'd surprised her once more with his quicksilver mood changes. Lips parted, she could only stare at the sharp angles and planes of his face.

"Look. I don't know if I can be away from Tokyo for another month. How about you? Can you stay with Jeff?"

"I can stay here part of the time. You asked for a leave of absence, for how long?"

"It's open ended right now."

They'd set aside their enmity for a few hours, but most of the tension had crept back in. Deflection time. "I'll get started on the arrangements for the dinner."

"If you can't —"

"I said I'd do it." She hadn't meant to reveal her frustration, but the man could be so infuriating. "Or would you prefer to arrange it yourself?"

"No."

The forceful way he emphasized the single word left her on edge. She spun on her heel and forced her feet not to dash from the room. In the library, she closed the door behind her with exquisite care.

Through a blur of tears, she slid into a seat beside an end table and picked up a book on Japanese culture Chase had given Pam as a gift. She dashed the wetness on her cheeks away with an angry fist and raised her chin. She refused to shed tears for that man.

A few inhalations helped calm her frayed nerves. Scanning the index, she found a chapter on Japanese customs and settled deeper into the chair.

Moments later, the front door opened and closed, and Jeff's giggles drifted through the house, followed by Lara's soft admonishments. Those two people filled up the empty rooms with joy and another feeling that she found elusive.

Much as she wanted to grab Jeff, shower him with hugs and kisses, and hold him close to her heart, she had to give Lara time to feed him first.

Forty minutes later in the family room, Jeff sprawled on the rug in front of the hearth, eyes closed, and a thumb in his mouth. The comforting heat and crackling sounds of the fire had wooed the tired little boy to sleep.

When Suzanne scooped him up, Jeff raised his impossibly long lashes and glowered at her.

"Bed time," she said.

Lower lip thrust forward, his little body stiffened. "Don't wanna."

"You can't sleep on the rug, Jeff. Someone might trip over you."

Weariness won out. He relented a bit and rested against her shoulder. In his room, she settled into the rocker and snuggled him on her lap, his fingers gripping her arm.

She wound the music box and strains of a song tinkled softly. She hummed along as Jeff burrowed his head in her neck.

"I love you, my precious boy." Tears tumbled from her eyes.

Jeff changed position and nuzzled his baby soft cheek against hers. A lock of hair fell over his forehead. His grip on her arm relaxed.

She wound the music box again. Still humming, she rubbed small circles on his back. The slow, rocking motions lulled them both into a quiet serenity.

A noise made her jolt awake.

The side of Jeff's sweaty face stuck to her skin. She tightened her arms around him and rose. Laying her precious cargo on the youth bed, she covered him with a quilt, rewound the box once more and closed the blinds.

Picking her way through the darkened room, she avoided stepping on the scattered toys and plowed into a wall of muscle. Chase.

He grabbed her shoulders and steadied her. One finger wiped away the dampness from her cheeks. Twice in one day she'd cried.

"I saw it all," he said. "You really love him."

"Yes."

"I love him, too."

"I know."

"He'll be a constant reminder of my brother."

"He looks like Pam — brown eyes, her grin."

"Her grumbling."

She forced one side of her mouth to curve up. "I think Jeff got that trait from your side of the family."

"Never, we're good-natured."

She choked back a laugh, not wanting to wake her charge. "Now that's a crock. You good-natured?"

"I can be."

His soft tone surprised her. He'd tensed when she'd told him about the court date. Not good-natured then. His moods changed faster than the weather in New York, too often for her peace of mind.

"Let's have some of that horrible herbal tea you like." He took her hand and led her down the hall.

She made a wry face. "Sounds like I'm making a convert."

"That could be." He draped an arm around her shoulder, and they started down the stairs.

The next afternoon, shadows crept into the solarium as Suzanne held the receiver to her ear and listened to Karla Lamb, Pam's friend, drone on and on. "Vic believes you misunderstood our relationship with Tad and Pam."

Their relationship? "I . . . uh, don't . . ."

"Something you said to Vic the day you and Chase brought the car back." Karla's voice, tense and unsteady, went on. "I think we should discuss this. How about lunch Tuesday?"

Suzanne's mind switched to her schedule of the week. "Sure."

"I know you're busy with Jeff and the lawyer and all, but clearing this up is important."

Even though Vic denied his involvement with Pam, it was possible he could be the other man in her life. "Just let me know where and what time, and I'll join you." She grimaced.

"How about noon at Bab's Tea Shop on Main Street?"

"That's fine. See you then." Suzanne hung up, but stared at the phone for lengthy moments. Had she imagined the sense of urgency in Karla's voice?

18

Morning sun played with the puffy clouds that drifted overhead as Suzanne and Chase stared at the mounds of grass that covered the new gravesites. Scrub jays twittered in the Douglas firs, then swooped down and snapped up bugs, only to perch on the granite headstones to enjoy their catch.

"I can feel Pam and Tad watching us," she murmured and pressed a hand against her abdomen, distress curling inside. "She's giggling because we haven't met until now. Their deaths accomplished what Pam's tactics to get us together couldn't."

Chase pulled her close. "She never mentioned that you and I didn't know each other."

"She'd often coax me into coming to Oregon, and later I'd find out that I'd just missed you. It wouldn't be the first time her schemes didn't work."

"You two were close, weren't you?"

"Of course. She was my sweet baby sister. Our family lived near Portland before she and I moved across the country. Oregon meant so much — rain and chilly weather were fine with her. Those years we were in New York, all she talked about was returning."

A mourning dove cooed from a branch high above them. Even the birds sounded sad today.

"How did you manage work, college, and taking care of Pam?"

Despite the fact that Suzanne basked in the warmth of Chase's silver eyes, her chin trembled. How difficult it had been to deal with her sister's rebellious nature. "Sometimes I wonder how I even squeezed in a semester at fashion school."

"You had no time for a social life?"

"Not really."

The pressure of his hands on her waist increased. "No dates, parties, or friends?"

"Not then." Her gaze sought the tops of the trees, anything to distract her from thinking about the financial hardship they'd endured after they'd arrived in New York.

He rested his head against hers. "Sounds as if you left mankind behind."

"I guess I did for a while. No time to feel sorry for myself. And why should I? If I could get us through the rough times, we'd both benefit."

"And you did." He loosened his hold without releasing her completely.

"I was grateful to meet a woman who thought I had potential — my 'patron saint.' Eugenie shared her swank apartment with us on Central Park West until we could afford a place of our own. I learned the boutiques business from the ground up, and with her financial assistance, I opened my first store. I've repaid her, at least monetarily, but without her belief in me, I wouldn't have made it."

He touched her cheek, his gaze fixed on her. "Oh, I think you would have succeeded one way or another. There's determination in that strong, sensitive chin. Suzanne Bratton would have been a success, even without a benefactor."

A tentative smile built up as amazement sank in. "Thanks."

His lips briefly met hers.

Her burden of grief eased a bit. Through a blur of tears, she stared at Tad's gravesite. "Your brother was very special. I always thought he and Pam had the perfect marriage. When Jeff arrived, Tad blossomed into a wonderful, caring father."

His sigh blended with the whisper of low

tide purring against the shore. "I'm glad you remember him that way. He had dark moments, especially in his youth. He injured a woman on Main Street while driving his pickup. Admitted to me he'd been 'drunk as a skunk.' Bleary-eyed, he couldn't make out the traffic lights.

"The impact slightly damaged the front end of his car, but the accident changed him psychologically. He started attending church and straightened out his life. Don't get me wrong, he still liked his booze, but only an occasional shot. It amazed me how drunk he could get on a single jigger of bourbon."

Suzanne chewed her lip. "Pam never mentioned Tad's drinking, only his good points. She loved him so much."

Sarcasm edged Chase's laughter. "If that was so, why did she have this 'other guy' in her life?"

A master at prodding her with a sharp stick, his words struck a painful chord. "I can't believe she did. Lara and I talked a few days ago, but she couldn't add anything other than Tad shouted about a man during their last argument. He accused Pam of letting him down in a crisis."

"I wonder what the crisis was. According to the accountant, the mill's finances could be in better shape. Other than that, what could Tad have meant?"

"We may never find out," she murmured.

"Maybe Karen and Vic know something. They were best friends."

"People don't always share their problems." She adopted a challenging tone. "Maybe I'll find out something on Tuesday when I meet Karen for lunch."

A dusty old truck drove along the nearby path and parked. An elderly couple emerged and made their way with slow, labored steps toward a gravestone. Once there, the woman fell to her knees, her sobs blending with the old man's to fill the lonely silence.

"We'll come back another day." Chase turned away and released Suzanne. "First, can I have a minute with Tad?"

Suzanne thumbed away a tear from her own eyes, nodded at his request, and started back toward the truck to give him privacy.

A glance over her shoulder showed him kneeling beside his brother's grave, one hand on the granite marker.

Her heart ached for him and for herself.

He didn't take long, catching up with her moments later.

As they ambled along in silence, she broached a subject that had troubled her lately. "Chase, if the judge should grant you guardianship, what about Jeff's religious beliefs?"

He lifted one eyebrow. "I occasionally attend church."

A smile tugged at her lips. "You know that's not good enough. He enjoys going to church, the singing, and the to-do the parishioners make over him. He needs consistency. It's important to nurture his inner spirit."

And with a few simple words, the quiet serenity of the morning evaporated. Tension climbed between them and formed a seemingly insurmountable barrier.

"Of course," he said in a tone that spoke less of his agreement and more of his volatile temper.

Why did she always react to his moods? Stepping in the middle of the path, she turned to face him. "There's no 'of course' about it." Her voice rose ever so slightly, not the least intimidated by his gruffness. "The question is simple. Will you take him to church every week? Be sure he attends Sunday school? See that he's taught all he should know about God?"

With an arrogant toss of his head, he retorted, "You know there are Christian churches in Tokyo. It's not as though I live in the backwoods."

"But will you see that he goes to church? Will you go with him?" She made an extra effort to lower her voice, when she actually wanted to yell. "You have to show him that his new father loves God. Children learn by example."

He sucked in a harsh breath through clenched teeth and exhaled. "You want to add another problem when you know I'm already overwhelmed."

She thrust her chin out and held the eye connection with him.

He looked away first, one hand rubbing the back of his neck. "Are you conceding the case?"

"No, but I won't agree to anything less than full commitment from you. A father is personally responsible for that part of his son's life, too."

Chase put a hand to his forehead, the look in his eyes as cool and remote as the North Star.

Another car entered the cemetery. The stalemate broken, they headed for the truck.

A wall of gray mist shrouded the landscape, another damp, fog-bound morning in Oregon. Pelicans soared past while a seal nosed along in the opposite direction. Chase jogged along the beach, grateful that the swarm of tourists wouldn't descend on the picturesque town for two months. He raised his eyes skyward. This small patch of Paradise belonged to him, at least for now.

Tokyo. He'd return there soon. Why didn't the thought please him? After his transfer from the company's main office in Anchorage, Alaska five years ago, he'd become accustomed to Japan and learned to like the culture. The promotion to general manager of sales and a substantial raise in pay didn't hurt, either.

He trotted to the back door. New problems seemed to crop up every day, adding to one that bugged him and needed his immediate attention. If Yamamoto wasn't interested in buying the mill and the property, should he authorize the purchase of the expensive equipment?

In the kitchen, he checked to see if the area was clear of scurrying women. The few hours spent at the house yesterday, he'd been able to dodge the flurry of vacuuming, the atmosphere like residing within a dust devil.

Suzanne cooked, called her Japanese friend for advice, provided dimensions for something she wanted built, and accepted deliveries. She and Lara prepared pickled radishes, marinated eggs, and cucumbers in special sauces.

He tried to snatch some of the mouth-watering delicacies, but Suzanne had cuffed his hand.

Jeff, who spent hours every day with the women, fed off their energy. He helped cut cookie dough for Lara's church festival, giggling when he spotted his own flour-dusted face in a mirror.

For whatever reason, Jeff held himself aloof from Chase. Time would heal him, and when he learned to trust again, his "Unca Chase" would be there for him, unless Suzanne took him away.

His smile edged up a notch. He had a new plan that would put him on an even playing field with her for custody, maybe even give him a wee advantage.

"Chase, would you catch that little boy for me?" Lara's face was flushed from rushing after Jeff and she mopped her brow with a tissue. "He needs his cough medicine."

Surprise made him pause. "Jeff's sick?" Why didn't he know this?

"Well, he started hacking yesterday. Miss Suzanne called his pediatrician, and since Jeff didn't have a fever, the doctor prescribed medicine."

"Where is he now?"

"Who knows? He runs off and hides

whenever I bring out the bottle."

Chase laughed. "Tad used to do that. He drove our parents crazy. Funny, I always liked the taste." He squeezed her hand. "Don't worry, I'll find him."

The sliding closet door in Jeff's parents' room stood open, his little face pressed against a few clothes that had dropped to the floor. Chase reached for him, but the rascal wriggled away.

"Gotcha." He scooped up the boy, draped him over his shoulder like a sack of pinecones and carried him downstairs.

Jeff snickered, the way he always did when someone outfoxed him.

Chase hugged and tickled him. He blew a raspberry on Jeff's neck, earning another wild giggle. And then he grabbed the boy as he struggled to escape again.

While Lara coaxed the spoonful of medicine into his mouth, Chase held Jeff's head.

Seconds later, the boy raced back up the stairs.

Lara shook her head. "I'm too old for this."

Chase took her seriously. "If you need help, we'll find someone."

"Oh, no, no." Lara cupped her cheeks. "I can handle him — for a while anyway."

He nodded. If the judge ruled in his favor,

he'd hire a Japanese housekeeper. But no one could take Lara's place. She genuinely loved the child.

Chase strolled into the dining room and halted in mid-stride. Wow. A low, black lacquered table replaced the mahogany one. Paper Shoji screens shielded one wall. Plump cushions sat on the floor, positioned over tatami-mats. The effect — instant, authentic Japanese decor.

"The room looks terrific," he said as Suzanne brushed past him, carrying flowers.

She pivoted. "Do you think it's too much?"

"Well, I'm sure Yamamoto doesn't expect this."

"Good. The element of surprise will be in your favor."

Disarmed by how pretty she looked — even with tousled hair, smudges on her brow, and wearing an old T-shirt and worn jeans — he made an effort to sound casual. "Have you dealt with Asians in the past?"

"No. My Japanese friend said the men aren't keen on women in business. But women run for political office and win more often than not these days, so male domination could be a thing of the past."

"The women are making headway on that score."

"I understand that men dine and party by themselves." She brushed a damp curl from her forehead. "I'll serve the food and stay in the kitchen."

"I don't see why you shouldn't sit at the table with us. After all, Yamamoto knows this isn't Japan."

She shrugged. "Whatever you say. It's your deal."

"We won't talk business tonight. It's been said Japanese men loosen up and let down their guard with alcohol. It's the only time in their rigid formal culture that etiquette is relaxed. I've heard they don't trust a man who talks too much and doesn't drink. A sober man holds back and doesn't reveal his true character, so I'll go along with the cultural practice for now."

"That makes sense."

"Thanks for your help, Sue." He curbed his urge to kiss those strawberry lips.

"I'm looking forward to meeting Mr. Yamamoto even though you said his English is limited. Good luck with your venture." She arranged the flowers on the table before scurrying off to the kitchen.

Pink cheeks and a glow in her eyes, she was gorgeous. Had she enjoyed the work and concern about the details of tonight's dinner? He hadn't pictured her this way, all domestic and willing to please.

Early Friday evening, Chase met the corporate jet. He'd hired a cab to provide transportation for his guest while he was in Emerald Point. What he hadn't anticipated was Takami Yamamoto's son, Kaz, accompanying the older man. Bright, knowledgeable, and a Harvard graduate, the prodigy looked about twenty-eight. He was taller than most Japanese men.

Dressed in expensive dark suits and topcoats, father and son epitomized the wealthy Japanese entrepreneur. Takami was much shorter than his son, rounded and well-padded across his middle.

This being the senior Yamamoto's first trip to the States, he seemed impressed by everything from the airport to the town, the thick forest of pines surrounding them to the large spaces between houses, and the variety of boats anchored in the cove. The sheer openness made a dramatic contrast to Tokyo's congested population.

The man's head rested against the seat, and within minutes Takami was snoring.

"I'm afraid the trip was too much for my father," Kaz apologized. "I'll check into the motel and put him to bed and then grab something to eat."

"Of course, you'll come with me —"

"No, no. No need for that. And tomorrow we're going on a sight-seeing trip around the area."

"But I thought I'd show you and your father the mill and forest."

"This is kind of a vacation for both of us."

"But you will join me at my home tomorrow evening for dinner?"

"That's very generous. Yes, we'll be there. And thank you for providing the transportation for us. Your kindness is appreciated as well."

"My pleasure."

At the motel, Chase smiled and extended his hand. "I'll see you tomorrow night."

Speaking a traditional Japanese greeting, Chase welcomed the Yamamotos to his brother's home. A movement at the landing drew his eye. Before descending the stairs, Suzanne smiled and inclined her head.

He recognized the type of outfit she wore. He'd been schooled in Japanese costumes and customs when he first took the job in Tokyo.

A white chemise, white cotton stockings, a kimono of embroidered vermilion silk, and a black satin cloak, called a *haori,* painted in a red, white and gold floral pattern flattered her face and body. An obi was wrapped around her waist and a pair of zoris graced her feet. Her copper hair, fashioned into an intricate knot, gleamed in the lamplight and framed her beauty.

Her fingers slid along the handrail. Poised and self-assured, she paused for a moment before gliding forward to join them. She seemed in her natural element, and had no doubt entertained often.

Though his insides vibrated with tension and awareness, he took her hand and faced their guests. He had so much to learn about this woman, something that takes years to do.

When Chase introduced her to Kaz, the young man's dark eyes lit up as they raked her from head to toe. Each man bowed low before taking her hand.

Kaz presented her with a wrapped box. "This is a small gift from my father."

"Thank you." She inclined her head in a graceful nod, accepted the gift, and placed it on the entry table.

When both guests removed their shoes, Chase followed their example.

Suzanne slipped off her zoris before leading the way into the dining room.

The elder Yamamoto halted in the doorway and rattled off something in his native language.

"My father is most appreciative that you have troubled yourself to welcome us," Kaz translated.

Chase liked his guests, but wanted to squelch the younger man's attention to Suzanne.

"It's our pleasure," she murmured. "This is a very special occasion. We hope you'll enjoy the dinner."

Kaz translated for Takami, who reached out to touch his son's arm. The older man's impassive face broke into a smile.

Delicate stringed chords of traditional *Koto* music set the soothing background mood as the men seated themselves on pillows.

Suzanne discreetly added a place setting for herself before kneeling with the grace of an angel to serve a clear soup garnished with tofu and watercress and placed small bowls of steamed rice by each plate. When she returned with a dish of pork tempura, Kaz murmured, "Thank you."

Her cheeks turned a delicate pink under the younger man's obvious admiration.

Chase tried hard to hide his scowl.

She sipped a fruity club soda while Chase

and his two guests drank from tiny sake cups. He was pleased to have Mr. Yamamoto's interest, but his son's fascination with the pearl Chase had only just discovered disconcerted him. He wasn't about to lose his prize and didn't want the competition.

The Asian music added a friendly atmosphere to the diner. Suzanne smiled at the easy camaraderie among the men.

Chase laughed a lot throughout the evening. Either he was enjoying the company of the Yamamotos, or he was a very good actor. Of course, it could be the sake. Several times he winked at her, once or twice with a brief flash of something more. Then his eyes would narrow, making her heart beat faster.

The elder Yamamoto made soft, satisfied sounds as he consumed great quantities of the meat, dumplings, and bean sprouts with green mustard. The men took turns refilling each other's sake cups, a mark of politeness and respect. Suzanne's friend had explained how Japanese men liked to dance, so after a light dessert of apples, bananas, cherries, and pineapple in gelatin, she asked Kaz if he would do the honor.

He inclined his head with a soft smile, the request seeming to please him. "You are very kind, but if you don't mind, I will ask my father first."

Her cheeks heated again. Had she made a gaff by not asking the older man first?

Kaz spoke to his father, who grinned with pleasure and nodded. The son rose, went to the sound system and turned up the volume. Spying a fan on a nearby table, he picked it up, and in a gesture of deference, bowed and extended it to the elder Yamamoto.

Takami nodded, accepted it, and rose with well-practiced refinement. After mumbling a few words to his son, he stepped back, his face an expressionless mask.

Kaz gave a slight shrug. "My father would like you to know that he wishes he could dance in the traditional manner, in a *yukata,* which is a men's robe."

Takami assumed a formal stance, his legs parted, he snapped open the fan. Despite his portly body, each movement flowed in graceful precision. He finished the dance and gave a deep bow to acknowledge his applauding audience. Seated cross-legged on the pillow once again, he wiped perspiration from his face with a silk handkerchief.

Urged on by Kaz, Chase rose to his feet in one lithe movement, loosened his tie, and removed his suit jacket. Not to be outdone, he performed a pretty decent routine, in a humorous imitation of old time rock and roll, bringing cheers and laughter.

She hadn't seen Chase's comedic side before, which didn't surprise her. The man had more moods than she could count. He could be zany one instant and serious the next without blinking. Loving and caring, and then fiery with anger a moment later.

At the end of his performance, he offered a perfect rendition of Mr. Yamamoto's bow to his audience, all the while grinning at their enthusiasm.

Kaz took his turn next. His lean body swayed with seductive rhythm to the music, while his gaze remained glued on Suzanne's, as though he performed for her alone.

She watched with polite interest, but his blatant regard made her uneasy. Half-way through the performance, she glanced at Chase and found him glaring, but not at the dancer — at her.

While Kaz bowed in response to their polite applause and retook his seat, she kept her gaze focused on the floor, the dishes, anywhere but at the two men vying for her favor.

"Would you dance for us?" Chase asked her.

The last thing she wanted was to bring more attention to her, but when she hesitated, the others offered encouraging words. Not knowing any Japanese dances and not wanting to imitate Chase, she went to the stereo and searched for something suitable.

And there it was. She'd taken hula lessons in grade school, so with trembling hands she played the Hawaiian song on the playlist.

Eyes closed, she swayed, allowing forgotten moves to resurface. Her hips undulated in slow motion, while her hands posed as the sun and the moon. The tempo increased as did her movements, and her heart pumped faster to the sweet sound of a love song. All stiffness in her body disappeared. She looked around.

Takami rocked where he sat, making flowing gestures to the melody.

Kaz's hands moved in time with the rhythm, head nodding in encouragement.

Chase, on the other hand, sat like a boulder, his gaze riveted on her. From the tight expression on his face, she couldn't tell if he enjoyed her dance or disapproved.

Kaz's black eyes were glassy, his face glowing with a look she wanted to attribute to the alcohol he'd consumed.

It was the weight of Chase's stare that drew her, though, and made her fidget. She wanted desperately to blame her racing pulse on the exertion of the dance, but the magnetic attraction for him was undeniable.

She escaped to the kitchen for more sake.

As the night wore on, both Yamamotos grew tipsy amid much laughter and conversation.

Kaz helped his swaying father stand while the old gentleman heaped lavish praises on Suzanne for the fabulous meal.

"I cannot thank you enough, lovely lady, for this wonderful evening," Kaz said, taking her hand and raising it to his lips. "You took many pains and made such an effort so our visit would be enjoyable."

"My pleasure," she murmured, pulling her fingers free.

Chase's appraising gaze left her tongue-tied. When he favored her with that adorable, boyish, one-sided smile of his, she turned away, blushing yet again.

He called for a taxi, and the men exited the dining room soon after to find their shoes.

Alone at last, euphoria filled her. She could feel it in her bones that the dinner party was a huge success. As she scooped up dishes and glassware, their guests' laughter echoed through the house.

Her spirits riding high, Suzanne stuffed the refrigerator with leftovers and filled the dishwasher. As she closed a cabinet door, footsteps echoed behind her. Keyed up and expecting a bit of praise for her efforts, she turned.

In a deep, raw-edged tone, Chase drawled, "I didn't realize you were such an accomplished flirt, Suzanne."

19

Suzanne's jaw snapped shut. After all she'd done for that man, the preparations and playing hostess, he dared accuse her of flirting with his business associate. Hurt, ready to smack him, she jammed her hands on her hips. "Flirt? Are you insane?"

Chase reached for her, his smile a curious mix of mischief and censure. "You outdid yourself with the meal, the dining room set, and your charm. I think I can live with a little innocent flirtation."

Oh, now it was innocent. *Make up your mind, Mr. Wonderful.* She met his gaze squarely, but slanted her body away from him.

"Kaz couldn't keep his eyes off you, more so after that hula. And his father — definitely charmed."

Her pulse sped up. "Jealous?"

"Maybe a little." His voice softened. "I'm only concerned about what you feel."

While she pondered an adequate response, dead silence surrounded them.

Then she choked out, "What do you mean, what I feel?"

He put up one hand. "OK, I know I have no right asking you that now. You've worked non-stop for two days, so you must be tired."

Digression? That meant he knew he was in the wrong, but was still agitated. Flames flared inside her, like dry tinder in a wildfire. "This has nothing to do with fatigue."

"Sorry, I shouldn't have put it that way."

"No, you shouldn't have." At times he ticked her off, but why get riled up when he'd be gone soon and out of her life? She tamped down her outrage, mentally tried to calm down, and deliberately stripped her voice of emotion. "I liked your dance. You did a great job with rock and roll."

"Not so."

"I disagree."

He brushed his hand down her cheek. "Why don't we turn in and leave the cleanup for morning?"

"Good idea." She flipped the kitchen light switch. With the exception of the second-floor hallway, the house was dark.

Taking her hand, Chase led her up the stairs. "Kaz asked if you and I had an understanding." He paused, as though expecting a reaction from her. "I told him we didn't."

Of course they didn't, so why did she itch to slap the smirk off his face? "Why would he ask?"

Chase stopped and turned to face her. "Because he's a gentleman and won't tread on another man's territory. That's not the Japanese way. He asked if he could take you to dinner tomorrow night."

She had scads of experience hiding her feelings, so through sheer willpower, she kept hurt and smoldering anger in check. "Well, he should ask me himself."

Chase shrugged, and they continued up the stairs.

"You can tell him no for me."

They reached the landing where he gave her a long, hard look. "Why not?"

"Because I'm still in mourning and have no time for a relationship. And there's no chemistry."

"You mean, like with me?" He reached out to run his thumb along her jawline.

Heat warmed her insides, but not in anger this time. "Maybe."

At Suzanne's door, he stepped into her space, backing her up against a wall. With both hands planted holding her head in place, he pressed his lips to hers. The flaming kiss sent shivers from her scalp clear down to her polished toenails.

Breathless, she succumbed to the moment.

He pulled away with a final touch to her cheek. "See you in the morning."

A moment later, his door shut with a soft click.

She stared after him, wondering what had just happened and when she had lost the upper hand.

In her room, she gazed out the window at the twinkling lights of a distant ship at sea. Such a lovely clear night. She pressed her fingertips against lips that still tingled from a kiss that had offered so much, and yet promised nothing.

At four the next afternoon, Chase found Suzanne in the kitchen sipping green tea. He wasn't sure how to approach her after she'd refused to have dinner with Kaz, but he wanted to share with her about the helicopter flight he'd arranged for the Japanese businessmen to survey the land and sawmill. "The Yamamotos seemed impressed with the property and the mill's operation. Tad's foreman, Zach, knew all the boundaries and proved to be quite knowledgeable. He's a definite asset."

"Glad it worked out." Her words were agreeable, but non-committal.

"I want you to wear your prettiest dress tonight. The Yamamotos invited us to dine out."

She shook her head. "No can do. Andy's plane arrives at six."

Chase eyed her. Great. *Another guy in her life.* "Bring him along."

"He'll probably be tired from the trip."

Yeah, excuses. Women were good at that. "You don't want to go."

She pinched the bridge of her nose and sighed. "I can't rush off and leave Andy in a strange house."

Pouring a cup of Lara's tasty java, Chase pulled back a chair and sat beside Suzanne. "OK. Let's ask him when he gets here. He might enjoy a little West Coast high society." *Why am I pushing her to join us when it only means watching Kaz try to insinuate himself into her good graces?*

She raised her eyebrows. "You're kidding, right? High society in Emerald Point?"

He'd have to pull back and not irritate her. "Well, it's not cosmopolitan, but there's a certain small town warmth and charm not found in big cities."

"You don't understand, Chase. I'm not

putting Emerald Point down."

He cocked his head. "Sure sounds like it."

She grumbled, "Shall we argue about this, too?"

He shrugged. "It seems your intent."

"Mine?"

"Yes."

She studied him for a few moments. "You're a strange man, Chase Garwood. Tell me, what brought on this bulldog attack?"

Good question. Who had irritated whom? Sometimes her no-nonsense approach made the hackles rise on his neck. Did he really want an argument? "Come with us. Please."

"Are you appeasing Kaz?" she snapped, her upper lip curling. "If I comply, will it be a repeat of last night? I hated the way he stared at me as though . . . as though . . ."

A vein pulsed in Chase's throat. This little tiff had the makings off a full-blown fight, one he didn't want. She had the right of it. Kaz had ogled her like a piece of very, very nice steak. But she'd accused him of conceding to Kaz.

His irritation took a sharp turn and veered toward provocation. "You're suspicious of my motives, like I'd sell you in order to sell the business. Newsflash, Suzanne. I don't need your help."

Affronted, her body took on the characteristics of an unyielding stone column. A moment later, all the tension disappeared. Her eyes narrowed with the focus of a laser. "Who put a bee in your toupee? Something other than me has made you testy. Now confess."

He scratched his head. Bewildered, frustrated, grouchy, his guts churning — no way would he admit how he felt about her, feelings that deepened by the hour. That would mean commitment . . . "I don't know. Guess I'm confused and unhappy about selling the mill."

"Then don't sell it."

"That's easy for you to say." He refilled his cup. "There's more, but now's not the time."

"Why not?"

He grabbed his forehead and ran his fingers through his hair. "I don't wear a toupee."

She smirked. "I know. I thought that would ruffle your vanity."

He took a sip of the black liquid. "You're a pro at getting under my skin."

She scooted her chair closer. "Back atcha," she said in a sweet, motherly tone. "Now tell me about your problems, Chase Garwood."

"I'll start with the biggest." He aimed his gaze at her. "You."

Suzanne fisted her hands. He thought *she* was a problem? Because of his feelings or because of Jeff's future?

A lock of ebony hair fell over Chase's forehead. The white shirt highlighted his deep tan, and the steel-blue tie added a new dimension to his gray eyes. A gorgeous man.

Breathless, she waited. Was the tightness in her chest caused by something other than a lack of oxygen? Would he say, "I love you?" Or, "You turn my guts inside out because I'm falling for you?"

No. That was her trying to foist her own wishful thoughts onto him. He only saw her as a distraction, or convenient diversion. She'd neither expected nor wanted a relationship.

Too late for her, since she'd already fallen hard. And now all the hurt she'd always protected herself from . . . She shook her head. No need to tell him that and add to his arsenal. "So, what's the problem?" Her attempt at sounding casual was a dismal failure.

"Wish I could put my finger on it. Tad. Pam. Jeff. You. Me. I'm good at sorting out things, but not this time."

"Any clues?" Did a woman wait for him in Tokyo? She refused to admit a sudden sting of jealousy.

He lifted one shoulder. "This house, this town, and what we've argued about."

"Stress brought on by the Yamamotos?" She hoped that was the reason. "By the way, what did they say about the mill operation?"

"There's excitement. I'd say they're in favor of the whole setup, but the Japanese don't make on-the-spot decisions. They're distrustful of contracts they'd have to take on. Tad signed a number of them for the mill and logging operations." Chase's vulnerable expression held a hint of disillusionment, his chin tilted down.

"Then there's the owl controversy. Years ago, many northwest towns were put into an economic tailspin and haven't fully recovered. Tad's foreman told me the Federal biologists changed the Endangered Species Act Protections for the northern spotted owl from threatened to an endangered classification. So, whatever that means to the industry . . ."

His voice lacked all emotion, as he went on. "The owl population continues to decline despite ninety-percent cutbacks on federal lands. The only good news is that steps have begun to deal with an aggressive cousin called the barred owl."

He pressed his fingers against the vein in his neck that had throbbed earlier. "If the Yamamotos are interested, there's an elaborate system of approval by managers and executives of the company. Each person avoids stepping on anyone else's toes. It's a cumbersome and slow process that could take weeks or months. Time I don't have."

She felt compelled to say this even if Chase didn't want to hear it. "The only solution — quit your job and run the business. Pam said it's a real money-maker. After seeing the household bills and mortgage, I'm convinced her lack of respect for money caused their failure to make ends meet. With your background, you'd do well at the helm." Before he could protest, she put up her hand. "I know. You don't want your own business."

"Unlike you."

A sense of self-satisfaction whispered through her that she'd accomplished her dream. "I always wanted to run my own company. Be the one who made decisions."

"Decision-making doesn't bother me, but being mired in a business does. Tad couldn't escape for even a few hours. He likened it to a prison at times." Chase interlaced his fingers and squeezed them tight until his knuckles turned white.

She glimpsed stark pain in those gorgeous eyes.

"Not doing the things I want — vacations, loaf in a hammock, gaze at the stars, and watch a sunrise. There are no hours to just be me."

Whoa. Had Chase Garwood just revealed a new and vulnerable side? "I can't picture you doing that. Is there time for leisurely stuff in your present job?"

"Unfortunately, no."

Ah. Ammunition. "Then I don't see the problem. What's the difference between running someone else's business in Tokyo, or your own in Oregon? I mean, if you can be miserable there, can't you be miserable here, too?"

He laughed. She hadn't heard much of that lately. "I don't run the overseas business now. I'm general manager in charge of sales."

"You said you were in line for promotion. A job as vice president comes with a lot more responsibility than you have now."

"True, but I could delegate more."

With a sniff, she muttered, "Like that would happen." She jabbed her finger at him. "Take over the mill. Branch out. You now have two possible outlets for your products — the company you work for and the Yamamotos. Make more of that fabulous furniture I saw at Vic and Karla's house. The carving's magnificent. And Lara told me that bench in the solarium is your creation, too."

"It's a reproduction of an antique —"

"It's exquisite. The demand for retro is high."

He shrugged, and his shoulders slumped. "Thanks, but . . . uh . . . it wouldn't work."

Chase viewed Suzanne's logic with grudging respect, not that he agreed one whit with her argument.

"I know our own needs and decisions are important, but Jeff's come first."

He stood and brushed her lips with his. "I'm holding everything in abeyance for now. What I do want to discuss is tonight. I already told Lara we wouldn't have dinner here."

She stiffened as though he'd thrown a pail of frigid water in her face. "You didn't hear what I said before, Chase." She stepped back. "I can't go with you and the Yamamotos tonight."

The fact that he hadn't been born with a cheerful, tactful nature had never bothered him before. But he'd make the effort. "Please come. I want you there."

20

20

"Suzanne?"

She clenched her fists and dropped into a kitchen chair. *How can I turn Chase down?*

Through a mist of conflicting emotions, his earnest plea shone through. Not pushy this time, just sweet and gentle coaxing. Too quick to forgive, but this man could arouse a sympathetic response from her without much effort. And that wasn't all . . .

The fresh, clean scent of him rendered her helpless to his charm. She glanced at her watch; the tiny dial blurred. "If Andy agrees, we'll go with you and the Yamamotos tonight. You're meeting them at eight?"

He nodded.

"That gives you and me a couple of hours to discuss some problems."

His gaze softened, and he took a seat beside her. "OK. It seems that's all we've done since we arrived."

She blew out a breath, and an ache in her

chest took its place. "Every day I return more boxes addressed to Pam. Clothes and knickknacks, ceramics, a silver figurine of a horse." She held her head, uncertain she could deal with the subject of her sister. "Pam had no interest in horses."

"Maybe it was meant to be a gift?" He lifted his eyebrows. "Her generous spirit always shone through."

She tsked. "Yes, but backed by Tad's hard-earned money. You should see the sales slip. I almost threw up."

"That's something we should talk about — the monthly expenses. The profits from the mill can't continue paying such exorbitant amounts."

"Of course not."

"I'm willing to pay half the running expenses until you decide what to do about this house."

Well, that offer was unexpected. "That's generous. And I can certainly cut corners."

He briefly closed his eyes, as though the topic had been difficult to bring up. "Collect the receipts and the accountant will take care of payment."

She nodded. "There are a dozen expenditures I still have to check out. Do you know anything about the Miracle House? Pam wrote checks every three months for five thousand dollars each time."

"I never heard of it. Maybe it's a charitable organization?"

She shrugged. "They also supported the church with a substantial contribution."

"I can help with that."

She leaned across the table. "You mean it?"

"It was important to them and Jeff, so why not?"

"But you're not into —"

"I've thought about what you said. If I'm Jeff's new father, I'll do everything possible for his spiritual future. And if that includes attending church regularly and learning more than I already know about the Bible, then I will. I believe in Jesus." He rubbed the heel of a palm across his chest. "Even if I haven't shown Him lately just how I feel."

Astonishing, in more ways than one. Even though she'd been named guardian in Pam and Tad's will, Chase sounded certain of the outcome of his lawsuit. A judge would yank a little boy from this country to live in a foreign environment with an unmarried man? Or did Chase plan to change that aspect of his life? Something she didn't know about?

"Maybe Pam's friends, Karla or Melody will know some of the answers to my questions." She rested her forehead on her palm. "I miss Pam and Tad so much, sometimes I can't breathe."

He stared at his empty hands for lengthy moments, his voice finally breaking the silence. "Me, too."

Suzanne grinned as Andy bounded down the stairs two at a time.

He'd agreed that a night on the town would be fun. Always impeccably dressed, he looked every inch the up-and-coming businessman in a navy silk and wool suit by a young, dynamic New York designer.

"Wow. You look great, Andy."

"Thanks." His innocent, boyish grin belied the romantic lover he appeared to be.

When Chase stepped into the foyer, wearing an elegant charcoal suit, all thoughts of dashing Andy fizzled away. Warmth infused her cheeks.

With a radiant glow of admiration in his silver eyes, Chase held her at arms-length. "You look fabulous." He touched her hair with fingers that whispered words he hadn't spoken, and his warmth enfolded her.

Her sophisticated jet-black dress with the semi-open back and swingy full-circle skirt contrasted with the simple neckline.

Aware of Andy taking in the scene, she laughed and moved away. "Come on, you handsome guys. Let's get to the Yamamotos' motel and paint the town."

"What colors?" Andy teased.

"Red, white, and blue."

"I'm with you," Chase chimed in.

As the men put on their coats, Suzanne looked up and halted. Jeff stood at the top of the stairs in his Spiderman pajamas, a forlorn look on his adorable face.

She exchanged glances with Chase, and then headed up, fingers gripping the handrail. At the landing, she knelt in front of Jeff.

"You come back?" he asked in a small voice.

Suzanne hugged him close. "Of course, we will. Uncle Chase and I have to go out tonight. When we get back, I'll come in and give you a goodnight kiss. OK?"

His mouth wobbled, and he seemed to fight back tears. "Mommy and Daddy didn't come back."

His clear articulation made pain charge into her heart, and she hesitated before answering. "No, they didn't. But we will. We're here for you always."

"You and Unca Chase live far way."

Jeff must have overheard them or had

some deep thoughts of his own. Neither Chase nor Suzanne would always be there for him — at least not together. "We'll talk about that when you feel like it. OK?"

His eyes dark and troubled, he nodded. "Come later? Hug Teddy?"

"I will." She brushed back the tousled lock of hair from his brow. "You know what? So you don't crush Teddy, when I get home, I'll put him on the shelf over your bed. Then he can guard you for the rest of the night."

He brightened. "And bunny?"

Not wanting to leave him, but knowing the others were waiting, she forced her voice to sound cheerful. "Yes. I'll see you in the morning, sweetie. Can I have a kiss now?"

He planted a noisy smack on her cheek.

She straightened the collar of his pajama top. "Shall I tuck you in?"

"No."

"Do you want Uncle Chase?"

"No."

She paused before rising. "Lara will be along in a few minutes, sweetheart. I love you."

He turned, and then stopped to give her a long, searching look before darting out of sight.

In the truck, Chase seemed pensive as he focused on the road.

Andy, bubbly as usual, kept up a constant chatter, asking a dozen questions and expressing an unexpected appreciation for the small town.

The restaurant was a few doors down from the motel. Good thing, since there was barely enough room in the truck for the three of them.

"Atmosphere," Andy mused, taking his fill of Main Street. "Like the fishing villages in New England. There's a warm acceptance from the few people I've met. The commuter plane pilot treated me like an old friend. And Lara's so caring and kind. I didn't bring a scarf. She told me the winds would chill my bones, and I should keep my throat covered. She dug one up from somewhere." He fingered the plaid tartan draped around his neck.

"Quite a difference from the people in New York, huh?" She smiled, feeling possessive and fond of Emerald Point.

"Yeah, but I'm used to them. Everyone there is so busy that no one takes time for pleasantries." Andy had a faraway look in his eyes when he added, "I come from a small town in Massachusetts, so I appreciate how wonderful this place is."

Chase pulled into the motel parking space

and strode to the Yamamotos' room. Shouts penetrated the door and he paused, reluctant to interrupt. It sounded as though Takami was unhappy with his son. He suspected it was over Suzanne.

Moments later, when the argument subsided, Chase rapped several times.

Kaz opened the door and greeted him with a smile. Chase returned the salutation. Though the Yamamotos were polite and pleasant, an undercurrent arced between them.

Back at the truck, Chase introduced Andy, and they all ambled down the street.

The crowded Seashell Restaurant and Nightclub, perched on a cliff overlooking the Pacific, evoked an atmosphere of fun and laughter. While they waited to be seated, the elder Yamamoto voiced his pleasure at the ship models, fishing nets, sea-faring artifacts, and the scenic walls featuring the lighthouse and bobbing boats at anchor. A forty-foot canoe made by the Tillamook tribe hung from the ceiling.

At their reserved table near the stage, Suzanne settled across from Chase. They ordered shrimp and lobster appetizers. Though the men toasted with mixed drinks or sake, she'd chosen a concoction of fruit and club soda.

Everyone talked and laughed while Kaz translated for his father.

Chase wondered about the easy camaraderie between Suzanne and Andy, who focused his attention solely on her. His thoughts froze on one specific fact. Did more than a business relationship exist between them?

Despite what he'd heard about the Ice Maiden, he no longer believed those tabloid stories, though she made little attempt to correct his initial notions about her past.

The hurricane lamps on the tables added a soft glow to Suzanne's copper hair. Giving each of them her attention in turn, she basked in the fun-filled looks the men cast her way.

A waiter took their orders. Controversy erupted between Kaz and Takami. Should they choose buffalo steaks or prime rib?

Chase hid his smile as the two bickered and finally decided on steak. Last evening he'd shrugged off Kaz's attention to Suzanne, but tonight the young Japanese man openly flirted with her. Takami's dark gaze followed his son's every move, flashing often with what Chase perceived as disapproval. Yep. Suzanne had sparked their earlier quarrel.

With the arrival of the food, Takami's entire demeanor changed. His stormy frown inverted itself with a show of delight as he inhaled the well-prepared food. His nose twitched at the succulent and delicious aromas.

A young woman in her mid-twenties took the stage, accompanied by a three-piece band. Her vivacious personality brought a new aspect to the oldies she sang.

But Chase remained honed in on Suzanne. His chest expanded with pride over the successful dinner party she'd arranged. He'd never known a more charming and gracious hostess. Any man would desire such a vivacious and beautiful woman. When she excused herself, it appeared several at this table thought so too. All but Takami's gaze followed her.

Something Chase refused to name quickened his pulse.

In the mirrored powder room, Suzanne dabbed on lip gloss, aware her cheeks were flushed. Though she'd enjoyed the men's banter, she couldn't account for the jumble of emotions that stirred inside of her.

Penny, the singer, darted into the room and went straight to the mirror to check her appearance.

"Nice crowd," Suzanne said.

"Mmm," Penny murmured as she powdered her nose and dabbed on lipstick. "The club's done real well this past week."

"That's probably because of your talent."

"Well, thank you," Penny replied with a wide smile, her voice bubbly.

Suzanne blotted her lips. "The men in my group enjoyed your performance."

Penny grinned. "I noticed those gorgeous hunks. Got any spares?"

"The only one I won't part with is the tall, dark-haired man seated across from me. Take your pick of the rest."

"You've left me with a great choice. They're all so handsome."

Penny's eyes appeared almond shaped, and on impulse, Suzanne asked, "Do you know any Japanese songs?"

"Only one, a favorite lullaby my grandmother sang to me."

"The Yamamotos just arrived from Japan. I know they'd be pleased if you sang it for them."

Penny nodded. "Be glad to. The guys in the band don't know the tune, so I'll accompany myself on the guitar."

"Great. Stop by our table later and I'll introduce you."

"Thanks. I will." After a last fleeting glance in the mirror and a brilliant smile, Penny left.

Back at the table, Suzanne smiled as the men still toasted each other. Sheesh, conquerors of the world.

Penny continued to belt out oldies and some newer danceable tunes. Then she announced, "I'm dedicating the next song, a lullaby, to the Yamamotos who are visiting from Japan."

She sang soft and low in Japanese, her eyes raised to the ceiling, as though she were immersed in the melody. Kaz smiled and waved to Penny, while Takami's eyes lit up at the unexpected tribute.

When her set ended, both men rose and clapped with enthusiasm. Suzanne beckoned Penny to their table and introduced them. Both Takami and Kaz shook hands with her and spoke in rapid Japanese.

Chase winked at Suzanne.

Her mouth twitched. *Chalk one up for me.*

When the band played a lilting love song, Kaz touched her arm. "Dance with me?"

His eyes burned with too much intensity, but she allowed him to lead her to the dance floor and into a fox trot. "I'm really attracted to you," he said.

She wrinkled her nose and smiled up at him. "It's the drinks. Liquor makes everyone look good."

He ignored her lighthearted teasing. "I'd

like to know you better."

How to turn him down without bruising his delicate ego? And ruining Chase's deal? No nice way to say she didn't want an affair, or whatever he had in mind. "That's not possible, Kaz. I'm leaving for New York soon."

"The problem isn't distance. It's the desire to meet."

His soft, seductive tone compelled her honesty.

"You're very likeable, Kaz, but —"

He studied her for a few seconds. "It's Chase, right? You're in love with him."

Unsure how to answer him, what she didn't want was Chase to have any inkling as to her feelings for him. "Maybe," she murmured.

He nodded, and his eyes lost their glow. "You are. I saw how you follow his every movement."

"I'm sorry."

"Don't be." He dipped her, and then gave her a rueful smile. "Chase is quite a guy. My father trusts him and that's a real compliment."

"My feelings are one-sided." She averted her eyes and hid the tears she ached to shed.

"I understand. It's his loss and mine, too."

Andy cut in at the psychological moment.

Whisked away, she felt safe, secure — more than an employer-employee relationship between them. He was a trusted friend.

The band played on. Penny's lyrics about broken hearts were the perfect accompaniment for Suzanne's melancholy mood.

After three songs and as many dances, Chase appeared and tapped Andy's shoulder. She melted into his embrace.

"Did you plan to dance with Andy all night?"

"Miss me?" she teased.

He gazed into her upturned face for the longest time, never missing a step before dropping a feather-light kiss on her lips. "If I said yes, I might turn your pretty head. The adoration of four men can be intoxicating for one woman."

One woman. She liked the sound of that. The rest of what he said didn't matter.

A question nagged at her about his reluctance to part with his job in Japan. She lifted her shoulders and finally found the courage. "Tell me, Chase." She met his silver gaze. "Does a woman wait for you in Tokyo?"

21

Suzanne's lashes fluttered down to cover her eyes before she looked away and pretended to study other dancers on the crowded floor. From his uplifted brows, Chase wasn't expecting such a personal question.

The music morphed from a slow and dreamy two-step to a spirited fox-trot that electrified the air. He didn't miss a beat. Whew. He twirled her away in an open break, and then she ended back in his arms again.

"Two years ago I would have answered yes."

Had she heard correctly? Unsteady for a moment, she exhaled. "What happened?"

"My fiancée followed the jetsetter crowd. Her American father owned a huge paper products company in Tokyo. She was young, beautiful, and flighty. I loved her, and thought she loved me. We had our wedding all planned, but a month before the scheduled ceremony, she eloped with an older guy, an English lord who oozed money and prestige. I couldn't compete, not that she gave me a chance. Her father broke the news of her elopement. If I were slammed by a tsunami, it would have been easier to take. For months, I felt as though I was ripping the scabs off my wounds."

"I'm sorry."

"I hope you're not. If I'd married spoiled Princess Wendy, who knows what state of mind I'd be in now?"

She grinned. "OK. I'm not sorry."

"When you and I first met, I acted like a jerk. I thought you were a copy of Wendy, but I couldn't have been more wrong." He looped her in a half turn, and pulled her close to his chest again. "I hope you'll forgive me."

Forgive him? Why not? "Sure. Consider it done."

"OK, I've confessed my past." His tone soft, persuasive, he added, "Isn't it time you shared yours?"

As the band played a wistful western tune, she considered his suggestion. "Yes, Chase, I think it's time."

The Seashell Restaurant hummed with

peppy music; the floor was packed with dancers. Chase and Suzanne returned to the table as the musicians started another set.

"No, no, you go. Music nice to dance." Takami waved them back to the dance floor where Kaz tangoed with Penny, and Andy had garnered the attention of a bevy of local girls. "Enjoy nice dance." He sipped his drink with smiling approval.

Chase and Suzanne returned to the dance floor, moving to a slower tune.

Chase danced close to her as he anticipated what she'd say about Derek. His feet moved in rhythm, but his mind struggled to comprehend the gravity of her words.

"Derek and I met at a social event where he immediately caught my attention. Handsome, and a talented actor, he could seduce women with his voice alone. I didn't date him because something just didn't seem right. He was too perfect." She paused and her mouth tightened. "When I think back, I remember him asking a lot of questions about my business and success. Would you believe he wanted to know the value of my company and the amount in my bank account? Of course, I didn't tell him."

Chase twirled her and caught her again.

"We'd dated a grand total of three times

when he began to talk about marrying me. I laughed it off as a joke. We barely knew each other. At first Derek laughed with me, but the marriage talk continued. And then he became pushy — more forceful, at which time I refused his invitations. That's when he started stalking me. I hired a bodyguard and he backed off for a while, but continued to call me every night. Like around midnight, after I'd gone to sleep. I asked him to stop, which did no good, so I unplugged my answering machine and phone. Annoyed, he began sending anonymous mail and emails to my home and business location. The man had me creeped out of my skin."

"He sounds like one of those crazies we read about after a shooting."

Suzanne took in a breath. "One night, my friends and I went to a nightclub. He found me there and threatened me. Said I'd marry him or else. When I asked what he meant, he started to cry and ran to the men's room. Norm, one of his friends followed. He raced back a few minutes later and yelled at me that I'd led Derek on. Norm said Derek had shot up heroin, had a gun and was threatening to kill himself —"

"My turn." Andy cut in on their dance and twirled Suzanne away.

Chase stood on the dancefloor for a long

moment, stunned by her revelations. Shaking his head, he returned to their table and struck a half-hearted conversation with Takami, while keeping tabs on the couple gliding across the dance floor in a lively foxtrot.

At intermission, taped music provided a soft backdrop for the muted conversations. Andy led Suzanne back to their table where she collapsed into a chair. "That's it. I've had enough."

"Not me. Mind if I keep dancing, boss?" Andy's grin made him look like a giddy teenager.

She waved him off. "Go on, big boy. Dazzle those ladies."

With a grin, he took off.

Chase leaned across the table and whispered, "Please excuse Takami and me if we speak Japanese."

"Of course." Though Suzanne focused on the dancers whirling in a tango, her mind was preoccupied with Chase. Had she told him too much? Made her appear too vulnerable? Did he believe her?

When Takami's eyes began to droop and his chin to nod, Chase grinned. "Too much sake," he whispered in her ear. "I think he's ready to leave for his bed." He rattled off something in Japanese, but Takami waved his hands and pried open his eyes. Then little by little his chin settled on his chest. He gave another startled jerk, and finally nodded, ready to go.

Chase signaled Kaz.

Kaz came over, face flushed and smiling.

"Your father would like to return to the hotel," Chase said.

Takami said something to his son.

Kaz grinned. "He says you can escort him back, and that Andy and I should stay and enjoy the music."

Chase, Takami, and Suzanne rose, donned their coats and headed for the door. Outside, in the crisp night air, Takami revived. He flitted down the sidewalk, light as a chubby bumblebee.

The sight was so humorous; she giggled and pressed a hand to her lips.

"Shhh," Chase warned, but his own mouth twitched as well.

At the door to Takami's room, he pulled Chase aside, his words slurred. "I would not allow such a beautiful, clever woman to escape. A man should have a wife. A charming hostess is an asset to any young man's future."

Aha. A shrewd man, even in his inebriated

state, and Chase wasn't oblivious to another hidden meaning behind Takami's advice — that if he locked down Suzanne, Kaz would have no choice but to back off.

Though she couldn't understand what they were saying, Suzanne tactfully focused on something above their heads.

He and Takami bowed to each other, and then the older man performed an even deeper bow to Suzanne before entering and closing the motel room door.

A burst of cold wind swirled around her, prompting her to snug the collar of her coat around her throat. "I don't like to see anyone inebriated, but he sure acted as if he didn't have a care in the world. And yet, when he's sober, he's very closed off. It seems he's only carefree when he drinks."

"I see that in my job all the time. Makes me want to practice abstinence."

Suzanne didn't comment, but she grinned.

He caught that mischievous look on her face.

On the short walk back to the restaurant, he pulled her arm through his. "You had a rough time with Derek. The press gave you a raw deal."

"You believe me?"

He stopped and drew her into his arms. "Anyone with half a brain would."

"A lot of people didn't. He was flamboyant and likeable. The tabloids ran the story of his suicide attempt, citing me as the reason. It didn't take long until my so-called friends deserted me. Except Eugenie. She's immune to society's pressures."

"I'd say she was the wisest of all. Put it behind you."

"That's easier said than done. My friends called me heartless, but later, they said *maybe* I hadn't caused Derek's irrational action. He was in financial difficulty. That's why he wanted to marry me, so I'd support him and his habits."

"Does he know you're here?"

"No, only Andy and Eugenie know. Neither of them would reveal my whereabouts."

"Good people."

"I know. I'm very blessed to have two loyal friends." She paused. "Then Ramon showed up right after the hoopla. He demanded a relationship between us. I refused. That's when he added a chapter about me in his memoirs. The tabloids loved the derogatory title he gave me. They snapped up Ice Maiden and made it a household name. My reputation took another dive." She closed her eyes. "You have no idea how much I hate that name."

At the restaurant door, Chase paused.

"Thanks for telling me, Sue. It's all I need to know. We won't refer to that name again."

As though liberated from a quagmire, Suzanne grabbed Chase's lapels and planted a solid kiss on his warm mouth.

"Sue," he murmured.

She danced away from him, and laughter slipped past her lips.

At the restaurant, Kaz and Andy sat at the only table that remained free of inverted chairs. The band members noisily packed their instruments and lowered the stage lights. That alone was more than a hint for the patrons to leave.

"We wondered if you'd come back for us," Andy teased with a wry smile.

"We walked Mr. Yamamoto back to the motel," Suzanne explained.

"That's what Kaz said." Andy grinned.

Kaz murmured his thanks.

Suzanne jabbed Andy's arm. "Where are all those girls you were romancing?"

Andy shrugged that off. "I sent them home, sobbing."

"One of these days, a woman will come along you can't resist," Chase teased. "Then you'll be in trouble."

"Maybe in twenty years or so."

Chase slapped Andy on the back. "Footloose, eh, man?"

"You got it."

After they walked Kaz to the motel, Andy pointed to an empty two-story building in the center of town. "Why is such prime property vacant?"

"A franchised hardware store closed its doors six months ago," Suzanne said. "Folks here like the small stores, so they didn't patronize the newer establishment."

"A great spot for a boutique," Andy marveled. "Look at the quaint windows. I can visualize the clothes displayed there. Bet you could rent it cheap."

She laughed. "I have enough headaches now."

Andy grinned. "Sorry, I can't go through a town without fantasizing about a new store. From what I've seen, there are only a couple of small dress shops. The younger crowd would go wild for our type of clothes."

"Do you want your own business some day?" Chase asked.

Andy's eyes shone like a kid with a new skateboard. "A string of shops. Fulfilling a dream takes money, and I don't have a rich uncle or a fairy godmother who could stake me."

Chase turned into the driveway of the

house. Lights blazed from every window.

Suzanne sucked in a breath. "Something's wrong."

They piled out of the truck.

Lara flung open the front door and met them on the steps. "Oh, Miss Suzanne. Mr. Chase," she cried. "I called the restaurant, but you'd left."

Suzanne choked out, "What happened?"

"It's Jeff." A sob caught in Lara's throat. "I checked on him about twenty minutes ago. He has a 104-degree fever and his cough is worse. I called his doctor."

"Oh, no," Suzanne whispered and bounded up the stairs, followed by the others.

The boy had tossed off his covers, his face aflame. He moaned and muttered about his toys.

Suzanne put her arm around the housekeeper's waist. "What did the doctor tell you?"

"I reached his answering service. He's out of town." Lara wiped at her tears. "The service operator said if we can't get the fever down within twenty-four hours, we should take him to the emergency room."

Chase scraped his hand over his face. "I don't think we should wait. Let's go."

With no experience to draw on, Suzanne

nodded.

Jeff sobbed, coughed, and couldn't catch his breath.

She wrapped him in a blanket, and Chase carried him down the stairs to the truck.

"Please call me as soon as you know something," Lara whispered. "I'll look after Mr. Andy."

The trip into town and the minutes until the emergency doors swung open seemed an eternity. A nurse whisked Jeff away, accompanied by Chase. Grateful for the distraction of answering questions and filling out forms, Suzanne attempted to focus, but her mind was on what was happening to Jeff. Poor baby, in the hands of strangers . . .

She dialed Mr. Pomeroy's home phone to ask if she had legal custody of Jeff. "I'm sorry to bother you at this late hour. We're here at the hospital. He's a very sick boy."

"You have the right to make any decisions for Jeff," he assured her.

An hour later, Chase introduced Dr. McKay to Suzanne in the waiting room.

"The test results show Jeff has lobar pneumonia," the doctor said. "He'll require antibiotics and fever-reducing drugs, also sponging and round-the-clock care. I left word with your doctor's exchange. I'd advise that we admit Jeff."

"He was coughing, but I never suspected pneumonia," Suzanne blurted. "Couldn't I care for him at home?"

"You could," the doctor said. "But I feel we'll stop the progression of the disease better and faster with professional care."

"I think he's right," Chase said. "We shouldn't take any chances."

She tried to still her restless hands. "May I stay with him tonight?"

"He'll be in the pediatric unit," the doctor said. "You can see him for five minutes every hour."

Her stomach churned like a cloud of moths fluttered there. "I should explain to him why he's here."

Dr. McKay stopped, a smile of reassurance on his mouth. "Right now, I think he's too sick to care."

"He just lost his parents in an accident," Suzanne said. "He'll be so confused."

"Children are more resilient than we think." The doctor checked his watch. "You can tell him later, or if he asks, the nurses can explain." He placed his hand on her arm in an attempt to comfort her. "Trust us to care for him."

Suzanne and Chase exchanged glances. When he nodded, she thanked the doctor, and then turned to Chase. "I'll stay with him tonight."

"I'm sure you can make yourself comfortable in the waiting room." Dr. McKay's cell phone rang, and he exited the room.

Who cared about comfort? That little boy, *her* little boy . . . She wanted to scream in frustration. *Dear God, please help Jeff.*

"I'll stay with you," Chase offered.

She shook her head. "Maybe it would be better if you went home and told Lara and Andy what we know so far. Get some rest and you can take over here in the morning."

Though worry lines framed around his eyes, his compassion shone through. "OK, if that's what you think is best. I'll stay for a while now. I'm concerned about you."

"He's so little. I don't think I could go on if I lost him, too." Her voice broke. If she said another word, a puddle of tears would likely dampen the waiting room floor.

Chase smoothed wisps of hair from her brow. "Jeff will be all right."

When he wrapped his warm, strong arms around her, the tears she'd dammed up flowed down her cheeks.

22

The first night and day in the hospital, watching over Jeff when they let Suzanne in to see him, passed in a blurred nightmare. Somehow, she got through the minutes and hours, although, the only lucid times she could recall were when she and Andy discussed the personnel problems at the boutiques.

"You have my full support," she told her young assistant. "Fire the current manager and hire a new one. We'll discuss your floating manager-salesperson suggestion when I get back. Your idea is good to have a replacement for days off and vacations. Great strategy. And talk to Marilee at Holden Enterprises about the overdue cosmetics shipment. She doesn't make promises she can't keep."

"Got it. You OK, Sue?"

"For the sake of my little boy, I have to be."

Andy's eyes lit up with a twinkle. "And don't forget that big guy who thinks the world spins because of you, too."

Chase? "Nothing permanent there, Andy. He reminds me of you, the perennial bachelor."

It was impossible to put Chase out of her mind, even briefly. A smile seemed beyond her ability that morning. What she really needed to do was sweep up the shards of her broken heart.

"Someday a gal will lasso me, and she'll have the last laugh."

As if that would happen any time soon. "You need someone to tie you down. That might make an even better entrepreneur out of you."

Andy's crooked grin appeared right before he pulled her into a hug.

On Tuesday morning, Chase dropped him off at the Emerald Point Airport for the first leg of his New York-bound flight.

Suzanne had gone home to shower and change clothes. When she arrived back at the hospital, she found Jeff had been moved to a private room.

Lara was napping beside him holding his little hand. Bless that woman for her thoughtfulness. She opened her eyes. "Chase brought me. He's here somewhere."

Her eyes slid closed again.

Jeff snored contentedly.

Suzanne went looking for Chase and found him in the chapel, kneeling in a pew. She joined him, her hand covering his. There always seemed a new facet to this man's character that needed to be explored. And when she heard his murmured prayers, her spirits soared.

The next day, Dr. McKay jotted on his clipboard. "The crisis is over. In a day or two, he'll be able to go home."

"Great news," Chase said.

Jeff reached out for Suzanne.

Leaning down, she hugged him tight. "How's my big boy today?"

"Wanna go home."

"As soon as the doctor says you're OK."

Jeff's grin, his first in days, brought a smile to Suzanne's face.

Would she ever forget how lost her little boy had looked when they'd first brought him to the emergency room? Now that he was better, he tried everyone's patience with his relentless pestering to go home. Jeff no longer needed her or Chase to stay with him every minute. Taking a moment to herself, Suzanne went into the waiting room.

Chase followed and pulled her into his arms. His kiss, though chaste, comforted her into feeling almost human again.

"I can breathe now."

"I know what you mean." He sighed. "For the first time, I realize what a huge responsibility it is to raise a child."

Did that mean . . . Her heart went into a tailspin. "I know. We're both ill-prepared for parenthood." After the scare with Jeff, would he give her the go-ahead to take the boy to New York? "I remember all too well how many problems Pam had in her early years."

Chase's eyes narrowed. "You think I changed my mind about Jeff? That I no longer want custody because I'm afraid of the responsibility?"

"Afraid?" She shook her head. "No. I thought maybe you'd realized that he'd be better off with me."

His lips compressed, he released her, and took a step back. "In a perfect world, Jeff would have both a mother and father. Ours isn't perfect. I haven't changed my mind, Sue."

She swallowed her disappointment and tried to quiet her nerves. Slim chance though it was, she might not have either Jeff or Chase in her life before long.

Putting all of that aside, she left Chase at the hospital and headed out to meet Karla,

Pam's friend, for lunch.

"I thought you might have to postpone this," the tall, gentle-voiced woman said. "Chase told us about Jeff. I called the hospital, but they said only immediate family could visit."

Though bone tired, Suzanne managed a smile. They covered a few pleasantries while studying the menu, but her mind focused on her reason for this meeting — to find out if Karla knew anything about the unknown man in her sister's life.

A waitress stopped by soon after to take their orders. Both chose a Caesar salad and clam chowder.

Karla caressed a carnation in a vase on the table as she spoke about Jeff. No longer the standoffish woman, she seemed friendlier and more compassionate now, and yet avoided eye contact.

Unsure what to say or how to broach the delicate reason for meeting with Karla, Suzanne chose to wait. Let her make the first move.

When the conversation lagged and the silence became awkward, Karla took a deep breath and jumped right in. "You . . . uh, I'm sure you're wondering what this is all about. Pam and Tad's problem —"

Suzanne toyed with the fork, unsure

whether she wanted to know the details.

"I gave it a lot of thought before all this happened with Jeff," Karla went on. "The day you returned the car Chase had borrowed, you said something that upset Vic. The more he considered it, the more it bothered him."

Suzanne eyed her. "You mean about Pam and her supposed lover?"

"Vic got the impression you thought he . . ." She ran her thumb around the edge of her water glass, still avoiding eye contact. "You don't really believe Pam had a lover, do you?"

"No, I don't."

"Well, you're right."

Suzanne frowned. How could Karla be so sure? "Lara, their housekeeper, said they argued and that Tad said —"

"Pam wanted to make him jealous. You see, he was at the mill so much, and she hoped it would push him to spend more time with her and Jeff." Karla's restless hands moved on the table. "It was foolish to try and maneuver Tad that way, but she wouldn't listen to me."

Unsure what to think or say, Suzanne leaned back in her chair. Was her sister so immature?

"You've no doubt found out by now that

Pam had a passion for pretty things. She ordered all kinds of stuff and spent all kinds of money."

"Yes, I know. I have the receipts." Suzanne sadly shook her head. "I've already returned a dozen boxes of stuff she'd ordered."

Karla nodded. "No matter how much money Tad made, he barely kept up with her spending. He worked double shifts and threatened to take away her checking account and credit cards. Pam thought if she distracted him with something else to worry about, he'd pay more attention to her."

Aghast, Suzanne made a conscious effort to close her gaping mouth. "That's so —"

"I know. Pam was such a delightful person, but she never really grew up."

Guilt sawed through Suzanne, settling with great weight and pain in her chest. "My fault. I raised her."

Karla smiled and touched Suzanne's arm. "I don't think so. You're so sensible. Something should've rubbed off on her."

Suzanne needed an anesthetic to dull her distress. "Lara told me they argued about a man the night of the accident. Do you suppose that contributed . . . ?" She trailed off. Her voice didn't sound like her own.

Karla squirmed as though she considered

the possibility too painful. "We'll never know."

More than upset by this disclosure, Suzanne also felt heartened that her loyalty toward Pam had not been misplaced. She pressed her fingertips to her temple.

"Pam really loved Tad," Karla went on. "The change in him broke her heart. She couldn't comprehend why he would spend every waking hour at work. She didn't realize it was because of her spendthrift ways. All she wanted was to make him aware of her again. And believe me, she tried hard, but he'd freeze and end up sleeping in the log cabin by the mill."

The waitress arrived with their food, putting a momentary end to their conversation.

A few sips of her soup and a bite of the salad was all Suzanne could manage to eat. Her appetite was lost.

Karla sipped her tea. "It distresses me that Pam might have pushed Tad into an argument that night, and then . . ."

The unfinished sentence left Suzanne swallowing hard. "Do you mind if I tell Chase?"

Her fork clattered on the table; Karla blotted her lips with a napkin. "Of course not. He should know."

When it came time to leave, the women

hugged. "Thank you for being Pam's friend and thank Vic for caring about Tad."

Tears sparkled in Karla's eyes, "Will you take Jeff back to New York?"

"You know Chase is contesting the will. He's suing for custody of Jeff. I can't make any plans until the court decides." She didn't mention another reason for not wanting to leave Emerald Point — her growing feelings for Chase.

On Main Street, several people waved to Karla and nodded at Suzanne. Their friendly gestures brought kindred warmth to her soul. In New York she had lots of acquaintances, but strangers surrounded her.

"I'd hoped the courts wouldn't be necessary." Karla took her keys from her purse. "Have you and Chase talked it through? If we can help —"

"He won't withdraw his lawsuit, and he wants Jeff as much as I do. That little boy is the last of our family, for both of us." Suzanne offered a weak smile. "Maybe you and Vic could convince him to let me keep Jeff."

"You must know him well enough by now." Karla shrugged one shoulder. "Chase is hard to convince about anything."

"Brothers cast from the same mold."

"Exactly. Maybe you and I can be friends

like Vic and Chase."

"I'd like that, Karla." She could use an ally in this town.

They hugged and vowed to meet again soon.

In the restaurant parking lot, Suzanne jumped in the truck and closed the door. A shadow appeared beside the window. The police chief signaled for her to lower it.

"Hi, Ms. Bratton."

"How are you, Chief?"

"I'm fine. I hear the Garwood boy's in the hospital. Is he OK?"

"He's better, thanks. A nasty case of pneumonia. I'm headed there now."

He pulled his hat lower. "I want you and Mr. Garwood to know we're still working on the cause of the crash."

Uneasiness stirred inside her. "Any news?" *Do I want to know?*

"We're checking local vehicles to see if any were involved in a recent accident. One could have had repairs and a paint job to hide any damage. We should finish the investigation this week."

"There must be thousands of vehicles in the area."

"Part of the job. If there is one, we'll find it."

Only a small-town police force would

make such an effort to find the truth. "Good to hear."

He touched his hat and stepped away.

Minutes later, Suzanne entered the hospital room to find both Jeff and his uncle asleep. Seated in a chair beside the boy's bed, Chase's head lolled sideways in an awkward position. He'd probably have a crick in his neck when he woke up.

Karla had let drop a few things about Chase, who'd received top honors in high school and college. He'd excelled at weightlifting, track, and swimming, but didn't have much use for spectator sports. No surprise. His shoulders and biceps were strong when he held her close. He had everything going for him — looks, physique, plus intelligence.

She pulled a plush squirrel toy from a bag and set it on the bed. When she touched Chase's cheek, he jolted awake. "Sorry, I didn't mean to startle you, but you looked so uncomfortable. How does your neck feel?" she whispered.

He rolled his head in slow circles. "Rough." Dark stubble shadowed his face. He looked haggard, but still handsome as ever. Somehow, he seemed more lovable when not so picture-perfect. She walked behind his chair and dug her fingers and thumbs into his neck. When she moved to his shoulders, those massive muscles rippled beneath her fingers.

"You have amazing hands." A pleasurable grin escaped before he tilted his head to search her face.

She waggled her eyebrows and teased, "You have a few amazing ways yourself. How's Jeff?"

He looked at the sleeping toddler. "I explained how he's a big boy now, and that you and I won't be here all the time. Only during regular visiting hours. He sort of accepted that."

"I was afraid to even broach the subject. It kills me to see tears in his beautiful eyes."

"I know." Chase paused. "What did Karla say?"

Suzanne told him about Pam and Tad's relationship, all the while massaging his neck and upper back.

Chase scowled. "Both of them were foolish. Tad shouldn't have avoided intimacy, but the thought of another guy —"

"I suppose most people would react that way." Knowing how childish her sister could be at times, she felt defensive toward the brother-in-law she'd loved.

Chase stilled her hand on his neck and drew it around to press a kiss on her palm. He arose and motioned for her to sit.

She shook her head. "Isn't it strange that Tad didn't tell you about their problem?"

He shrugged. "Not really. As an older brother, he knew he was my hero. You don't ever make yourself seem like less than a man."

"Yeah," she whispered and brushed his hair from his forehead. "You worshipped him."

"Think so, huh?"

"Know so."

"I can't wait until we take Jeff home," Chase said.

The boy stirred and opened his eyes.

Suzanne caressed his warm cheek. "Feeling better, sweetheart?"

Jeff nodded. "Hungry."

"Oh, that's good. Are you hungry as a grizzly bear?"

"Yep." A slow grin crossed his darling face.

"I'll see if the nurse can rustle up something you'll like, maybe pudding or ice cream?"

Jeff nodded at all of her suggestions. When he'd eaten two chocolate puddings and the nurse promised him more later, then ice cream for dessert after dinner, his eyes slowly closed again.

Only then did Suzanne and Chase slip from the room.

■ ■ ■ ■

The smell of sand, kelp, and the sea made Suzanne's nose twitch. Chase sauntered beside her along the stretch of beach. Clouds rolled overhead, oblivious to the darkening sky. A storm brewed, marching straight for them from across the Pacific.

"You're as strong as the wind and as wild as the ocean," she told Chase. They'd been teasing each other, saying outrageous things.

"Ho. Ho." Chase tossed one of Lara's chips in his mouth and crunched. "You're so beautiful, I'll have to have my eyes lasered so I don't lose my sight."

She giggled and jabbed his arm.

Chase added another silly tribute. "The scent of you reminds me of fields of flowers blossoming in the sun."

"Pretty heady stuff," she teased, "coming from a man who wears eau de pine tar."

His husky laughter charmed her. "I see very little of the lumber we sell. I have the easier end of the job." He turned to her, kissed the side of her neck, then glanced down and stopped. As though magnetized, his golden half-heart had tangled with hers. "Looks like you hooked me."

"Like a fish?" She reached to untangle the charms.

He watched her struggle with the hearts. "What happens if we can't get these apart?"

"We might stay hooked together for the rest of our lives." She desperately wanted to see the reaction in his eyes, but didn't dare meet his gaze.

"Would that be so terrible?"

She clenched her hands at her sides.

"Sounds crazy, huh, Sue?"

"Yeah," she murmured, not daring to breathe.

"I really care about you," he admitted.

She didn't have the strength to suck in air. "I care about you, too."

He smiled. Then, as though he'd thought of something unpleasant, his lips flattened. Those amazing gray eyes grew shuttered, and he pulled back but only as far as their chains allowed. "I have some important calls to make before we visit Jeff again."

The golden charms miraculously parted.

Thunder rumbled and flashes of lightning lit up the solarium as Suzanne dialed Pam's friend, Melody Kelly, and confirmed their lunch date. Maybe she could shed some light on the large checks Pam had written.

After a series of phone calls, Chase left

the house, his shoulders slumped.

Suzanne let out a yelp as she stared at a small package delivered that morning. At the sight of the vivid crimson book jacket with hearts, cupids and arrows, a smile tugged at the corners of her mouth. *Warm Hearts, Cold Facts.* She hugged the book written by her benefactor, Eugenie Haven-Hall, the only person who'd stuck by her during those trying times.

Her heart thudded as she flipped through the pages. When she spotted her name coupled with Ramon's, she worked her way back to an earlier chapter, searching for Derek's name. Scanning the pages, a smile curved her lips as heat slipped into her cheeks.

Sometime later, she whispered, "Thank you, Eugenie, for setting the record straight. You're a wonderful friend." Putting the book aside and staring wide-eyed at the plants, she really didn't see them. Sounds of the house — Jeff's chatter and the clank of pots and pans — surrounded her, but she didn't really hear them.

Joy scattered through her like bits of driftwood.

Chase found Suzanne in the solarium, surrounded by schefflera and golden pothos, wearing a wide smile on her beautiful mouth. "Sue," he murmured.

"Hi, Chase." Tears shimmered in her blue eyes. Joyous ones, he assumed, given her smile.

"What's happened?" He wanted to share in what seemed to be good news.

Share. The word implied something he hadn't thought much about before they met. He knelt on the rug in front of her and tipped up her chin with his finger. Lord, so precious, sweet, warm and giving. His hands shook, and he was rattled to the very foundation of his psyche. *Sharing.*

"Do you remember when I told you about my friend, Eugenie, the only person who reached out to me when my world crumbled?"

He nodded.

She held up a book. "She wrote this and laid out the simple facts in a straightforward fashion, not the sensational drivel made up by the tabloids. I'm vindicated. Would you like to read it?"

He drew her to him and sheltered her head against his shoulder, letting her happiness soak his shirt. He grabbed his handkerchief and blotted her cheeks. "If that's what you want, I'll read it. But I told you I believe you. And I'm glad you feel better about all that happened."

She grinned at him. "Sometimes you say the sweetest things."

"You are those sweet things." The words popped unbidden, but he truly meant them.

"Lara left a while ago with her sister for some serious shopping in Pleasant Valley. Afterwards, she'll visit Jeff until we get to the hospital."

He jumped up and held out his hand. "Come on. Let's go see our little boy."

Though sharing was new to him and he liked that, he wouldn't tell her about the phone calls he'd made to business acquaintances on the East Coast, or their cordial, yet less enthusiastic feedback. He felt sure he could make a living in New York, but not in his current line of work. And not receive the fabulous salary he now commanded. Was there an alternative?

He shook his head. Depending on the results of the custody battle, precious little time remained for him and Suzanne.

23

Melody Kelly picked up Suzanne in her beat-up car which was held together with rust and an Our Father prayer. She headed for Main Street, skirted a row of commercial buildings and mom-and-pop stores, and parked at the back door of one sporting a sign that read Fred's Fresh Fish.

"All those questions you asked. I have some of the answers," Melody said.

Suzanne frowned. Answers in a fish store? "Great."

"Pam volunteered here and gave a lot of money for its upkeep."

Suzanne pointed to the sun-faded outline of a tuna on the brick exterior.

Melody laughed and pulled open a heavy door. No sign of fish or the smell associated with them.

"This is Miracle House. It was converted to a rehabilitation center for the homeless and some veterans. We bought exercise equipment, cots, and even set up a soup kitchen so the men get at least one warm meal each day. We're housing an abused woman and two babies in a motel down the street. She's eager to find a job and a permanent place to live."

Suzanne glanced around. Clean, everything neatly folded, blankets stacked high. Several wheel chairs and canes stood in a corner as though waiting for someone to claim them. Six men, some old, some not, played cards at tables set up around an open space.

"Pam gave her heart and soul to this place. Put on her apron and served, even though she had a maid at home. She organized fundraiser dances, and most of the wealthy people in town attended. She was a blessing to these folks with her hard work."

My wonderful sister was more than a pretty face. Pam had a heart filled with love for her fellow citizens. And she didn't throw Tad's hard-earned cash away. She used a lot of it to help those less fortunate. Suzanne blinked back tears. "I'm amazed."

"The director lost a leg in Desert Storm and volunteers his time here. Would you like to meet him?"

Suzanne pressed a hand to the dip in her neck and caressed the half-heart necklace.

A chill chased down her back. "No. I don't think so. I'm not sure I could keep from becoming a blubbering mess."

"I thought you'd feel that way. We have Pam to thank for this worthy endeavor."

"I had no idea she gave so freely of her money and time." And because of her good heartedness, she obviously placed the relationship with her husband in a precarious position. "I think I've seen enough. Can we go?" Her sister's positive achievements made Suzanne's spirits soar.

Melody started toward the door. "I think it's important that you see a few more places. We should visit the church hall."

"Don't tell me. More volunteer work and cash?"

"You got it." Melody opened the door.

Sunshine bathed Suzanne's face, but that couldn't match the inner glow that warmed her heart for the precious sister she'd lost. "Maybe we can save that visit for another time. You've more than answered my questions."

The sound of the surf pounded in her ears, and the fresh breeze added to the rewarding afternoon. The briny air smelled so pungent; she could almost taste it. "I'll tell Chase about this. Thank you for the enlightenment."

Melody drove to the Garfield house. "Does this help you understand what your sister was all about?"

Suzanne nodded. *Not quite.* Besides wanting more attention from Tad, why would Pam spend a fortune on expensive trinkets and designer clothes?

The grandfather clock in the solarium chimed four times. Suzanne had nodded off and awoken with a stiff neck.

Two days from now she'd hop a flight to New York, her time with Chase at an end until they met again in court.

The thought of him as an enemy because of the custody battle sharpened the ache in her chest. Depending on the judge's decision, they could very well end up hating each other. A sigh rose from her throat.

A deep masculine groan broke into her pensive thoughts. She followed the sound to the sofa. Chase sprawled there, asleep. When did he come in?

She studied his profile. His strong jaw lay slack — as though the weight of the world had slipped from his shoulders while he dozed. She swallowed hard, burning the image of his handsome face and body into her mind.

Boutiques and business relationships

wouldn't keep her warm at night, but maybe these memories of Chase would sustain her.

The phone rang, and his eyes popped open. "Don't answer."

"It could be important, maybe about Jeff."

He let out a heavy breath and reached for the receiver. "Hello, Kaz." His free hand on his forehead, he stared at the ceiling. "I understand. I . . . yes, that is good news." Then moments later, "I'll certainly consider your company's offer."

Her stomach churned.

"Give me a couple of weeks. I'll be in touch. Thanks for the call. Yes, I'll tell her." He replaced the receiver in its cradle and stared at it as though it were some alien object.

Suzanne couldn't have spoken if she'd wanted to. The mill would be sold. One more memory of Tad and Pam gone.

"Kaz sends his regards to the loveliest lady on the West Coast." Chase's voice cracked midway through the sentence, as though something clogged his throat. "Things are winding down here." His eyes were half closed, as if he couldn't bear looking at her.

Suzanne's mind whirled with the implication that their relationship would soon end. "It looks that way." Probably sounding more controlled than she felt, she added, "I spoke with Karla and asked her to look in on Lara and Jeff while you and I are gone. She agreed. I know she loves our little boy."

"It seems odd to think about returning to Tokyo. We only have one day after Jeff comes home from the hospital tomorrow to make him understand what's happening."

Energy slowly seeped from her. She was perishing, but wouldn't share her feelings. "I've talked about it in bits and pieces to him, but I'm not sure he understands that we both have to leave at the same time." She hesitated. "Will you be back for the hearing?"

This was the first time in days that either of them had mentioned Jeff's future. *I won't cry.*

"I'll be here." He still didn't look at her. "I never told you about my mother, did I?"

A tentative smile built as surprise sank in. He'd changed the topic. That was unexpected. "No, you haven't."

"My world transformed on my twelfth birthday. Mother divorced Dad, and our family split apart. Dad got custody of Tad, and Mom took me with her to San Diego. I hated her for that. She'd always been a disinterested parent, but once we were there, the situation got worse. Her only interest was to pick up men, a whole succession of them. It was as if I didn't exist anymore."

He hadn't shared much of his past. Why now?

His eyes narrowed as they seemed to focus on a distant point. "I needed my father, a hero figure. Only on rare occasions did she allow me to visit him and Tad." Chase's impassive face, stone-like, resembled Washington's on Mount Rushmore. "She never told the truth. And when she didn't outright lie, she ignored me."

His laughter held no joy. "I gave her as much trouble as she gave me. Had a few run-ins with the cops — more to get attention than for any logical reason. They had lots of experience with troubled kids, so they took me under their protective wing, and I learned from them how to be a grownup. Occasionally I would meet an aggressive cop who didn't look at kids the same way."

"Did you ever commit any serious offenses?"

"Nah, I was smart enough not to get into any real trouble. I have to thank the good cops, though, those who cared that I turned out OK."

She had a new appreciation for his willingness to share his less than sterling youth. "I have a feeling you'd have done well even without their help."

The mischief glowing in the smile he gave her was filled with playful, annoying clown like antics — something he probably perfected as an unhappy child. A handsome lawbreaker who derived pleasure out of forcing his mother to be confronted by the police.

"Did your mother plead your case?"

"No, but she had to promise to keep me out of trouble, which really bugged her."

"I hope Jeff doesn't take after you."

"He could do worse."

"Yes." She said a silent prayer for the boy.

Chase sat up. "I didn't trust my mother, and after that I viewed all women the same way. Sometimes I thought about running away, back to Dad. Even though she didn't want me, she wouldn't give up the monthly child support my father sent. The main reason she held onto me."

He paused and took in a breath. "Five years ago, she died in a plane crash along with her latest conquest. And then my disastrous relationship with Wendy reinforced my feelings about all women."

Suzanne closed her eyes, now confused. "And you're telling me this, why?"

"I want you to understand."

"Is this about commitment?"

He grabbed his lip with his teeth. "Relationships don't last, Sue. I say this because of my parents, Tad and Pam, and many of my acquaintances. If you and I decided to see each other — that would be maybe two or three times a year. And only after a lot of planning."

She tossed her head. "No relationship could survive those circumstances."

"Exactly," he said.

"While we were apart, we might find other people we'd become attracted to. And . . ."

"Yes." He met her eyes. "You know I love you."

Whoa. She felt a tug at her heart. Exhilaration flooded through her, right before realization set in. This wasn't a happy ever after. This was goodbye. Her hands pressed against her chest did nothing to lessen the pain.

If he could share her feelings with her, so could she. "And I love you, Chase."

His fingers spread like a fan against his breastbone, mirroring her pain. "Maybe it would have been better, easier, if we hadn't admitted that."

In a soft, halting voice she asked, "Easier for whom?"

"I need you, Sue. I've also seen my share

of unfulfilled love, and that makes me question that desire and the possessive feelings you invoke."

She clenched her hands together against the temptation to reach for him. They had to talk this out. "Before I met you, I swore off having a man in my personal life. I thought I could survive in a world without caring. You changed that. You changed me — and for that I'm grateful. I would have been a sorry example of womanhood if I hadn't struggled through all of this with you."

"But?" he prompted.

Tears welled up, the sharp, stinging kind. She forced herself to look away. "A long-distance relationship wouldn't satisfy either of us. It might be exciting for a few months, but then the time between meetings would be lonely, and the distance too long, too far to sustain a relationship. Not only that, but I'd be fighting against the religious tenets I've come to embrace, and that's something I don't think I can deal with." She lowered her voice. "And, of course, there's the inevitable letdown when we discover our feelings didn't last."

"You believe they wouldn't last?"

A slow death lingered in her future. Without him she'd only be half-alive. But with him . . . "We're both saying the same thing with different words."

A haunting sensation of sorrow filled every pore of her body. Dammed-up emotions flooded through her. Feelings burst inside, shattering her into shards of glass, the tiny pieces, digging into her flesh from the inside made her want to cry out in anguish. Why was love so difficult? Why did it have to hurt so much?

She battled against the driving impulse to say, "Let's follow God's plan. Let Him guide us." That was risky. She didn't know if she could survive giving him her heart if he left her in the end.

"There's a lot more we should talk about."

She crawled over, knelt before him, and then placed her fingers across his lips. "I know." A horrible ache tore at her chest, like a hot poker drilling into her flesh.

He reached for her and rocked her gently in his arms.

After the days in the hospital, Jeff came home to hugs and kisses from Suzanne and Lara. Chase took a more dignified approach by shaking the youngster's hand and helping him open the presents that awaited him in the playroom.

Making up for the endless time spent

cooped up in the pediatric ward, Jeff scattered cars and his garbage truck, and growled at his stuffed animals. Suzanne played games with him and when he grew tired, held him on her lap in the rocking chair.

"Mommy? Daddy?" He tripped over the words, yawned, and tears welled up in his brown eyes.

Her head spun, and she swallowed hard. *Dear Lord, give me the right words to comfort him.* "They told you about heaven, didn't they?" she said, attempting to keep her voice light.

He nodded. "Where Jesus is."

"Yes. Did they tell you that someday all of us will meet again?"

He nodded.

"Jesus wanted your parents to join Him."

"Why?"

A question she needed answered as well. "Because they were good people and believed in Him."

Fear widened his eyes. "If I'm good, Jesus takes me there? Like poor kitty?"

She shuddered. He remembered the dead cat in the street. Strange that he hadn't mentioned it since then. "Yes, like the kitty. Jesus knows when it's time for you to join your mom and dad."

"Not take me now?"

"No." *Lord, help me.* "Because He wants you to grow up and then —"

"Heart." He touched his chest. "I'm in their heart."

Whew. She released a tortured breath. "Yes. And they'll always be in yours."

Jeff grabbed her hand, fighting off sleep. "Want them here."

Me, too. If I could only . . . "I know. But until you go to meet them, Uncle Chase and I will take care of you. We love you, sweetheart, and will always look after you."

"You and Unca Chase?"

"Yes. One of us will be with you as much as possible."

His little face twisted. Too much for his mind to absorb.

"If you ever have a problem, we'll help."

"They gone." He pressed his face to her shoulder and sobbed as though his heart would shatter.

Suzanne couldn't hold back her own tears. *Please, Lord, be here for Jeff and me. I need to know how to deal with this.*

24

The morning sun smiled on Suzanne and Jeff through the French door as she pulled his chair closer to the kitchen table and cuddled his restless body. They laughed as birds twittered and scurried about to pick up twigs for their nests. Springtime in Oregon — a wondrous time of year.

She spread a large calendar on the table and pointed to the days marked with red hearts and a big old sun. "Your uncle and I leave tomorrow, but we'll return the tenth of April. We'll be gone the days marked with red hearts. You and Lara can check them off."

Jeff brushed his hand over the hearts. "You back then? Fingers?"

She held up nine fingers. "Uncle Chase will be back from Tokyo, and I'll return from New York when the big sun in this space shines on you."

Unsure how he would react to their leaving, he surprised her with an "OK." Quick as lightning, he wiggled out of her arms and bounded up the stairs.

The rock slowly lifted from her chest. It felt as though hummingbirds fluttered in her stomach, the vibrations setting off a rush of unexpected joy. Jeff had begun to accept that at times only Lara would be with him. Their little boy showed signs of growing up.

The phone rang, and she reached for it.

"This is Chief Ray Trent. How are you, Ms. Bratton?"

"Good, thanks. You have news?"

"Yes. I'd like to see you and Mr. Garwood in my office." He sounded as though his breath hitched.

A moment of dread spread through her. "Chase should be back from the mill in about twenty minutes."

"That's fine. See you as soon as you can make it."

Suzanne checked on Jeff in his playroom. He hummed, tossed his cars and trucks, and laughed out loud when a plastic one hit him on the head.

She trotted down the stairs. In the solarium, Lara dusted furniture and sang along with a western tune playing on the radio.

A blaze of cymbidium orchids, in shades of pink, yellow and maroon, graced one corner. Such a beautiful, cozy place to relax. When it came time to leave Emerald Point permanently, she'd miss this room the most.

Thirty minutes later, she and Chase entered the police chief's small office. A printer spewed out paper, his full attention focused on each page. Then he looked up. "Please have a seat."

They each took a chair in front of his desk.

"We've finished our investigation into the accident and finally located the pickup involved."

Suzanne covered her mouth to stifle a gasp.

Chase hunched forward, his hands clasped, knuckles white.

"A young boy, just seventeen, admitted he sideswiped the Garwood car."

Chase sat back. "Does that mean — ?"

Trent wiped his brow. "We can't say for sure what it means. It may have contributed to their going off the road and down the gully. Or maybe not."

Chase eyed the chief. "Who is he?"

"I believe you know him. Rick Kelly."

Suzanne half rose, but then slumped back into the chair. "Melody and Grant's son?" she whispered.

"Yes."

Chase shook his head and grimaced.

"What happened?"

The chief winced. "Rick's girlfriend dumped him that night. Her house is about a half mile past Vic and Karla's. He was crying and didn't see the Garwood car until after he grazed it. Claims he stopped, but the Garwoods drove on. This information coincides with where we found paint chips from the pickup. Farther down the road is where their car left the pavement."

Suzanne couldn't still her twitchy hands.

"The next morning when the kid heard about the crash, he panicked. Took the pickup to a repair shop up the coast, and they fixed the fender and repainted it. Did a good job. You could only tell it had been damaged if you knew where to look."

She took a calming breath. "But you found it."

He gave a half-smile. "I have an assistant who's good at sniffing out details."

I'm numb. She'd only seen the Kelly boy at church. Hold on . . . Now she remembered. The same teen almost knocked her down the day of the funeral. That had been her fault. She'd stepped off the curb without looking.

Chase cleared his throat. "Can we see him, talk to him?"

"You won't do anything rash —"

"Of course not." Chase rubbed his hands down his thighs. "My brother had a similar accident at that age. Right here in Emerald Point. The judge gave him a break. I just . . . I don't know . . . maybe if I talk to Rick, see if he remembers anything."

"I released him to his parents."

"When did they find out?" Suzanne asked.

"This morning."

She leaned forward. "What happens now?"

Trent grabbed a pen and twirled it through his fingers. "Rick will go before the judge later today. He has no traffic violations or record of any kind. I'm sure all that will be taken into account. He's a good kid."

"A woman can do that to a guy," Chase grumbled.

Suzanne pressed her lips together. It was one more example to reinforce Chase's poor opinion of women.

The chief continued. "We like to give each child a chance to redeem himself. Because Rick tried to cover up his part in the accident, he's been through a rough patch. As have you both."

Chase nodded, rose and thanked the chief. "Do you have the Kellys' phone number and address? I'd like to see them now."

"I have the phone number," Suzanne said.

Trent jumped up and stared at Chase. "I'll come with you."

Suzanne put up her hand. "No need for that, Chief. There's been enough heartache without us adding violence." She stepped toward Chase and cupped his elbow. "He's a peaceful man."

Chase's eyebrows shot up.

The chief wrote directions to the Kelly house and handed Chase the slip of paper.

They thanked him and left the office.

While Chase drove, Suzanne phoned the Kellys.

"They're upset" she said after the call ended. "Please don't say anything to hurt them more."

He shot a quick look toward her as she stared ahead through the windshield.

"As if I would."

At the Kellys' small white bungalow, adorned with spring buds and a turquoise entry door, Suzanne and Chase stepped from the truck.

Her knock produced an immediate response. Melody stood before them, eyes overflowing with tears. Her husband, Grant, appeared haggard as he stood behind her, one hand on her shoulder. Rick hovered off to one side, his face red and contorted.

Melody choked, "We're so sorry."

Suzanne hugged her.

Chase grasped Grant's hand. "We don't want to intrude, but I thought maybe Rick might remember something significant about the accident."

The teenager rushed past his parents to stand in front of Suzanne. "I'm so sorry." Tears swept down his cheeks. "I haven't slept since it happened."

Though Suzanne struggled with her emotions, she patted his back. "We know you feel bad. We didn't come to harass you. Jesus would want us to extend forgiveness." *Where had those words come from?*

The teen's head jerked up. "You forgive me?"

Suzanne drew him to her. "As you would forgive us." She turned and stepped away. "Chase?"

Color had left his cheeks. He rolled his shoulders, released a sigh, and then his arms enfolded Rick.

The long, emotional moment went on for a while but eventually they all moved to the living room. As Chase spoke, a sensation of warmth and understanding drifted over Suzanne. Rick related the happenings of that fateful night in a torturous voice, while his parents looked on with tear-streaked cheeks.

"The chief saw the tire marks on the road where I jammed on the brakes." Rick stuttered over his words. "He measured the distance from the accident to where their car went over the side . . . about a quarter mile farther down the road. He thinks something more could have happened than just my pickup touching their fender."

Chase cleared his throat. "Could you see into the car? Do you remember anything out of the ordinary?"

"No, it was dark. I only saw a flash of headlights — too late. It happened so fast, and then they were past me. I was shook up and stomped on the brakes. Got out of the truck with my flashlight and saw my scraped fender."

"Did you hear anything?"

"The chief asked me that, too. Now that I think back, I heard a thump, but it wasn't loud."

"You probably wouldn't hear much of in impact from that distance." Chase sat back with a strange finality.

Rick wiped a hand over his face. "I'll never forgive myself for trying to cover up my part in the accident."

"I know it must be traumatic for you to talk about what happened." Chase squeezed the bridge of his nose. "I don't hold any of it against you. It was an accident. And I want you to promise me something."

Rick seemed confused, his gaze darting from Chase to his parents. He nodded. "Sure. Anything."

Chase scuffed the carpet. "Put this behind you, Rick. But if you can't, if it continues to haunt you, and if you need therapy, let me know. I'll be glad to help."

The Kelly family stared at Chase with disbelief that quickly turned to hope.

Melody stepped forward. "Bless you, Chase, for understanding."

Chase grinned. "Thanks. I think I'll need a lot of blessings in the next few weeks." He let his gaze drift toward Suzanne.

He had turned out to be all she'd hoped for and so much more. What a great guy.

Her heart seemed to tilt. The pride she felt for this man was worth any amount of sadness and emotional suffering she'd have to endure once she was away from him on a permanent basis.

A half hour later, after they prayed together, Chase and Suzanne left the Kelly home hand in hand.

When they got to the truck, she whispered, "Amen."

Emerald Point's tiny new park on the edge

of town was a young boy's dream. Laughter filled the air as youngsters swung from rung to rung on the monkey bars and whizzed down the slides.

Suzanne had joined the small group of mothers who'd also brought their children for a fun time that bright spring day. She listened to the ladies' chatter, and kept one eye on Chase, who pushed Jeff's swing. She purposely avoided looking his way, sensing that something deeply troubled him, which so far, he'd refused to divulge.

Jeff braved the slides and the view from the wooden fort, but then chose to return to the swings. He pumped his little legs, shouting, "Higher. More."

Chase flinched each time the boy shrieked.

Whatever his mind must've been focused on, Chase only responded after Jeff yelled a second time.

She hadn't seen him like this, so immersed in thought. Maybe she could help.

With a wave to the ladies, she headed for the swings. When she reached Chase, she whispered, "What's wrong?"

One hand pushed the swing and the other curled at his side. "I guess I have to tell you. It's only fair."

She stepped back. What now? A new problem added to the others that plagued her? "Tell me." She urged.

"It's about . . . Jeff."

She rubbed her wrists, and a wave of nausea swept through her. Something bad. She could tell from the way Chase's mouth twisted. Almost afraid to ask, but something pushed her. "What?"

"Before we part this time, you should know about my plans for work and how they'll affect Jeff's custody."

There, in the sun's warmth, she shivered as though a wintry blast from the North Pole whipped across her shoulders. In contrast, perspiration beaded the back of her neck. She didn't want to think or even attempt to guess what he was about to say.

Jeff's little head bobbed, ready for a nap. She released him from the swing and picked up his limp body. He fought sleep, his chubby hands brushing against his eyes.

"Time to go." She started toward the truck. Chase followed. With Jeff safely in his car seat, she turned and waited.

Chase tucked his hands in his pockets and shuffled his feet against the concrete pavement. What could he possibly have to tell her?

"When we meet before the judge, you should know that you and I now have an even playing field when it comes to . . .

custody."

Fearful that she'd burst out crying, she merely stared at him.

He rubbed the back of his neck. "My attorney plans to advise the judge of a new development. I'm going to transfer back to Alaska, so my home base will no longer be a problem. If I gain custody, Jeff and I won't be returning to Japan."

25

Suzanne glanced back at the Garwood house as the taxi pulled away from the curb. A part of her heart remained among the tall Douglas fir branches dancing in the brisk wind. *Goodbye for now, sweet Jeff.*

The tide-swept ocean crashed against the rocks that had withstood the pounding twice each day for millennia. With the grace of God, they would continue to do so for centuries to come. If only Jeff's life could go on in such a perfectly stable setting.

Mist condensed on the cab's windows and blurred her vision. Like her grief, she wanted to wipe it away.

Chase must have heard her sniffle, for he covered her hand with his. When they arrived at the Emerald Point Airport, he assisted her from the taxi before grabbing both of their carry-on bags.

Nerves stretched taut as banjo strings, Suzanne whispered, "Thank you."

Minutes after they entered the small commuter plane that would take them to Portland, the aircraft lifted into the air and headed north. Outside the window, cloud cover soon enveloped them, obscuring the ground below. Surreal, as though the rest of the world ceased to exist. Her lungs didn't function with any degree of normality until the small plane landed safely on terra firma again.

She wiped a tear from her cheek, only now realizing how much she'd come to love Jeff. And how difficult it was being away from him.

Now that Chase had leveled the playing field by his decision to transfer to Alaska, her outlook on the custody battle had tanked. Her fears multiplied. Still, her sister and brother-in-law had named her to be Jeff's legal guardian. Wouldn't their wishes carry weight in the judge's decision?

How quickly her life had changed. After such a short time, Oregon had begun to feel like home again. Jeff was her son in so many ways. And Lara, such a dear, sweet lady, had become much more than an employee. They'd formed a friendship.

And then there was Chase. Love was the last thing on her radar when she'd arrived for the double funeral. Any thought of forging a romantic relationship had left her shuddering from revulsion . . . and yet, somehow, some way, Chase had wormed his way into her heart like no one before.

Now she faced a very real risk of losing all of them.

After a smooth landing at Portland International Airport, they exited the plane. The time she dreaded had arrived. Chase to Japan and she to New York. She'd miss him, oh, so much.

Chase, holding his boarding pass, started to say something, but closed his mouth and turned away instead.

A sense of overwhelming loss left Suzanne immobile in the middle of the concourse, watching the love of her life walk away, perhaps forever.

A dozen steps farther, a tiny miracle brought the light back into her eyes. Chase stopped, turned around and retraced his steps. "Hey, I've got some time to kill before my flight and your plane doesn't leave for another hour. What do you say we grab some coffee?"

Fearful she might choke if she tried to swallow anything, Suzanne nonetheless grasped at the chance to prolong their time together. "Sure."

At the coffee bar, they sat at the counter

and ordered drinks. After they were served, he lifted his coffee cup to hers. "I guess this is it."

"Why is it when you look back, time seems to have flown by?" And why, when the hourglass was down to its last grains of sand, did she feel the need to bare her soul to this man?

"Always does."

With much to say and little time left, the words of her heart stuck in her throat. Taking the coward's way out, she resorted to tracing the swirls in the granite counter top with her fingertips and fumbled for a neutral topic. "Uh, Lara is so good to look after Jeff without either of us there. She's a treasure. Do you think he'll be all right?"

"Yeah, he'll be OK."

She stirred her coffee with a shaky hand. Might as well ask him or keep wondering . . . "Was there, uh, anything you wanted to discuss?"

Saying goodbye was never easy, especially when it really meant the end of their relationship, if it could be called that. Neither of them had ever acknowledged it.

He leaned forward, his gaze boring into hers. "Yeah, I want you to know I'm glad we finally met."

His words filled her with bittersweet

disappointment. "Me, too. Pam can rest easier now."

"No, not yet." With his coffee cup firmly held in both hands, his gaze remained riveted on her face. "No one will rest until Jeff's custody is settled."

A shiver skittered through her as she searched his face. Like the tone of his voice, his expression was ambiguous, neither hostile nor friendly.

Perhaps spending these last few moments with him had been a mistake. They certainly had crushed her already low spirits.

A tinny voice blared out the arrival on the loudspeaker announcing her flight. Too bad she was leaving Oregon instead of arriving.

The thought brought a frown. She loved New York, loved the hustle and bustle of one of the busiest cities in the world. The Big Apple made her feel alive. Her business thrived there.

But she'd learned to love the little town, too. The house and the ocean. Playing on the beach. It hurt her heart to recall Jeff's sweet little face and how he'd looked so forlorn when they'd kissed him at bedtime last night. Her prayers had included a fervent wish this would be the last time she'd have to say farewell to the precious little boy.

Only the Lord knew what the future held, but she'd prayed more in the past few weeks than in all the years since she'd started attending church again.

When her flight was announced, she breathed a sigh of relief. Enough with the maudlin thoughts. This was it. The Lord would prevail.

Chase tossed a bill on the counter, picked up their bags, and followed her to the terminal security checkpoint. She turned to him, put her hands on his shoulders and gently kissed his cheek. "Thank you, and have a safe journey."

He set the bags down and offered a smile that didn't quite reach his eyes. "You, too." He kissed her lips. "Have a safe trip."

Hurt by the distance he'd forced between them, all the while knowing it was for the best, Suzanne choked back the sadness that squeezed her chest and walked through the gate without looking back. "Goodbye, my love," she whispered, her eyes filling with the tears she'd refused to shed in front of Chase.

Thy will be done, dear Lord.

26

Tokyo's skyscrapers didn't hide the open expanse of water from Chase's view. Standing in front of his office window, the bustling harbor had always had a calming effect, but not this time. For some reason, his gut kept telling him to beware. He glanced at his clenched hands, forced them to relax, and tackled the mountain of paperwork waiting for him.

The sound of the door opening, and an achingly familiar scent brought his head up.

Wendy stood just inside the room, her golden hair billowing. Her back was against the wall, her head angled to one side to showcase that long, swan-like neck he remembered so well, and those plump, wine-red lips were slightly parted and glistening. She could have been a model in a photoshoot.

Or a witch stirring her cauldron.

The irreverent thought brought a snort of

laughter, which he quickly covered with a cough.

Wendy's electric blue eyes narrowed at his reaction. The frown spoiled her carefully concocted entrance. She hesitated for a moment, but quickly regained her confidence, glided his way, a picture of seduction.

"Hello, Chase." That well-modulated voice had once made his heart race.

But this woman, with a wave of her hand, had swept him out of her life as though he were merely dust particles. She'd taught him a valuable lesson in the process, and he'd learned well. One he would never forget.

"It's good to see you." Her hand found his arm, her fingers sliding up and down the sleeve of his suit jacket.

He eased away, only micro-inches, but enough to leave her hand hanging awkwardly in the gap. "Good to see you, too," he said realizing the only good part of seeing her was that it made him realize how much Suzanne meant to him and how very little she did.

Limp, her hand dropped to her side. "Can we talk?"

Chase shrugged. "Sure. Go ahead."

Those perfect nostrils flared ever so slightly. "Not here. Not now. Meet me tonight at our favorite place."

"Tagasuki's?"

She nodded. "Seven. Drinks first, and then dinner."

"Fine." Except it wasn't fine. It sounded a bit too much like old times. Wendy was up to something. He just didn't know what. And wouldn't until tonight.

Her smile suggested a beautiful cat that had just eaten a bluebird.

"May I assume your husband will attend?" Chase wanted a third person there, someone who would ensure he didn't succumb to her charms and her duplicity again.

"No." The smug smile disappeared, her lips compressing into a slash of haughtiness. Ah. There she was, the Wendy he remembered.

"OK." The single word seemed necessary but he wasn't sure why.

She left him with a feeling of uneasiness, a doubt that perhaps wasn't as strong as he thought. But something in him wanted to know why she'd dumped him. Had he not been enough . . .

The remaining hours passed in slow motion, even though he kept delving through the many contracts awaiting his review and approval. As the time grew closer for their dinner meeting, his thoughts tumbled in free-fall. The old sensation of anxiety brought on another headache and too many unanswered questions.

At the window once more, he stared out, not seeing the cargo ships as they plied Tokyo harbor.

Help me, he wanted to shout. But to whom?

Suzanne's soft voice whispered in his mind. For a moment, he was certain he could feel the pressure of her hand squeezing his.

The Lord's Prayer. The only answer. He slipped to his knees and pressed his hands together. *I need your help, Jesus. I don't know if You will listen. Please let me know Your plan for my life. Have I avoided relationships because of Wendy or because after her betrayal I felt I could never be enough? And if I love Suzanne how can I take Jeff away from her. But Lord, he's my nephew too. I feel like I'm in a boat in a storm. Only You can rescue me.*

He ignored the phones and the occasional tap at the door. A glance at his watch told him the time had come to face the past. And the future?

Squaring his shoulders, he sucked in a deep breath, and opened the door to peer down the hall. His fellow employees had already left for the day. Silence followed him into the elevator, across the parking lot, and to his car. Somehow, he navigated the heavy, early rush-hour traffic to the restaurant and even found a parking space reasonably close.

Giving himself a pep-talk, he cautioned himself to man-up. He knew Wendy, probably better than she knew herself.

At the door of Tagasuki's, Chase removed his shoes and then gave his name to the maître d' who led him to a private room.

Wendy was already there, reclining on a pillow. The blue of her dress exactly matched the color of her eyes. A dream. She was still as beautiful, maybe more so, than when they first met.

She smiled and waited for him to acknowledge her.

Not in this lifetime, Instead, he straightened his shoulders, stepped forward, and lowered himself to the floor on the other side, his long legs crossed in the sunken area beneath the table.

"Chase," she whispered, and patted the cushion seat beside her. "I've missed you."

He met her eyes, but said nothing.

Pressing a cigarette to that lush mouth, she inhaled deeply and released the smoke. "I'm truly sorry for what I put you through.

It was foolish and cruel. Can you forgive me?"

He leaned back, his upper lip curling as he recoiled from the smoky haze that wafted toward him.

She blinked and her eyes filled with uncertainty, as though suddenly unsure of what she planned to say. And that's what this was all about — her plan.

"Aren't you going to speak to me?" she pleaded.

"You're the one who wanted to talk. I don't have much to say." He could talk until donkeys no longer brayed, but she only heard what she wanted.

She reached across the table to touch his cold fingers.

He withdrew his hand, surprised by the revulsion that swept through him. Not just from the cigarettes.

Her pretty forehead creased. "I'm trying to tell you something . . . important."

"Go ahead." he prompted.

The waiter arrived to pour Wendy a refill of whatever drink she was having before turning to Chase for his order.

"Lemon Perrier." Why didn't he request something alcoholic? His mind flashed back to Suzanne. No, he wouldn't change his order.

Wendy's quizzical look didn't faze him one bit.

"We could order dinner," she said.

"Go ahead, if you want to. I'm not hungry."

She waved the waiter away.

They were silent until his drink arrived. Chase swirled the liquid in his glass, the ice cubes clinking in frozen rhythm. "What is it you want to tell me?"

"I left my husband." Wendy stared at him as though trying to read his mind. "Our marriage didn't work."

No surprise.

He twisted on the pillow and leaned forward. "Did he find someone younger?"

Disapproval emanated from her in waves. "It wasn't like that."

"Really?"

She shifted — squirmed seemed a more apt description. "You, uh, you're different."

"What? Did you expect I'd be waiting for you? Welcome you back with forgiving arms?"

Her mouth formed a perfect *O* before her hand swept the air. "Well . . . more than this."

With an openhanded gesture, he said, "What is it you want, Wendy?"

"You."

Good to know his instincts remained true. He studied her with a whole new level of disgust. "And you think I still want you in my life?"

He took another sip of his drink. Lord, it was good to face her without the false courage provided by liquor. Another grateful tribute to Suzanne.

Time to end this farce. He could look at her now with candid eyes and appreciate her physical beauty, but nature's generosity couldn't hide the ugliness of the person who dwelled inside that body. All the affection he'd felt for Wendy during the year they'd spent together was gone, leaving him to wonder whether he'd truly loved her. Otherwise, how would he clear his soul so easily?

Supernatural strength flowed through him. Pride lifted his chin, even as a calming peace drifted over him. "Wendy, what we had seemed so right at the time. This is now. You threw me away like garbage. It took me a while to get over your betrayal, but I did. Seeing you again, I know what we shared wasn't love. Even the sparks are gone. You see I finally understand what love is, because God is with me now."

Her mouth opened but no words formed.

"Well, the Lord's always been with me. I was just too arrogant to realize it."

"But . . . but . . ."

"I don't want you, Wendy. I don't even like you." In a swift movement, he rose from his seat and kicked aside the pillow. "And if you're alone now, it's probably what you wanted, and angled to get. Your own choices put you where you are now."

In the aftermath of his declaration, he tossed a handful of yen on the table, gave her a final glance, and walked away to reclaim his shoes. Outside the restaurant, he sucked in a deep breath and relished his freedom.

Overhead, the night sky, clear of pollution for once, twinkled with a million stars.

He smiled, gratitude zinging through him. *Thank You, Father, for the gift of clear thinking and the courage to say what needed to be said.*

He ambled toward his car, feeling lighthearted and free from the hatred and sorrow that had plagued him the past two years.

27

Chase turned off the bedside lamp and listened to the distant sounds of Tokyo, echoing the symphony of sadness in his heart. Tomorrow, early, he'd board the commercial jet to Oregon.

Give up the boy.

The sudden thought sprang unbidden, and struck him like a boulder. Jeff needed a mother to love and hug him, and Suzanne was best suited for the job. If the boy were older, the situation might be different. Besides, it gave him the perfect reason to stay involved in their lives.

Suzanne's face breezed into his mind with perfect clarity. His desire to see her and talk with her again, coupled with his growing need to hold her in his arms, weighed heavy on him. In the past days, since they'd parted at the Portland airport, time had blurred one into another. Dinners with prospective clients seemed endless food and drinking sessions. Busy and brightly lit Tokyo — not what it used to be. At least not to him. He ached with a loneliness he hadn't realized before.

Now, since gaining closure with Wendy, Suzanne filled his waking thoughts, and more than a few of his dreams. Sue. Sweetheart. She'd shown him an astonishing new world, and what had he done? He'd walked away only to realize he wanted her with wild desperation, needed to hold her, to feel her warmth, to hear her sweet chuckle.

He considered a dozen options, explored a hundred avenues, but none seemed right. His inner turmoil mounted until a moment of reckoning lit up like a lightbulb that flashed on above a comic strip character's head. An idea . . . could it be? Could he pull it off?

It would mean he'd have to step off the earth, throw caution to the winds. All of those crazy clichés people use when searching for an answer to an impossible problem.

He could take a chance, something he would have never considered yesterday or even hours ago.

In her New York apartment, Suzanne squirmed in the chaise lounge, unable to find a comfortable position. Or perhaps it was her state of mind — excited and devastated at the same time. Soon, she would see Chase and little Jeff again, albeit for one of the last times to soak up all the joy of their company. The following day, she and Chase would meet in court to decide her precious nephew's future. It was hard enough to have Chase step out of her life. Could she survive losing Jeff, too?

Her racing pulse and aching heart told her no.

And yet, while her personal life had fallen away, her business life was in full swing. The boutiques were thriving. Andy had continued to blossom and show outstanding management skills. Everything she touched seemed to turn to gold. If only . . .

"Chase," she whispered.

His name on her lips set goose bumps racing over her skin, the wonderful kind that made her pulse throb. A vision of him sweeping her up in his arms haunted her. Could she handle a long-distance relationship? No. He didn't want commitment, and watching him walk away again would shatter her already damaged heart into a billion particles of hopeless, helpless despair.

Losing Jeff as well —

Perhaps it would be better to have nothing at all. That might be the only way to survive.

The judge's decision would determine visitation. If she won, Chase would no doubt want to see Jeff. She certainly would if their roles were reversed. They would never say a final goodbye, and the wounds would reopen time and time again.

Another thought collided with the others, one she'd pondered for several days — generated by the impulsive need that hummed and burned along her nerve endings.

The time was fast approaching to do something. Even if Chase rejected it, regret would haunt her forever if she didn't at least offer the suggestion.

Decision made, she let a plan take form in her mind, the same one both she and Chase had dismissed at the onset of this impasse. Perhaps with the new twist, he might consider it now.

28

Karla met Suzanne at the Emerald Point airport and drove her to the house. They'd spoken a number of times on the phone in the past weeks and as a result, she now considered Karla a valued friend.

Exhausted from the lengthy trip from New York, Suzanne tried to focus on inconsequential things, anything that would distract from the heart-wrenching discussion she would have with Chase tonight.

Flashes of lightning zigzagged across the Oregon sky as she arrived at the front door and inserted her key into the lock.

The house was quiet in the early evening twilight. Lara, in all likelihood, had already retired to her room. That left Chase. Karla said Vic had picked him up earlier that afternoon.

She sped up the stairs, heart beating frantically, not daring to look for him. Every nerve in her body twitched as she padded past his bedroom. She wasn't ready to face him. Not yet.

Murmurs carried to her from the far end of the hall where a light shone from the open door of Jeff's playroom. One high voice squealed with excitement. A second, lower voice rumbled with laughter.

Drawn by invisible threads, her feet carried to where she found the two males she loved most in this world.

Chase and Jeff lay on their stomachs, side by side, immersed in a picture book. Knees bent, each made tiny circles in the air with their bare toes.

Jeff giggled at something Chase said, and they rolled onto their backs and laughed.

The boy was the first to spot her. "Aunt Sue." He jumped to his feet and flew to her, wrapping chubby little arms tight around her legs. "You come back."

"Of course I did." She bent over to kiss his silken cheek.

Her gaze lifted and fastened on the dark-haired man who sprawled on his side and watched their interaction. He looked wonderful, even with dark circles under his eyes.

"Hello, Chase."

"Welcome home, Sue."

"Thank you." Words failed her as they often did around him. One of his superpowers was the ability to turn her brain into mush. Not that she could speak with a lump the size of Texas in her throat . . .

Jeff stretched out beside Chase again and patted the space next to him on his other side, chanting, "Read to me. Read to me."

Unable to deny him, she plopped down onto the rug next to Jeff while her heart danced with both joy and heartache.

He reached for his favorite book, the story of a mother and father bear and their mischievous baby. He knew every word.

"You Mommy," he said to Suzanne. Turning to Chase, he announced, "And you Daddy."

Over Jeff's head, she met Chase's eyes. Seeing his softened silver irises, the lump choking her grew larger.

She began to read, her voice husky. Chase joined in for the role of the Daddy Bear, and Jeff squeaked his part. Before the story ended, his lashes began to lower. He tried to lift them again as he fought off sleep.

" 'Nother story," he mumbled.

Chase chucked the boy under his chin. "How about we stay here with you while you go to sleep?"

"OK."

Chase slid his hand across the rug past Jeff's head and threaded his fingers with

Suzanne's. A bolt of electricity charged through her.

"Let's drop the case tomorrow," she said. "We can love and share him."

Chase cleared his throat. "How do you propose we do that?"

She grabbed her lower lip with her teeth. It was now or never. Acceptance or rejection, she had to say it. She gave Chase a soft smile. "What if Jeff and I came to stay with you for a while in Tokyo?"

A flush crept up his face, astonishment and disbelief in his eyes. "What about your business and everything you've worked so hard for?"

"I'll do . . . something with it. Maybe I could be Andy's fairy godmother."

Chase shook his head.

Her mind played a funeral dirge, and for one awful moment, she thought her heart might stop. Chase didn't want her.

"The 'for a while' won't work, Sue." His grip on her hand grew firmer, determined.

"What do you mean?" *Do I really want to know?*

"I'll take my chances, quit my job, and go to New York with you and Jeff."

Suzanne sucked in a breath, almost overcome by mingled surprise, shock and joy. "No, no, I can't let you do that."

"No?" Chase's face shuttered.

Jeff stirred between them. "Don't wanna go New York or Tok-ee-o," he muttered. "Wanna stay here."

Suzanne and Chase stared at each other. A chuckle left his lips. She joined him and soon the three of them were giggling.

"Out of the mouths of babes." Suzanne couldn't believe she'd spouted a cliché.

"Each of us was willing to give up our livelihoods to be together," Chase said. "Why don't we try what Jeff suggested?"

The constriction in her chest eased. "Lara told me when I called yesterday that you didn't accept the offer to buy the mill, so maybe you could run it for a while. I can rent the empty building in town and open a new boutique here. I called the owner a few days ago." She grinned. "He's anxious to rent the property and gave me a very reasonable price."

"It's worth a try." Chase's voice was low and gentle. "I'm game if you are."

They leaned on their elbows and stretched across Jeff. Their lips met and clung.

"Like a fairytale." A voice spoke from the doorway. "Everyone lives happily ever after."

Three heads popped up.

Lara clutched her robe with her hands. "Why did it take you two so long to see what I saw the first time you came into the house together?"

"I guess some people can't see the forest for the trees," Chase said.

Heavens, another cliché.

Lara grinned and nodded. "I'll tuck Jeff in if you two want to . . . um, discuss this some more."

Chase helped Suzanne to her feet and pulled her close. "That's an excellent idea, Lara. I knew there were more reasons why we thought of you as the perfect housekeeper and friend."

"For sure," Suzanne added.

They kissed the sleepy boy under Lara's watchful gaze. And then there were just the two of them.

"This might work," Chase said.

"Oh, yes," Suzanne murmured.

"I know this crazy attraction" — he motioned his fingers between them — "will work. What I meant was my staying here in Emerald Point to run the mill. Maybe create some furniture as you suggested."

"Ah."

"And if it doesn't work out . . ." His mouth caught hers. "Staying here, I mean, we have other alternatives."

"Uh huh."

When he lifted his head, joy and love

glowed in his beautiful eyes. "We have dozens of choices, places, chances for work and a future, as long as we have each other and our little boy."

"For as long as you want," she murmured.

Chase's eyes dazzled her. "I want forever."

She gave a tiny sigh, and he covered her mouth with his. Like a match touched to nitroglycerine, excitement exploded through her. "Chase, Chase," she whispered in a blissful sigh.

"Easy, sweetheart." With throaty laughter, he buzzed her neck. "Sue, my darling." His breath was hot against her lips. "I love you."

"I love you, too," she whispered.

He backed toward the rocker, pulling her with him, and then settled her on his lap. "You drive me crazy. Let's see if we can get the minister to marry us soon."

She nodded, happiness winging its way into her heart and soul. "How soon?"

"Like tomorrow, or the next day."

With a glance at Jeff's treasure trove of toys, she focused on the three plush animals. Mama bear, Baby bear and Papa bear. Maybe one day she and Chase would add another little bear. Joy burst inside her.

"You've stepped over the threshold of love, my beautiful Suzanne. You belong here in my arms," Chase said. "I don't plan to ever let you go."

Suzanne snuggled closer, knowing her future with Chase and Jeff would be filled with joy and sadness, laughter and tears, and with enough love to last a lifetime.

Right now, though, in this treasured moment, she felt the approving presence of the Lord and his wondrous peace.

Thank you, Father, for Your blessings.

A DEVOTIONAL MOMENT

Having predestinated us unto the adoption of children by Jesus Christ to himself, according to the good pleasure of his will, to the praise of the glory of his grace, wherein he hath made us accepted in the beloved. In whom we have redemption through his blood, the forgiveness of sins, according to the riches of his grace; Wherein he hath abounded toward us in all wisdom and prudence; Having made known unto us the mystery of his will, according to his good pleasure which he hath purposed in himself. ~ Ephesians 1: 5-9

People are sometimes given a place in a family not of their birth. Though adopted, they get the same rights, protection, and an inheritance as natural-born members of the family. This is how God's family works. He has given us the free will to join His family if we accept salvation. We will be His children, with all the rights, protections, and an inheritance that is everlasting.

In **Ice Maiden's Meltdown,** the protagonists are battling over a child. Each believes they can offer the best life. As they work together to ensure the child's future, they come to an understanding about putting the needs of another first, even when it is to their detriment. With love for the child, they find that peace comes when they put aside differences and work together.

> Have you ever felt alone, out of place, or abandoned? Even when you have a large family, it is easy to feel as if you don't count as much as some other members of the family. When you're a member of God's family, you can rest assured that He loves you, will treat you, will count you and will help you just as much as all the other members of His family, His flock. Whether you've been a Christian for a day, a year, or you're a revert, You will be part of the family completely. So when you feel out of place, unloved, unworthy or forgotten, remember you are not forgotten. You are part of an eternal family whose Father loves you more than you can imagine.

Lord, help me to give my worries and concerns to You, so that You can give me the best solutions. In Jesus' Name I pray, Amen.

ABOUT THE AUTHOR

Emily Grey finds happiness writing romantic stories that touch the heart.

The employees of Thorndike Press hope you have enjoyed this Large Print book. All our Thorndike, Wheeler, and Kennebec Large Print titles are designed for easy reading, and all our books are made to last. Other Thorndike Press Large Print books are available at your library, through selected bookstores, or directly from us.

For information about titles, please call:
  (800) 223-1244

or visit our website at:
  gale.com/thorndike

To share your comments, please write:
  Publisher
  Thorndike Press
  10 Water St., Suite 310
  Waterville, ME 04901